DEATH DINES OUT

CLAUDIA
BISHOP

BERKLEY PRIME CRIME, NEW YORK

DEATH DINES OUT

A Berkley Prime Crime Book / published by arrangement with the author

PRINTING HISTORY
Berkley Prime Crime edition / December 1997

For information address:
The Berkley Publishing Group, a member of Penguin Putnam Inc.,
200 Madison Avenue, New York, NY 10016

The Putnam Berkley World Wide Web site address is
http://www.berkley.com

ISBN: 0-425-16111-0

Berkley Prime Crime Books are published
by The Berkley Publishing Group, a member of Penguin Putnam Inc.,
200 Madison Avenue, New York, NY 10016.

PRINTED IN THE UNITED STATES OF AMERICA

10 9 8 7 6 5 4 3 2 1

For John, Lyn, and John Robert,
who love the Florida house

The Hemlock Falls Mysteries

1 pretty little town in upstate New York
1 picturesque inn overlooking Hemlock Gorge
2 talented sisters even better at solving crimes
than they are at their day jobs
1 (or more) murders . . .

A WINNING RECIPE FOR MYSTERY LOVERS!

Don't Miss these Hemlock Falls Mysteries . . .

MURDER WELL-DONE

Looking to get re-elected, ex-senator Alphonse Santini has brought big-time politics to the little town. And while politics makes strange bedfellows, the dead-fellows being made are even stranger . . .

A TASTE FOR MURDER

One of the year's biggest events, the History Days festival takes a deadly turn when a reenactment of seventeenth-century witch trials leads to twentieth-century murder . . .

A DASH OF DEATH

The Quilliam sisters trail the killer of two Hemlock Falls women who won a design contest. Celebrated style maven Helena Houndswood was furious when the small-town women won. But mad enough to murder?

A PINCH OF POISON

Hedrick Conway is a nosy reporter who thinks something funny is going on with a local development project. But nobody's laughing when two of his relatives turn up murdered. For Hedrick, and the Quilliam sisters, this could be one deadline they'll never meet . . .

MORE MYSTERIES FROM THE BERKLEY PUBLISHING GROUP . . .

DOG LOVERS' MYSTERIES STARRING HOLLY WINTER: With her Alaskan malamute Rowdy, Holly dogs the trails of dangerous criminals. "A gifted and original writer."—Carolyn G. Hart

by Susan Conant

A NEW LEASH ON DEATH
DEAD AND DOGGONE
A BITE OF DEATH
PAWS BEFORE DYING

DOG LOVERS' MYSTERIES STARRING JACKIE WALSH: She's starting a new life with her son and an ex-police dog named Jake . . . teaching film classes and solving crimes!

by Melissa Cleary

A TAIL OF TWO MURDERS
DOG COLLAR CRIME
HOUNDED TO DEATH
FIRST PEDIGREE MURDER
SKULL AND DOG BONES
DEAD AND BURIED
THE MALTESE PUPPY
MURDER MOST BEASTLY
OLD DOGS

SAMANTHA HOLT MYSTERIES: Dogs, cats, and crooks are all part of a day's work for this veterinary technician . . . "Delightful!"—Melissa Cleary

by Karen Ann Wilson

EIGHT DOGS FLYING
BEWARE SLEEPING DOGS
COPY CAT CRIMES
CIRCLE OF WOLVES

CHARLOTTE GRAHAM MYSTERIES: She's an actress with a flair for dramatics—and an eye for detection. "You'll get hooked on Charlotte Graham!"—*Rave Reviews*

by Stefanie Matteson

MURDER AT THE SPA
MURDER AT TEATIME
MURDER ON THE CLIFF
MURDER ON THE SILK ROAD
MURDER AT THE FALLS
MURDER ON HIGH
MURDER AMONG THE ANGELS
MURDER UNDER THE PALMS

PEACHES DANN MYSTERIES: Peaches has never had a very good memory. But she's learned to cope with it over the years . . . Fortunately, though, when it comes to murder, this absentminded amateur sleuth doesn't forgive and forget!

by Elizabeth Daniels Squire

WHO KILLED WHAT'S-HER-NAME?
MEMORY CAN BE MURDER
REMEMBER THE ALIBI
WHOSE DEATH IS IT ANYWAY?

HEMLOCK FALLS MYSTERIES: The Quilliam sisters combine their culinary and business skills to run an inn in upstate New York. But when it comes to murder, their talent for detection takes over . . .

by Claudia Bishop

A TASTE FOR MURDER
A PINCH OF POISON
A DASH OF DEATH
MURDER WELL-DONE
DEATH DINES OUT

I have taken a number of liberties with the geography and institutions of Palm Beach. The curious will not find the Combers Beach Club, the Florida Institute for Fine Food, or Beach Road as they are described in this book. The characters are just as imaginary.

My thanks to my friends the pros: Dana Paxson, Nancy Kress, Nick DiChario, Duranna Durgin, Sally Caves, and David Greer Smith. My thanks also to the Culinary Institute of West Palm Beach and the friendly people there.

CAST OF CHARACTERS

Vacationers at Palm Beach

Sarah "Quill" Quilliam—manager/owner, the Inn at Hemlock Falls
Margaret "Meg" Quilliam—her sister, a master chef
Tiffany Taylor—a wealthy patron of gourmet cooking
Verger Taylor—her ex-husband, fourth richest real estate developer in America
Corrigan and Evan Taylor—Verger's sons by his first marriage
Cressida Houghton—Verger's first wife
Ernst Kolsacker—Verger's business partner
Franklin Carmichael—Verger's lawyer
Luis Mendoza—caretaker/manager, The Combers Beach Club
Dr. Robert Bittern—Psychiatrist

The Florida Institute for Fine Food

Master Chef Jean Paul Bernard—*directeur-general*
Linda Longstreet—administrator
—various chefs, students, waiters, and waitresses

The Lunch Bunch

Birdie McIntyre—a widow
Selma Goldwyn—a widow
Beatrice Gollinge—a widow

The West Palm Beach Department of Police

Jerry Fairchild—chief of detectives
Trish—his partner
Ange Wisc—a policeman

DEATH DINES OUT

PROLOGUE

The fourth day of the blizzard, Sarah Quilliam seriously considered unpacking her luggage. There was no way the Syracuse airport would open the next day. She and her sister, Meg, were going to miss their flight to Palm Beach. Snow piled high around the foundations of the Inn at Hemlock Falls. The waterfall in Hemlock Gorge had frozen to a small trickle, and the road to the Inn was drifted over.

There were no guests. The Inn was closed and would be closed for another week. The waiters, *sous* chefs, and receptionist had been sent home days before. The staff that remained was getting very, very irritable. There was nothing to do except squabble.

"You two might better have stayed home anyways," Doreen Muxworthy-Stoker said. Somewhere in her fifties—Doreen wasn't telling, and she never had filled out an employment application—she was the Inn's head housekeeper. They were all sitting around a table in the Inn's dining room: Doreen; Meg, the gourmet chef and Quill's partner; John Raintree, their business manager; and Quill herself.

Quill looked crossly at the snow whipping against the floor-to-ceiling windows overlooking Hemlock Gorge. "The storm's due to break sometime tonight," she said. "I'll bet we'll make it out."

"Sure you will," John said easily. He was Quill's age, in his mid-thirties, and three-quarters Onondaga Indian. He'd been brought up in Hemlock Falls and was one of the few people Quill knew that loved cold weather.

"I'll bet we won't," Meg said gloomily. "Just think—somewhere a couple of hundred miles outside this lousy weather, the sun is shining, the roads are clear, and the air is warm. And we're *stuck!*" Meg had recently taken to collecting T-shirts emblazoned with mottoes, selecting sayings appropriate to her mood. Today's read RUNS WITH SCISSORS.

"You shouldna took the money," Doreen said. "You take the money, you're committed. You gotta go. Tolt the sheriff this morning he'd have to get the sled dogs out and take you."

"Myles isn't sheriff anymore, Doreen," Quill said. Doreen knew this very well. Davy Kiddermeister had taken over as Tompkins County sheriff when Myles went back to his job as a private investigator. Doreen just plain didn't like this change, so for her, it hadn't happened.

"You shoulda married the sheriff last year," Doreen continued stubbornly. "He woulda stayed home."

"We *are* getting married, Doreen," Quill said tartly. "Sometime soon. And it wouldn't have made any difference to his career choice anyway."

"You two had better get to Florida," John said. "Or I'm going to redo our business plan for this year, ditch the restaurant and hotel business, and go into charity work myself. How does the Hemlock Falls Charitable Institute for Victims of Cabin Fever sound?"

Tiffany Taylor, ex-wife of the fourth richest real estate developer in America, had succeeded in recruiting Meg and Quill to help with a week-long charity function in Palm Beach. From what Quill had gathered, the charity was for phobic women—and some of them had sounded in a pitiful state. Tiffany had alluded to suicide attempts.

The working conditions were ideal. Meg and Quill were booked first class to Palm Beach. Tiffany was putting them up at the Combers Beach Club, a luxury condo that had been part of her divorce settlement. Quill was obligated for one lecture—Fundamentals of Innkeeping—Meg for three cooking classes. For Meg, the real attraction had been the ball and banquet slated for the end of their week. She would cook one dish, and one dish only: potted rabbit. And Tiffany promised that the editors of *L'Aperitif*, the gourmet magazine that awarded the highly prized ratings for America's chefs, would be there.

"There's no doubt," she'd told Meg with vigorous assurance, "that you'll get back that third star. None at all."

Meg, who'd lost the third star in an imbroglio several years ago, would walk on hot coals to get it back. The prospect of a week in the sun in the midst of a New York winter with light duties and a huge paycheck paled beside the chance to get her potted rabbit into the magazine editor's stomach.

The swinging doors leading to the kitchen opened and Myles came in. He was wearing a heavy parka. Snow sprinkled his dark hair. His face was red with cold. He bent down and rubbed his cheek against Quill's. "It's clearing to the east," he said. "The airport's open. Looks like you'll be able to go."

Meg grinned, jumped up from the table, and did a little dance. "Third star, here I come!"

CHAPTER 1

Margaret Quilliam stretched out on the lounge chair facing the ocean and exhaled with exaggerated pleasure. "Bliss," she said. "Absolute bliss. It's ten degrees above zero in Hemlock Falls and here we are, cocooned in salty sea air precisely at body temperature. We couldn't have asked for more, Quill."

Quill contemplated the view in a contented frame of mind. They were lucky to be getting paid to live here for a week in this kind of luxury.

The Taylor charity had sounded worthy. An institute for phobics, Tiffany Taylor had said. The first of its kind and completely privately funded. Quill didn't recall precisely what type of phobics were the focus of the fund—but Tiffany had made them sound in desperate need of help.

Quill took a fourth—or was it fifth?—swallow of Meg's version of Planter's Punch, then wished she hadn't. She was dizzy. It couldn't be jet lag—Palm Beach was a four-hour flight from upstate New York. It must be the punch. She'd warned Meg about the punch.

She set the drink carefully on the patio deck, then linked her hands behind her head—more to steady it than to relax. Her hair was damp and frizzy with the humidly. She patted futilely at it and closed her eyes. That was a mistake. She was dizzier than ever. She blinked and sat up. "What the heck did you put in that drink?"

"The punch?" Meg waved her glass in the air, beaming. The moon rose behind her, high and white among the palm trees. The ocean bumped gently against the shore in front of them. To Quill's left, the condominium pool shimmered aquamarine over the in-ground lights. Meg brought her drink close to one eye and, peering through the lucent pink, said, "Mango, orange, and pineapple juice. A touch of cranberry. Cherries, oranges, and mint."

Quill looked dubious. "No rum?"

"Of course there's rum." Meg was indignant. "The very best rum. Dark rum. Light rum. Coconut rum. Something called Island Very Strong Rum. Rum." Meg subsided, muttering, then resurfaced. "I know a swell song about rum. Want to hear it?"

"No."

"It goes like this." Meg cleared her throat and began to sing. She was thirty to Quill's thirty-four and for twenty-nine of those years (Meg's vocalizing had started early on) Quill had never known what drove her sister to sing. She was awful. Her voice wandered, gypsy-like, through the keys. Her tone was thin and buzzy, like a Dremel drill or a very large bee.

"Away, away with rum, by gum, it's the song of the Temperance Union. We never eat cookies if they contain rum."

"Meg."

"For one little bite turns a man to a bum . . ."

"Meg!"

"Now ever have seen you a sorrier disgra—a-a-ace . . . than a man in the gutter with crumbs on his face!"

"Be QUIET down there!" The voice, male, floated somewhere above them.

Meg peered fuzzily into the night sky. "Okey-dokey," she said.

Quill heard the distant *thunk-bang!* of a glass patio door. Tiffany Taylor had mentioned the crabby tenant on the third floor. She'd also mentioned the condo rule against renters. "Nobody'll mind," she'd said, "as long as you're quiet. And you aren't renters, exactly. After all, *I'm* paying *you.*" And she'd given that tinkling, artificial laugh. Ugh. Quill shook herself. "Time for a cup of coffee, Meg. Stay right there." She glanced upwards; there were no irate faces hanging over the third-floor balcony—at least not yet. "And don't sing a word."

"Where're you going?"

"To get coffee. And hide the rum." The handle of the French door to the inside was smooth and weighty in her hand. Everything about the condominium was like that: polished, substantial, the best of its kind. The bleached oak floors were like pale mirrors. In the living room, buttery leather couches formed a U facing the French doors. The occasional tables were marble set on intricately detailed gilt bases. The island dividing the living room from the kitchen was made of a single slab of whorled mahogany.

Quill crossed the hardwood floor to the kitchen, the surface cool against her bare feet. Neither one of them had expected much from the kitchen itself: Quill because she'd guessed that most very wealthy people in Palm Beach ate at restaurants, and their hostess Tiffany Taylor was among the wealthiest; Meg because she was a professional cook and never expected much of anything from other people's kitchens.

They'd been surprised. The appliances were restaurant quality, and the shelves were fully stocked. The Subzero refrigerator held eggs, cream, butter, yeast, vinegars, and essential vegetables like onions, carrots, celery, and fresh herbs. The pots and pans were mostly copper—harder to clean than stainless steel (which made them inefficient for professional cooks) and expensive (which made them impractical—neither Meg nor Quill would ever make enough money to be in the Palm Beach league). But the cookware came in the right variety of sizes—from sauté to stock pots. And the knives were superb.

Quill filled the kettle with spring water and set it on the gas stove. Coffee would be too stimulating; they had a full day scheduled for tomorrow and both of them should get a good night's sleep. Tea would be better. She bent down and opened one cabinet door after another: pasta machine, still in the box; cappuccino/espresso machine—the three-hundred-dollar kind—which looked unused; a Cuisinart. The cabinet under the microwave held tins of ground coffee, boxes of flavored teas . . .

. . . and a videotape, labeled SARAH AND MARGARET QUILLIAM: PLEASE VIEW.

Quill set the videotape on the counter. They'd already received multiple faxes, print packages of the week's agenda, and too many phone calls about Meg's classes and Quill's lecture from Tiffany's underemployed secretary in New York. Whatever was on the tape—Tiffany at her Louis Quinze desk giving them wardrobe advice—Tiffany suggesting variations on Meg's potted rabbit recipe—Tiffany introducing Quill to the latest hairstyles—Quill didn't want to see it just yet. She sighed and set the tape on the countertop, then rummaged through the teas for something decaffeinated. She'd make the tea and then stick the tape in the VCR. She hoped the tape wasn't too long. And she really hoped that she hadn't made a mistake about this trip. "It's the charity," she said aloud. "I'm not so sure about this charity."

Meg, who'd wandered in from the patio, perched on one of the wrought iron chairs around the kitchen island. "It's for women with phobias, right?" She burped. She was looking a little green. She'd drunk two glasses of her own punch.

Quill took the kettle off the boiler and selected a packet of tea. Chamomile should settle them both; neither of them were used to rum. "I think so. Tiffany sort of slid over the specifics."

Meg picked up the videotape. "What's this?"

"Who knows? Tiffany's Travel Tips. But we'd better look at it before she gets here. There's a video player with that huge TV in the library."

Meg pointed to a small shelf near the corner window.

"In the kitchen, too?" Quill walked to the small television set and peered at it. "By gum, you're right." Meg stretched across the counter, handed over the tape, and Quill slid it into place. She tapped the PLAY button and the screen sprang into life.

"It's that news show, *Hot Tip*," said Meg. "Yuck. That's one of the sleaziest . . ."

"Hush, Meg."

"And that guy's the creepy interviewer Bernie Waters . . . and *that's* . . . "

"Verger Taylor," said Quill. "Uh-oh."

". . . exclusive interview with the most successful real estate entrepreneur of this or any other decade." Bernie Waters grinned whitely into the camera. "Verge—can I call you Verge? Tell us about this so-called charity that Tiffany's cooked up."

The camera zoomed in on Verger Taylor's heavy-featured face. Quill instantly mistrusted the sincere blue glow of his eyes.

"It's unfortunate, Bernie, the lengths to which my ex-wife has gone to embarrass me and destroy the good things I've worked for on behalf of the good people of Chicago."

"What good things?" Meg demanded. "If he's talking about the Taylor Towers, he can forget it. Architectural monstrosity is NOT the word! All that pink marble overlooking Lake Michigan? It's a womb with a view."

"Hush, Meg."

"My lawyers inform me that anyone, anyone participating in this fiasco may be liable for damages. And you know me, Bernie, I've been up and everybody was my best friend. When I was down . . . I was down so far I couldn't get arrested. I have taken it, and I suppose I'll have to take it in the future. But I'm not taking it now, not from this broad. Anyone dealing with the ex–Mrs. Taylor and that charity down in Palm Beach is going to have to answer to me and my lawyers."

The tape ended abruptly.

"Good grief," said Meg. "What the heck was that all about? And who do you suppose put the tape there?"

Quill drummed her fingers on the countertop. "Verger Taylor, of course."

Meg scowled. "It wasn't Verger Taylor. It was one of the other chefs cooking for the banquet Saturday night. Trying to scare me off."

"Don't be silly, Meg. Of course it was Verger Taylor. Who else would know that we'd be staying here at Tiffany's place? She didn't even want the people at the condo to know, since it's illegal to rent or something. Which reminds me. About your singing . . ."

"Maybe you're right." Meg ran both hands through her short, dark hair. "On the other hand, maybe *I'm* right. You know how competitive the cooking business is. I know chefs who'd poison their rivals if they thought they could get away with it. Planting that videotape is small potatoes. Cooking is war, Quill."

"Then let's go home. Right now. God forbid you should get shot with a turkey baster or clubbed with a rolling pin or . . ."

"We can't go home! Quill, I've got to get that third star back. And stop that drumming. It's driving me nuts."

Quill placed her hand flat on the marble. It was her left hand. Myles's engagement ring winked at her. For a brief moment, she felt a cowardly desire to give up and go home to Hemlock Falls. "I think that from all accounts, Verger Taylor can be a pretty vindictive guy. He put the tape there to intimidate us. It's not going to work, right?"

"If it's Verger Taylor who did it. I think . . ."

"I know what you think. That everyone in a toque is out to get you. Nuts. I think we should reserve an opinion until we talk to Tiffany."

Meg grabbed at her hair. "If it is Verger Taylor, that's a different problem to worry about. What if he sabotages the banquet? Or my cooking classes? You know what he's like. The Meanest Man in Chicago. Who wants to get mixed up in that? Maybe we should go home!"

"Meg. Settle down. We can't back out on Tiffany because her ex-husband's vindictive."

"You're right," Meg admitted. "I wished I liked her better, though. I hate to say it, but if my career's going to go down in flames I'd rather it was for a better purpose."

"I didn't like her very much either," said Quill. "But it doesn't matter. Here's what matters. Are you ready?"

"Yes," said Meg sulkily.

"Cooking matters. Let me worry about the Taylors. You worry about the potted rabbit that's going to get you that third star back. Besides, Meg, Tiffany can take care of herself. She started out as a pro golfer. And those women are tough. She isn't going to need us to run interference for her." She pulled the tape out of the machine and read the label again. "On the other hand, Verge the Scourge is one tough cookie, too. I wonder how he got this in here. I thought the condo was part of Tiffany's divorce settlement."

"Quill?"

"Yes, Meg."

"Any way you slice it, this is going to be a horrible week." Meg's expression was woeful.

"The punch was definitely a mistake."

"I don't mean that. I mean, you're right that I made

them too strong. I had two, you know. But I'm paying for that.'' She burped woefully. ''I'm suffering.''

''Mm,'' Quill said unsympathetically.

''Our mistake was that we didn't ask enough questions about this charity. I don't like Tiffany Taylor. And I sure as heck don't like what we've heard of her ex-husband. We were dopes. Boobs. Greedy-guts. We've let ourselves be talked into disaster. We saw the chance for a nice, warm vacation at the worst time of the year. And we haven't been away from Hemlock Falls since we opened the Inn, so we temporarily lost our minds. It's going to be,'' she burped again and said hollowly, ''a big, horrible mess. And it'll end in disaster. Did you see the article in the newspaper at the airport?''

''Just the headlines. I was hoping you didn't see it.''

''I was hoping YOU didn't see it. 'Tiffany's Revenge'? That one? The one that said this charity for phobics was a bunch of hooey?''

''It was a tabloid,'' Quill said hopefully. ''You know what they're like. 'Dwarf Rapes Nun, Escapes in UFO.' They're full of baloney. So this isn't necessarily a bogus charity. I mean this Dr. Bittern. He's supposed to be a real psychiatrist, isn't he?''

''Hah. Where did it say he was a psychiatrist? And if he is a psychiatrist, what if his degree's from the Arkansas School of Psychiatry and Plastics Recycling? Quill, forget the star. I want to go home.''

Quill sighed. There had been a tacit understanding between Tiffany and Quill that part of her own responsibilities were to see that her volatile sister survived precooking nerves. ''It's going to be fine. We'll ask Tiffany more details when she gets here.'' She squinted at the kitchen clock. The clock was made of stainless steel, with wrought iron hands that indicated the time of day in a very vague way, since there weren't any numbers. ''What time is it, anyway?''

Meg looked at her watch. ''It's sometime after eight. And that's when she said she'd show up. Sometime after eight tonight. I hope it's a long sort of sometime; I don't feel all that terrific. I think I'll lie down for a bit. Everything's going sort of swimmy. And I'm hearing weird noises. Why in the heck did you force me to make those drinks?''

''I did *not* force you to make those drinks. You insisted on making those drinks. Planter's punch, you said. Just the ticket to celebrate our arrival.''

''Rum punch.''

''Rum punch, then. And you shouldn't have gulped them down.''

''I was hot. And thirsty. And giddy. Do you hear bells, Quill? Or am I going clean out of my mind?''

Quill listened. The scented air was filled with a subaural chiming that reminded her of expensive department stores. ''It's the doorbell. It must be Tiffany. Stay right there.''

''They are making me cross. Very, very cross. Bells,'' Meg said glumly. ''The ringing and the singing of the bells, bells, bells . . .''

Quill left Meg to her Poe and went down the long corridor to the ornately carved front door. The hall was painted a soft, suffused peach. The recessed lighting in the ceiling made the air around the walls glow. Impressionist paintings from one of the minor schools hung at carefully selected intervals along the walls. Whoever had picked them had a good eye. Her hand on the doorknob, Quill stopped, astonished. The perennial garden at their Inn shone at her from the wall to the right of the front door. It was one of her own acrylics—part of a series she'd produced in a brief burst of activity four years ago. She remembered that particular piece well. Myles had sat with her in the garden. It had been a rare afternoon, peaceful and contented. Her agent in New York had asked for more.

The key scraped in the lock and the door opened. ''Darling Quill!'' Tiffany cried. ''Sorry to barge in. But you didn't answer me! I was beginning to think the plane had crashed! Do let me in, there's a sweetie. It's broiling out here.''

In the past three years, Tiffany Taylor's face had made the cover of major women's magazines in the United States and Europe. First because of her marriage to Verger Taylor (his third, her second) and then due to the divorce (spectacular and sordid). She was tall—well over five nine—with the Barbie-doll rounded slenderness that belonged to professional athletes with personal trainers—or women who could afford liposuction. She had a straight little nose, high cheekbones, and what the gossip columnists called a ''Paris mouth,'' full-lipped and sullen. Her changing hair color was as notorious as the numbers of her plastic surgeries. Today's was white blonde.

Tiffany was dressed in what Quill—having spent close to an hour waiting for her luggage in the crowded West Palm Beach airport—was already coming to recognize as The Palm Beach Outfit: hand-tailored khaki trousers, blue-striped shirt, navy blazer, and a three-hundred-dollar straw hat with a black grosgrain ribbon around the crown. The hat was hand-tailored, too, from a small shop in one of the arcades off Worth Avenue. Quill knew the price of the hat because Tiffany's secretary had included that information in one of the endless stream of memos.

Tiffany halted her forward rush and frowned. ''My God! It's so humid in here I can't breathe! The air conditioner must have broken down again. You'd think that for what I paid for this place . . .'' She hurried down the hall, squeaking a little in her agitation. ''I'm so sorry, sorry, sorry that you two arrived to this *sauna*. Oh, that damn ol' Luis. He's supposed to check on the place every single week, but if you're not here to climb right up his backside . . .''

Quill, hurrying after her, nearly knocked her over when Tiffany stopped abruptly at the edge of the living room.

"The *windows* are open," Tiffany said accusingly.

"Well, yes," Quill admitted. "I opened them. This air's so lovely after our winter that . . ."

"But your hair! The leather couches!"

"Surely not," said Quill. "We're in Florida, and it seems a shame to . . ."

"Ugh! Ugh-ugh-ugh!" Tiffany ran past Meg and closed the French doors with a firm and determined air. "There. That will help enormously. We'll just give it a minute to cool down. Goodness!" She sat down on the leather couch, crossed her legs and took a cigarette case from her purse. She patted the sofa. "Come and sit by me, both of you."

Quill sat opposite her on a leather chair. Meg settled at the kitchen island.

"How was your flight?" Tiffany lit the cigarette with what looked like a diamond-encrusted lighter, dropped the lighter with a clatter on the marble end table, and inhaled deeply.

Quill took a deep breath. "It was fine. But our reception here was a little odd."

Tiffany cocked her head and eyed Quill through a cloud of cigarette smoke. "Was Luis rude to you?"

"We didn't meet Luis. But someone left us a videotape of an unpleasant interview with Mr. Taylor."

"Which one?" Tiffany tapped her cigarette into a cloisonne bowl on the coffee table. "If it was the *60 Minutes* one, then it was somebody on my side. Mike Wallace gave Verge a great going-over."

"It was an interview with Bernie Waters."

"Oh. Then that was Verger himself. Done at the home office in Chicago, right? Beating his chest. Trying to scare you off, I suppose. He didn't, did he?"

"Why is he so angry?" Quill asked.

"Why is Verger anything? He's an asshole, that's why."

Meg knocked her bare heel rhythmically against the leg of the bar stool, a frown on her face. Tiffany turned and looked at her. Meg had changed into the newest addition to her T-shirt collection as soon as she'd arrived in Florida: IT'S MS. BITCH TO YOU. "Love the message, darling. I'd like to send one to Verge. Well." Tiffany exhaled, stubbed out her cigarette, and settled back onto the couch. "Let's see how you two look." She ran her cornflower-blue eyes over Quill, stopping at her hair. She raised an eyebrow. "I didn't even give you a chance to tidy up," she said with extravagant self-accusation. "And Dr. Bob will be here any moment. You go on ahead and fix it. Don't mind me."

Meg raised her eyebrows. "Dr. Bob? You mean this Dr. Bittern in charge of your charity?"

"Yes. He's dying to meet both of you."

"I'm dying to meet him," Meg said darkly.

Quill ignored these warning signals from Meg and dabbed at her hair. Maybe she should have worn it up. Tiffany was wearing hers up and the humidity hadn't so much as plastered wisps around her perfect little ears. Maybe she was one of those glamorous, voluptuous blondes who refused to sweat. Maybe all the collagen in her face had migrated and plugged her sweat glands up. She was also one of those blondes who could wear anything with flair, and Quill, who was too slender, felt lanky in her cotton skirt and espadrilles. "I am not going to change a thing," she announced to no one in particular.

"Dr. Bob?" said Meg, her gray eyes boring into Tiffany's blue ones. "About this Dr. Bob? Is he a real shrink, or what? Does he have anything to do with why Verger Taylor's trying to run us out of town?"

"You chefs," said Tiffany. "So dramatic. Come and sit here, sweetie. It hurts my neck to turn around. But before you do, be a darling, Meg, and fix me one of your famous gin and tonics."

"I'm not famous for making gin and tonics," said Meg succinctly. She beat a furious tattoo against the chair leg.

"Stop thumping, Meg," Quill said. "It's driving me nuts."

Meg continued thumping. Quill thought she recognized the rhythm to "Dead Skunk in the Middle of the Road." Meg gave the chair leg a final, ominous thud and slid from the stool. She swayed slightly on her feet. "I'm a famous cook. A famous cook who wants to know about this Dr. Bob's qualifications."

"Little squiffy, darling, are we?" Tiffany said coolly. "Enjoying my liquor?"

Meg drew a deep breath. Tiffany obviously hadn't understood the attitude implicit in Meg's T-shirt motto, but she was about to understand it clearly now.

Quill sprang up from the couch. "I'll make the drink. Sit down, Meg. Tiffany, please. You left the most wonderful cheese and crackers for us. Let me get you some."

Meg wandered to the leather chair facing the couch and curled up cross-legged. She eyed Tiffany owlishly. Tiffany pulled a jewel-encrusted compact out of her purse and examined her face critically in the little glass mirror. Quill, fuzzy on how much of each should go into a gin and tonic, poured substantial amounts of both into a glass, filled it with ice, and set it in front of their hostess.

"Thank you, sweetie." She returned the compact to her purse with a snap. "I haven't had a chance to talk with either one of you for ages, just ages. Did you hear what Verger tried to pull on me last week? About the beach house in Cannes? Can you believe that bastard *refuses* to let me use it? I mean, I'm allowed in May. May! What in God's name do you find in Cannes in May? Tourists!"

"Hard luck," Meg said. "Now, to get back to this Dr. Bob—"

"My dear!" Tiffany waved both hands distractedly. "My dear! If you knew what this divorce has done to me! I've been through tornadoes, blizzards, a tidal wave, a volcanic eruption, two hurricanes, a typhoon, and an earthquake that registered seven-point-one on the Richter scale. The divorce was worse. Far worse. If I didn't have this little affair coming up this week, I'd be in a rubber *room* somewhere. You two are saving my sanity. That's all I can say.'' She ran one scarlet-nailed hand through her champagne-colored hair and downed the gin and tonic with the other. ''Verger was a *bastard.* Just a *bastard.* He was a bastard when we got engaged, a bastard on the honeymoon, and a *super* bastard in bed. Bastard, bastard, *bastard.*'' She looked vicious. ''And the world's going to know just how much of a bastard. I've got them all lined up. All the wives of his so-called friends. They're all going to be here for the therapy sessions this week . . .'' She caught Meg's astonished face and said crossly, ''That's right there on the agenda. Right after your cooking classes or whatever. My secretary should have mailed you that weeks ago.''

She probably had. Quill, who hated going through mail, hadn't read anything but the maps, the airline tickets, and the check.

''Anyhow. I've invited the press to sit in—in the interest of getting information to those poor ol' women who can't afford to come, of course . . .''

''You've invited the press? To therapy sessions?'' said Quill.

''And why not?''

For a moment, nobody said anything.

Quill poured herself a cup of tea and sat next to Tiffany on the couch. ''Volcanic eruption?'' she asked, just to fill the silence. ''You've been through a volcanic eruption?''

''Hawaii,'' Tiffany said. ''A combination fund-raising and site selection trip for my little hospital. I'd planned to build it on the side of Haleakala mountain, with a marvelous view of the Kiluea Iki crater. But it blew up. Barfed lava and whatnot all over the place. You wouldn't have believed it. Red hot molten rock simply poured down the side of that mountain. It hit the ocean and smack—giant sauna. Clouds of steam everywhere. Marvelous, really, but my architect thought it might upset the patients."

Meg looked at Quill and raised her eyebrows. "So you decided to place it here, in Palm Beach," Meg said. "A hospital for phobics."

"Well, it's a lot calmer, really. You only get hurricanes a couple of months out of the year."

Meg's expression was innocently inquiring. "Any of the patients suffer from hurricane phobia?" She closed her eyes dreamily. "What would you call somebody who's terrified of hurricanes? An aeoliaphobe?"

"A what?" Quill demanded.

Meg gestured vaguely. "Winds. Aeolian is Greek for winds."

"My charity is for women afraid to marry wealth again. I told you that. It's not a phobia, they tell me. I may have told you that. But Dr. Bob straightened me out. It has to do with identity crises and that sort of thing. So Hawaii would have been perfect. I mean—between the ambiance and the beach boys, you can't get much more therapeutic than that. But the volcano worked out for the best. Things like that always do. For instance, I don't know if I could have gotten Meg to come to Hawaii to cook for my fund-raiser. It was hard enough to get you to come to Florida for two weeks."

Meg sat up straight. "It's a hospital for whom?"

"Women who've married wealth, gotten divorced, and are afraid to marry for money again," Tiffany said patiently. "I can't tell you how many of my dearest friends have gone through simply agonies. Agonies. One of them got a job in publishing rather than marry again."

"Shaw," said Meg, with a told-you-so look at Quill. "Old George Bernard himself. He asked Mrs. Siddons or somebody to go to bed with him for a million pounds and she smiled and said she'd think about it. And then he asked her to sleep with him for twenty pounds and she got indignant and shrieked, 'Sir! What do you think I am?' And he said 'Madam. We've established what you are. We are just trying to establish the price.' I knew it. Quill? We're here under false pretenses.''

''It wasn't Mrs. Siddons,'' said Quill, momentarily diverted. ''It was Mrs. Patrick Campbell. Mrs. Siddons lived a hundred years earlier.''

''What are you talking about?'' Tiffany said crossly. ''We're not talking about hookers, here.''

Meg grinned ominously. Quill was recalled to the task at hand, which was to keep the volatile Meg from annihilating Mrs. Taylor. She got up and fetched Meg a cup of strong tea. Meg took it, drank half in two swallows, and glowered.

''You wouldn't have, would you?'' Tiffany persisted.

''Wouldn't have what?'' asked Meg.

''Gone to Hawaii to cook for my fund-raiser.''

''I wouldn't have crossed the street for the fund-raiser if I knew what it was for—wealthy women who are afraid to marry wealth again?''

Quill sent a hasty prayer to whatever gods were in charge of Meg's temper. ''What Meg means, Tiffany, is that we're busy most of the year—''

''That's not what I meant,'' Meg said doggedly. ''What I meant was that a bunch of rich women who've gotten their big bucks from—''

Quill raised her voice. ''Early November's about the only time we could close the Inn and not lose a ton of money. And a week is the maximum time Meg can spend away from her kitchen without freaking out. So, no. We probably wouldn't have gone to Hawaii. Not if you wanted seven days of celebrity cooking lessons capped by a celebrity-cooked banquet. Between celebrities and jet lag Meg would have had to check into your hospital.''

''It's not for stress. I've told you what it's for. Women who are afraid to take a chance on mar—''

''Phooey,'' Meg interrupted rudely.

"You have doubts about it. I can see that. Both of you. Well, if you don't believe in the charity now, you will after you've met Dr. Bob." Tiffany's perfectly taut brow didn't wrinkle with sincerity, which it should have, since her tone was passionate with it. Quill remembered reading that in a full face lift, the surgeon peeled the skin off the forehead, severed the frown muscles, and pulled the extra skin over the skull. Tiffany's brow couldn't wrinkle if she wanted it to.

"It's not doubts, precisely," Quill began.

"It's doubts," said Meg flatly. "We've been seduced by the beaches and swimming in warm weather when everybody else at home is armpit-deep in snow. But we're getting unseduced fast. Of course we don't believe in a charity for wealthy women who have divorce phobias. Charities are for people in need."

"Exactly. Charities are for people in need. And need occurs at all levels of society. At all levels of income. Do you have any idea how neglected women such as myself and my friends are? Do you realize the kind of abuse we've taken from people like Verger?"

"Gee, no." Meg's own forehead wrinkled quite satisfactorily, which, Quill knew, frequently presaged an eruption quite as volcanic as Kiluea Iki's. "Unless your mother sold you to him at an early age, you had something to say about marrying him, didn't you? Plus, I can't say as I have a whole lot of sympathy for people who got the second-best Rolls in a settlement." She grabbed her head. "Aaagh! The bells!"

Tiffany glowed. "It's Dr. Bob." She uncrossed her legs and got up gracefully. "You're sure you don't want to do something about your hair, Quill?"

"Shall I get the door?" asked Quill politely.

"He'll use his key." She cocked her head, listening. Quill heard the door open, then the click of shoes on the wooden floor. Tiffany extended her hands. "And here he is. Darling!"

"My dear."

CHAPTER 2

Quill had imagined Dr. Bittern as a slick, smooth Richard Gere look-alike. He wasn't. The doctor (psychologist? psychiatrist? osteopath?) was small and shaped like a fire hydrant. It was hard to tell how old he was. (Quill was discovering that in Palm Beach it was hard to decide how old anybody was. Florida seemed to be the appearance-surgery capital of the world.) Dr. Bittern had silvery white hair—very thick—wire rimmed glasses, and a small black goatee. He stopped several feet in front of Tiffany, crossed his hands on his paunch, and beamed at her with the smile of a happy baby.

''Kiss, kiss,'' Tiffany cooed, pecking the air on either side of his cheeks. ''And here is our cook.''

''Chef,'' Meg corrected belligerently.

''Meg, may I introduce Dr. Robert Bittern? And Dr. Bob, this is Sarah Quilliam, Meg's sister.''

He inclined his head and, to Quill's surprise, gave Meg her proper title. ''Maitre Quilliam. An honor. And Ms. Quilliam? I have seen your art. It is wonderful.''

''Thank you—um—Dr. Bittern.''

He gestured toward the couch. "May I?"

"Please," said Tiffany. "Please. Dr. Bob . . ." She fluttered down next to him. "I am so glad you're here! I was just trying to explain the importance of our work to the girls . . ."

Meg made a noise like a steam kettle.

Tiffany acknowledged the reaction with a vague smile and murmured, "Women, then, and I can't do it half so well as you. No, not a tenth so well as you. If you would?"

"Perhaps a cup of tea, before we begin?" Dr. Bittern sat erect, his back several inches from the couch cushions. His voice was precise and his feet were tiny.

"Meg?" Tiffany all but snapped her fingers.

Quill looked at her sister. Meg looked back. For a moment, Meg's reaction hung in the balance. Suddenly she grinned, shook her head, and got up. "What kind would you like, Dr. Bittern? Black? Green?"

He waved a perfectly manicured hand in the air. His hands were small, too. "Something peaceful. Scented. Not too strong."

"Jasmine," said Meg. She walked behind the couch toward the kitchen, then turned and made a horrible face at Quill.

Quill cleared her throat. "You were telling us about the charity, Dr. Bittern."

"Excelsior," said Tiffany.

"I beg your pardon?" Quill said. It had sounded like a sneeze.

"Excelsior," said Dr. Bittern. "To indicate life's journey. One must move past the past. One must move onward, upward, to the pinnacle of experience."

"Tennyson," said Meg, setting a cup of tea on the marble slab in front of Dr. Bittern. "Same guy who wrote about Lancelot cleaving the heads off his enemies. 'My strength is of the strength of ten, because my heart is pure.' Whack!" She drew her finger across her throat execution-style and wiggled her eyebrows.

"That is a different poem, I believe," said Dr. Bittern gravely. "But yes, the name comes from the pen of that noble poet."

"So you're not an illiterate phony anyhow." Meg settled cheerfully on the arm of Quill's chair. "What kind of phony are you?"

"Hey!" said Tiffany. "Hey!"

Quill shoved her elbow sharply into Meg's leg. "Meg was up all night," she lied, "with a particularly difficult recipe . . ."

"No, I wasn't," said Meg. "But before I get involved with this thing I want to know what it's all about. If I'd known it was some screwy fund-raiser for a bunch of gold diggers, I would have stayed home."

Dr. Bittern cocked his head with a faraway expression, as though he was listening to a strain of music only he could hear. He crossed his hands over his paunch—a gesture Quill was beginning to recognize as very characteristic—and beamed impartially at the three of them. "Ms. Quilliam's objections are familiar to me—if somewhat infelicitously stated." He looked at Tiffany. "This is the sort of question we must anticipate from the press. I am, of course, prepared to answer."

"Good," said Meg. "I am prepared to listen."

A scuffling sound came from the patio outside. Quill turned her head. Three figures loomed against the glass. One of them was very tall. Quill had seen that face before—not fifteen minutes ago on the TV screen in the kitchen.

"Oh my God!" Tiffany shrieked. "It's Verger!"

The French door banged open. Verger Taylor stamped arrogantly into the room. With him were two young men. He came to a full stop and thrust his head forward. His fierce blue eyes raked over Meg and Quill, then rested on Dr. Bittern with the intensity of a mongoose after a snake. "You!" he said. He whirled on the balls of his feet. "Goddammit, Tiffany. I've had about enough of this. You're gonna cancel the whole goddamn thing—or you'll regret it. You got that?"

"How did you get in here?" Tiffany hunched back into the couch. "Who let you in here? I had the locks changed! Luis? Was it Luis? I'll kill him!"

"Not as much control as you thought you had, Tif? Told you it'd be different out there after being married to the Verbster." Taylor grinned nastily. He was tall—three or four inches over six feet—with the neck, shoulders, and belly of a defensive tackle who'd been benched too long. He was dressed in part of a three-piece suit in banker's gray; the vest hung open over a rumpled white shirt and his trousers belled over a low-slung belt. The suit coat was nowhere in evidence. He clutched a balled-up newspaper in one fist. "Verger Taylor," he grunted finally to Meg. "You this celebrity chef, or what?"

Tiffany's voice rose several decibels. "Isn't that just like you, Verger? She is not an 'or what.' She is not a thing. She is a woman. This is Margaret Quilliam, Verger, one of the few female three-star chefs—"

"Two star," Meg corrected with glum punctilio.

"—whatever—in the country. And I will not, I repeat, will not have you demeaning her with your macho, sexist, piggish attitudes."

Keeping his eyes on Meg, Verger swung his head rather like a bull that's been bitten in the ear. "What the hell, Tiffany."

"What the hell yourself." She hissed like a snake. "And you look at me when you talk to me, you bastard."

Verger's eyes flickered over Meg's dark head then took in her shorts and the newest in her T-shirt collection. He rolled his eyes, sighed, and shook his head. "It's taken Tif a while to get over the divorce, you see?" He gave Meg a grin meant to be complicit. "She's discovering what I told her—it's impossible to replace the Verbster. Lotta women'll tell you that." He hooked both thumbs through the buckle of his alligator belt and hitched up his trousers.

Tiffany screamed, "If you're not out of here in two seconds, I'm calling the cops!"

Verger sneered. "Ask for Captain Phillips. Old buddy of mine."

Tiffany spat, "Tell me what you want, then, and get out." Her face crumpled. Her eyes teared. "Can't you just leave me alone? I'm having a nice, quiet time with my friends . . ."

"Bullshit." His eyes flickered over Dr. Bittern. "Goddammit, Tiffany. This guy's a phony." His face reddened underneath the leather of a Florida tan. "I've warned you about this shitface before."

"Goddammit yourself," said Tiffany icily. "You leave Dr. Bob alone. He's a far, far better man than you will ever be."

Quill looked at Dr. Bittern, who seemed quite unperturbed by Verger's venom. Perhaps, like Sydney Carton, he was into self-sacrifice, but Quill doubted it.

Tiffany squalled suddenly, "What are you doing here, anyhow? How did you get a goddamn key? This condo's mine. Get out of here. And take those two little bastards with you."

"Who are these two guys?" Meg interrupted in an overly casual tone. "I know who you are—Verger Taylor. Anybody who watches CNN knows who you are. But who are they?"

Verger swung his head; his head and shoulders moved together, as though his neck were nonexistent. He used his height and weight like a club, Quill thought. Not a nice guy at all. She moved closer to Meg. "Can I get anyone anything to drink?" she asked brightly. "Would you like some planter's punch, Mr. Taylor? And what about your friends?"

"Those two aren't his friends," Tiffany said sulkily. "They're his sons. That's Corrigan"—she jerked her chin in the direction of a slight, blond boy of nineteen or so—"and the other one's Evan. And they're not staying long enough to have a drink."

Evan resembled his father in height—but the paternal genetics stopped there. He was dark, probably in his mid-twenties, and casually elegant. His voice was a pleasant baritone. "Sorry to barge in like this, but Dad has a couple of questions." He clapped his hand on his father's shoulder. "Take five, Dad. We'll get this sorted out. And I think a drink's a good idea."

"Yeah?" Verger's glower darkened.

"I do." Evan smiled at Quill. "We just need to talk a little bit. You're Sarah Quilliam?"

Quill nodded.

"I'm glad to meet you. My brother's glad, too. Aren't you, Cor?"

Corrigan blushed attractively, hunched his shoulders, and nodded.

Evan sighed and shook his head. "Graceless as Dad, bro. Believe it or not, Ms. Quilliam, we're here to talk things over. Like gentlemen. Right, Dad?"

"Sure," said Verger. "What about that drink?"

Evan sat down next to Quill. He smelled like soap and fresh air. "I had a professor at Yale who said that there is nothing in the human condition that is not ultimately compromisable. I've believed that ever since I heard it. There isn't any reason why all of us can't discuss Excelsior sensibly."

His father made a noise like a sneaky, angry dog.

"Dad?" Evan's smile was engaging.

"Okay." Verger slouched onto a kitchen stool. "Okay, kid. This is why I brought you along. You wanna negotiate with this little tart? You negotiate."

Tiffany went "huh" in a resigned way.

Evan leaned forward, his elbows on his knees. "Tif. We've had some good times, haven't we? At the beginning. When you first married Dad."

Tiffany's mouth thinned. "I've been in absolute hell since I signed the damn marriage certificate."

"Tif, that's just not true. Remember that trip we took? On the *Seamew*? Just the four of us?"

"What I remember is that I was goddamned seasick for two goddamn weeks."

"And remember how Dad took care . . ."

"I remember shit! I have had enough of this." Her voice rose to a shriek. "And you people here are witnesses to how these guys have harassed me for three years of the most miserable marriage a woman ever went through and are harassing me still." She closed her eyes, took a deep breath, and the color receded from her face. She waved her hand at Meg. "Get these people something to drink. Then maybe they'll get out of here."

"What I'm going to get," said Meg, "is a nap. And after the nap, I'm going to get a taxi to the airport. I'm going home. I refuse to get smack in the middle of a family squabble."

Quill stood up. Meg was right. She couldn't imagine anyone less of a victim than Tiffany Taylor. And she couldn't say "nice to have met you all," because it hadn't been.

Tiffany snapped, "Where do you two think you're going?"

Quill forced herself to smile. "I'm sorry, Tiffany. This kind of thing just isn't right for either Meg or me. We were hesitant about it from the start—and honestly, I don't think you'd be happy at how things would turn out if we stayed. We'll pay our own way back to New York."

Verger gave a whoop of triumph.

Tiffany's cornflower blue eyes were narrow slits. "The two of you aren't going anywhere. Meg signed a contract. Remember?"

"I didn't sign on for this," Meg said. "This is a circus. And you misrepresented that charity."

"I don't think—no, I don't think that you can afford a lawsuit." Tiffany's voice was sweet.

"Sure, she can," Verger said. "I'll pay for it."

''Fat chance,'' Meg snapped.

Tiffany shook her head. ''Oh, but all that time spent taking depositions and whatnot? She's a cook. And that's what cooks do for a living—cook. And she can't cook if she's in court.''

Meg's face went pink. She took a deep breath. Quill braced herself.

Dr. Bittern stood up and said gently, ''All this dissension. Please. If everyone would just sit down?'' He gestured toward the couches. ''Please.''

''Good idea, doc.'' Evan Taylor nodded vigorous approval, followed by Corrigan, who so far hadn't said a word. Verger drew a large cigar from his vest pocket and lit it, grinning unpleasantly.

Dr. Bittern inclined his head toward Quill. ''If you would, Ms. Quilliam, I will help you serve some wine. And we will all take a moment to calm ourselves.''

Verger spat tobacco leaf on the floor.

In the midst of a charged silence, Quill took a bottle of Pouilly Fuisse and the wine cooler from the refrigerator. Dr. Bittern set wineglasses on a tray. He uncorked the bottle, set it on the tray, and carried it back to the living room. He set the tray on the coffee table, poured six glasses, upended the empty bottle in the cooler, and passed the glasses around. Meg refused with a curt shake of her head.

''There,'' he said. ''We are set. Now.'' He sat down primly next to Tiffany. ''What seems to be the chief trouble here? We will sort it out. You, Mâitre Quilliam, thought that perhaps you would combine a nice vacation with some charitable work? And you, Quill, loyal to your sister, have accompanied her. You, Mr. Taylor, are afraid that this charitable work will in some way embarrass you?''

''Damn straight,'' Verger grunted. ''Look at this damn thing.'' He waved the crumpled newspaper at them. ''You know what this goddamn headline says? ''Spurned Wife's Last Laugh!'' This charity's a joke.

Lemme tell you right here. Right now. Nobody laughs at me. Nobody.''

''People have laughed at you for years, Verger,'' said Tiffany. ''Years.''

''We will not pursue this,'' Dr. Bittern said firmly. ''What we will pursue is calm. Life is a journey. For those who are depressed, who are unenlightened, it is a downward journey. But for those whose eyes are on the stars . . .''

''Bullshit. My eye's on what's going on right in front of my nose.'' His gaze rested on his ex-wife. ''You still going through with this?''

''You'll see who my friends are, Verger. You'll see. Everyone's coming this week. Simply everyone. You can't bully me anymore, Verger.''

''Right. I wouldn't count on it, if I were you.'' Verger tossed his cigar in the sink. ''Evan, Corrigan. We're going.''

Evan shrugged, smiled at Quill, and joined his brother and father. Verger went to the French door, opened it, and turned back to confront them. His eyes reflected red in the light of the lamps. ''I stopped by to tell you, Tiffany, that this shit's gotta stop, and Evan thought he could goddamn reason with you and look what happened. So listen up. I see one more newspaper article about your goddamn therapy club, I'm taking this condo, the Palm Beach house, the Westchester house, and I'm gonna goddamn burn them down. You got that?''

''You wouldn't dare. You wouldn't dare.''

His teeth flashed white. ''Try me, sweetie. Just try me.'' He swiveled heavily on his feet. ''And as for you two. Quilliam, isn't it? I've checked out that cute little place you've got in New York. There's a nice fat mortgage on it—what was the balance, Evan?''

''Dad, I really don't think . . .''

Verger snapped his fingers.

''Three-hundred-fifty-three thousand,'' said Corrigan.

''At seven and one-eighth.'' He blushed apologetically. ''Sorry.''

Verger cocked his head at Quill. ''You two prepared to pay that out if the note's called? You think about it. Think about it hard.''

Tiffany leaped to her feet. ''You wait just a minute, Verger.''

The door slammed and they were gone.

CHAPTER 3

Meg hung up the phone with a sigh.

Quill had opened the French doors to the morning air. Sun streamed across the floor. The view of the Atlantic was dreamlike. Little flags that indicated the presence of scuba divers bounced along the water side of the sea wall. Three fishing boats floated peacefully on the water beyond the buoys marking the channel entrance to the Port of Palm Beach. The Combers Beach Club was located on the west end of Palm Beach key. There were two stacks of three-story-high condominiums. Both stacks faced the Atlantic on the west and the channel on the north. Singer Island—Palm Beach's poorer cousin—lay straight across the channel. Quill, who'd placed a kitchen stool in front of the open French doors so that she could watch the water, wriggled her bare toes in the sunlight. "What does Howie say?"

Meg sipped coffee. Her dark hair was ruffled. She was still in her nightgown. Quill, who had been swimming in the heated pool, rubbed her face with a towel and looked with concern at her sister. After a moment, she got up, picked the stool up and carried it back to the island separating the kitchen from the living room.

"Well, he didn't like getting up this early."

"Did he give you an opinion?"

"He's a lawyer. He'll have to go to the office and look up the contract I signed. So I didn't get an opinion; I got an impression. But it's his impression that I'm stuck." She smiled. "I'm stuck unless I want to spend a whole pile of time in court. And Howie thinks I'd lose."

"What about Verger's threat to call in the mortgage?"

Meg tugged at her hair. "Howie will check with the bank. He says it'd be unusual, the bank selling just the one mortgage out. But it can be done."

"Good grief. Where the heck would we get three-hundred and fifty-three thousand dollars?"

"From another bank, of course. But Howie says that takes time, and that Taylor can force us to pay on demand. You know what this is like, Quill? Those old Victorian melodramas. 'I can't pay the rent.' 'You must pay the rent.' Jeez. What have I gotten us into?"

"We're both in it," said Quill cheerfully. "What do you want to do?"

"Stick with it for the moment, I guess. Howie says it is much more likely that I'd get sued for breach of contract and lose than we'd forfeit the Inn. And the publicity would be awful for my career." She sighed. "Those people seem to spend their lives on the front pages anyway. Quill, I think they like the attention!"

"You could be right."

"You're not stuck, though. Why don't you go on home? I'll stay here."

"Okay."

"Quill!"

"Just kidding. Of course I'm not going to leave you to these hyenas."

"Evan didn't seem that much of a hyena," Meg said.

"He didn't, did he? And brother Corrigan looked okay. Maybe a little shy. Which marriage are they from?"

Meg shrugged. "Who knows? God, Quill. What a crew. It's almost as bad as the McIntosh wedding at the Inn. We got through that with only a couple of bodies."

"And we'll get through this. Body-free, unless Tiffany loses it altogether and shoots Verger. If she does, I'll be the first to testify in her defense. Evan seemed sympathetic. Maybe what I can do today while you're with chef whatsis is look him up and talk to him. Maybe he can keep Verger from burning the place down around our ears." She recalled Taylor's specific threat and added glumly, "Literally. Just let me get showered and dressed, and we'll go on to the culinary institute." She went down the hall to the bedroom that had been reserved for her use and rummaged through her suitcase. "What's on the agenda for today?"

"What?" Meg appeared at the door. They'd had an amiable squabble over who should take what bedroom. The master suite—which Meg had insisted on leaving to Quill—had a splendid view of the ocean. Oversized sliding glass doors led to a small stone patio circled by planters filled with impatiens, bougainvillea and gardenias. Beyond the patio, green lawn swept to the sea.

"I said, what's on the schedule for today?"

"Oh." Meg's face brightened. "It's not too bad, actually. I'm meeting with Maitre Jean Paul Bernard to go through the banquet menu and discuss the cooking classes. I've always wanted to meet him. His soufflés are outstanding. Just outstanding. And I heard through the grapevine that he's developed a variation on my marinade for potted rabbit that's incredible. He's amazing, Quill. It's his versatility that's so impressive. I mean—he's meats *and* desserts, which is a rare combination."

"But I meant more in the line of how I should dress. Florida casual? New York chic? Beach bum? What?"

"Well, we're touring the institute. And we're meeting Linda whosis . . ."

"Longstreet."

"Whatever. And she'll show us the facilities and go over the guest list, so I suppose you should wear whatever you want to wear. It's nothing very formal. I told them we'd be there at ten, but it's quite casual."

"What are you wearing?"

Meg glanced down at her nightshirt. It was the purple one with the puppy logo and the message IN DOG YEARS, I'M DEAD. "I don't know. All I brought were my T-shirts. And my tocque, of course."

Quill sighed. "One of us should look like we know what we're doing. I'll have to put on a suit."

"Poor Quillie. Are you sure you don't want to go home?" She grinned in response to the look on Quill's face, turned on her heel, and disappeared. Her voice floated down the hall. "Don't answer that. I'll be ready in ten minutes."

Quill pulled a cream linen suit from its hanger and found a black scoop-necked bodysuit to go with it. The humidity was doing violent things to her hair, and after a brief struggle with the mass of curls, she combed it out and scooped it on top of her head. She checked her briefcase to make sure she'd kept all of Tiffany's directions. By the time she emerged from the bedroom, Meg (dressed in black trousers and a T-shirt that read LOOK BUSY! JESUS IS COMING!) was wandering disconsolately around the living room. Quill recognized the attitude: precooking nerves.

"Have you got your menus?"

"Yes."

"And your chef's gear?"

Meg picked up her tote bag. It was packed with her knives, her hat, and her tunic. "Yes."

"Don't brood. We'll get through this. You'll be magnificent. Even if it is pearls before swine."

"I'm homesick."

"You can't be homesick. We've been here less than eighteen hours."

"Seems like years. What do we do now?"

Tiffany's New York–based secretary had sent a sheaf of instructions relating to the condo, the car, and their itinerary to the Inn three weeks before they'd left. Quill snapped open her briefcase, pulled out the memo, and referred to page three, which read:

> *Monday* A.M. Car has been left for you with Luis, the concierge. His office is to the left of the parking lot as you exit number 110. It will take you fifteen minutes to get to the institute, depending on traffic.

A clearly drawn map was printed at the bottom of the page.

"Okay," said Quill. "First, we find Luis."

Outside, the sun was glorious: warm, radiant, and effulgent gold. Quill's mood lifted into euphoria. Her early morning swim had left her feeling relaxed, and the weather was like a caress. Feathery white clouds drifted along the edges of the horizon. "I wish Myles were here right now."

"Thursday. He and Andrew will be here Thursday." Meg tugged at her hair absentmindedly; her mind was already dealing with clarified butter and pinches of spice. "How are we supposed to get there? Are they sending a car?"

"We're supposed to find Luis. And then I'm going to drive us."

Meg stopped dead. "You're going to what?"

Quill put her hand at the small of Meg's back and propelled her gently forward. A sign to the left of the parking lot read: OFFICE—LUIS MENDOZA, MANAGER. A small, hand-written sign below it read: COMPUTERS RE-

PAIRED. "The map's really clear. And how bad can Florida traffic be?"

"Quill. No offense, but if there's a worse driver in the seven states between here and New York, I would like to meet him. Or her. I am not, I repeat *not*, going to ride with you to an unknown destination in a car you haven't been in before. And that's flat. We'll get a cab."

"We don't need a cab. Look. This must be Mr. Mendoza." She waved at a young man with black hair and olive skin who'd come out of the office. He was dressed in a royal blue shirt with the Combers Beach Club emblem on the pocket.

"How do you know that's Mr. Mendoza?" Meg whispered. "It could be somebody else. And Luis Mendoza's the name of a famous boxer."

"It says 'Luis' on his name tag, he's carrying the kind of teeny screwdriver they repair computers with, and he's obviously a computer-repairing concierge with the name of a famous boxer. Which is what the sign says." Quill waved as they approached. "*Buenas dias, Señor.*"

"*Buena.*" He nodded politely to them. "You are guests, here, madam?"

"Yes. Mrs. Taylor's guests. I'm Sarah Quilliam, and this is Margaret Quilliam. We're here for a car, I think."

"We're here for a taxi," said Meg firmly. "If you could call us one, please, Mr. Mendoza, I would appreciate it very, very much."

"They just call me Luis here." He grinned. "And Mrs. Taylor's car is a very fine one. I doubt that you'd need a taxi."

"We need a taxi," Meg said.

"What kind of a car is it?" Quill asked.

"A Mercedes. The small one. The one Señora Taylor doesn't like."

"A Mercedes?" Meg said. "She doesn't like a Mercedes?"

"The color," said Luis expressionlessly. "It's black. Where are you going?"

"The Florida Institute for Fine Food," Quill said.

"The address?"

"Ummm . . ." Quill referred to the paper. "One Sea View Drive."

"Ah. One moment, please." He vanished inside his office, leaving the door open. Quill and Meg followed him in. The office was small, but efficiently furnished. A row of metal filing cabinets stood against one wall. Long benches ran the length of another. PCs, laptops, desktops, and printers lay in various stages of assembly on the benches.

Luis's desk was in the center of the room. There was a sleek IBM computer, printer, and external hard drive on it, and nothing else. He sat down and key-stroked rapidly. Quill, who was a little afraid of computers, admired his apparent expertise. The printer began to hum and spit out a colored map.

"Here you are," Luis said. "I just bought Find It! software. Amazing, isn't it? Tells you the quickest way to get to the institute."

"Thank you," Quill said. She took it. The instructions were different from those on the memo from New York.

"Now, if you'd like to wait just a minute, I'll bring the Mercedes around for you."

"A Mercedes," said Meg again. "Good grief."

"There, you see?" Quill smiled with what she hoped was a lot of confidence. They walked out of the office together and back into the sunshine. "One of the best cars ever if you have to be in an accident . . . not," she added hastily, "that there's going to be an accident. Look, Meg. Here's Luis's map. We take a left out of the parking lot, go to the light, and straight on through to Forty-fifth Street. We take a right on Forty-fifth, go down six blocks, and take a left again into the institute. Left-right-left. What could be simpler?" She reexamined the map from New York. "Even simpler than that is Interstate 95. That'll get us there in ten minutes."

''With you driving, quantum physics could be simpler.''

''Oh, ha.'' She clutched Meg's arm. Luis drove a small sports car out of the garage and pulled up in front of them. ''Oh, Meg. The car!''

''What about it? It's black. It's dinky . . .''

''It's a 380 SE! And it's incredible! Meg, please. No taxi. I've always wanted to drive one of these.'' She grinned happily at Luis, who grinned back. He got out of the car and handed her the keys.

Meg shook her head. ''You? And a Mercedes? You're kidding.''

''I am not kidding. You remember when I was driving a cab in New York?''

''There are a lot of traffic police who remember you driving a cab in New York.''

''Well, one thing that experience taught me is to appreciate fine machinery. This is one of the best-made cars in the world.''

''You've been my sister for how long?''

''Too long.''

''And still you constantly surprise me. Okay. No cab. But if I'm late to this meeting, Quill, you're dead. And if we crash, you're even deader.'' She rolled her eyes at Luis, who made a sympathetic clicking sound. ''Tell us to go with God, or something.'' She tossed her tote bag into thc boot and slid into the passenger seat. Quill opened the driver's side door, slid in, and sat down with a feeling of awe.

''May you go with God,'' Luis responded in an accommodating way. He leaned over the door. ''And watch out for the traffic on Broadway. It's a killer.''

''The freeway looks faster,'' Quill said.

Luis looked alarmed. ''I don't think . . .''

''This car's got an automatic shift,'' Quill said. ''Darn it. Watch out for the what?'' She moved into reverse. Luis leaped out of the way. She put her foot on the accelerator and shot backwards.

Meg twisted around and said briefly, "Missed it."

"Missed what?"

"Never mind. Just slow down, Quill. If the map is right, we've got plenty of time."

"The traffic," Luis called. "Be careful! Don't take 95!"

"Ten minutes," said Quill confidently. "Tops."

An hour and a half later, Quill pulled into the parking of the Florida Institute for Fine Food and came to a shaky halt.

"We're late," said Meg, her voice tight.

"I know we're late."

"It wasn't your fault," Meg said carefully. "I understand that it wasn't your fault."

"Meg, I've never seen such traffic in my life. Not even in Times Square. At rush hour."

Meg leaned back in the seat. The top was still down, and ninety minutes in the hot Florida sun had turned her face pink. "Lunatics," she said, staring upwards. "Crazed kids going a hundred miles an hour. Stroke victims going twenty miles an hour. Vacationers pulling U-turns on a four-lane expressway. Truck drivers cussing in at least three different languages. Even LA was never like this. Now, Quill, if you don't mind, I have just a few suggestions about driving in this type of—"

"I mind." Crossly, Quill put the car into park and eased herself out of the front seat. She took a couple of deep breaths and said with a brightness even she found artificial, "Look how lovely this place is, Meg. It's all pink stucco. And it's right on the ocean."

"I don't give a hoot about the stucco. You either listen to me, or we spend the rest of the week in taxis. Which will totally destroy any profit we could have hoped to make out of this trip."

"We won't take the freeway next time."

"We'll take a cab next time. And the time after that. At least we can cower in the back seat together. I was afraid to close my eyes. I was afraid to keep my eyes open. I was petrified!"

"You couldn't be," said a hurried voice in Quill's ear, "the Quilliams?"

Quill jumped and turned. A pleasant woman with an anxious face took several steps backward. She was somewhere in her twenties. Her dark hair was pulled back in a ponytail. She wore a cardigan sweater and a long cotton skirt. Quilt wondered about the cardigan. The temperature was in the upper eighties and climbing. "I'm sorry if you're not the Quilliams, but I've heard about the way you squabble." She flushed, embarrassed. "I mean . . ."

"It's okay," said Meg. "We're the Quilliams."

"I'm Linda Longstreet?" she said, as though she questioned the fact. "You aren't Sarah and Meg?"

"I'm Sarah. Please call me Quill. And this is my sister, Meg."

"Thank goodness. Thank goodness. I was so worried. So worried. I thought something happened to you."

"We took I-95," said Meg grimly.

"Oh. At this time of day it shouldn't be too bad."

"It gets worse?" said Meg. "It can't possibly get worse."

"Oh, sure it can get worse. But please, come in. We've all been waiting. And waiting." She bit nervously at a forefinger. "And of course the electrical power would decide to play tricks on us this morning . . . But now you're here and everything's going to be just fine. Just fine."

"I'm really sorry," Quill said as they walked across the parking lot. "But we were trapped by an accident, and there was no way to call."

"What's wrong with the electrical system?" Meg asked. "Are the ovens down? Are the refrigerators down?"

Linda stopped in the middle of the lot. "It's not as bad as last week," she said reassuringly. "We didn't lose a thing. The food's just fine. I think.'' She looked around, bewildered, seemed to recall where she was, and headed toward the building again.

''And this is just an introductory meeting, isn't it?'' asked Meg. ''I mean—you didn't have anyone waiting for us. Did you?''

Linda stopped again. Quill had never seen anyone as easily distracted. ''Well, they all left after the first hour, I'm afraid. Except for Chef Jean Paul. And he can't leave, you know, since he works here. And lives here. He's got an apartment over the Food Gallery.''

''All left?'' said Meg. ''All who?''

''Well, there were the folks from Carpe Tedium . . .''

''From where?'' asked Quill.

''It's a choral group. They rewrite songs from the forties for the nineties. Retired people, mostly. They sing stuff like 'Come to Me, My Melantonin Baby' and 'Prozac Lane'—instead of 'Primrose Lane,' you know? Here we are, just up these steps.''

Quill followed Linda up a short flight of steps to a cool, green atrium. A large fountain splashed in the middle. An ice sculpture of a swan had been placed on the lip of the fountain. It dripped forlornly in the heat.

''That was the only casualty today,'' Linda said brightly.

Meg gave Quill a frantic look. Quill said, with determined good humor, ''Linda, this building is lovely!''

''It is, isn't it?'' said Linda, without looking around. ''If I could just get some reliable electricians . . . We'll just go through here, through Le Nozze.''

''So this is the institute's restaurant,'' said Meg.

They paused inside the door. The dining room was deserted at that hour, but preparations for lunch were under way. The tables had been set with yellow and blue pottery place settings. The clatter of pots and the smell of garlic came from the archway of a vast lighted room at the far end of the dining area. Quill got a quick impression of polished wood, French blue wallpaper, and tile floors. "It's great."

"It's cold," said Meg. "Is everything in Florida air conditioned?"

"Oh, yes. Basswood," said Linda. "The wainscotting, that is. And the striped wallpaper's from—oh, I can't remember." She halted, her hand on a door marked STUDENTS ONLY PLEASE. "Look, I'm afraid Jean Paul's in a bit of a snit."

"He is?" said Meg.

"Well, we wanted to surprise you. I mean, your reputation and all. So he had all of his fourth-level students—there's only six—prepare a sample of each of his soufflés. He's famous for his soufflés, you know."

"Soufflés," said Meg. "Oh, no."

"And they were *timed* you see, to be presented at precisely ten-ten, since he thought you would be here at ten o'clock and no chef, he said, is ever very late to meet another chef because it would be famously rude . . ."

"Wow," said Meg. "They all sank?"

Linda's expression was woeful. "They all sank. If you'd only been half an hour late, it would have been okay, because the clocks were all wonky from the power outage and it was really ten-thirty-five." She tipped sideways suddenly. Quill grabbed her before she could fall over. "Sorry. I forgot I was standing up. And he sent the audience home."

"He had an audience?"

"The Carpe Tedium people. I think I mentioned that before. They've been marvelous about fund-raising for the institute, and of course three of them are on the board of directors. Jean Paul wanted to give them the special honor of meeting you and eating his souffles . . . Well." Linda took a deep breath and shoved open the door. "I guess we'd better face it."

"Oh, lord," Meg muttered. She shifted her tote over her shoulder. "You know, Linda, maybe if I called Jean

Paul on the phone and gave him a chance to cool down . . .''

''Too late,'' said Linda. ''He saw you pull into the parking lot. Through the kitchen window on the third floor. I think he's still there, in the charcuterie kitchen. But everyone else has left. It's just up these stairs, here.'' She turned and trotted up, puffing a little in agitation.

''There's something very anxiety-making about going up stairs to meet a cranky chef,'' Quill muttered. ''You can't go too fast, because it's up. So you're going slowly, slowly to your doom. I'll just bet it isn't Jean Paul at the top of these stairs, it's Verge the Scourge himself, holding our mortgage in both hands, in pursuit of my fair white body.''

''Shut up,'' Meg hissed. Then, as she followed Linda through a heavy, metal door, she said in an artificially hearty tone, ''Mâitre?''

The kitchen was empty. Long windows lined the outside wall, giving a spectacular view of the ocean. Three large stainless steel bakery ovens banked the walls to the left of the windows; two heavy stainless-steel doors and several oak-faced storage bins lined the wall opposite. They'd entered though a door in the fourth wall. This wall was made entirely of glass, presumably so that an audience could look in and watch the professionals at work.

A large center island dominated the room. The shelving underneath contained pans of all kinds: narrow aluminum cradles used to make Parisian breads, Bundt pans, tiny tart tins. Saucepans of various sizes hung from brackets suspended over the marble-topped island. On the top of the island were a dozen or more deflated soufflés, like parachutes collapsed after an invasion of midget paratroopers.

''Oh, dear,'' Quill said.

''Chef Bernard?'' Meg called.

''The bread closet,'' Linda said. ''He ends up there at least once a week.'' She sat on one of the high stools lining the island and picked morosely at a puddle of chocolate. A spoonful dripped onto her cardigan.

"Well, where is the bread closet?" Meg asked briskly.

Linda pointed to a wooden door set between two double ovens. Meg shrugged, pulled a face at Quill, marched over to the door, and tapped lightly on it. "Mâitre?"

The door swung open. Chef Jean Paul Bernard sat inside on a barrel labeled FLOUR. He was tall and thin, with the mournful eyes of one of the larger breeds of hounds. He had mutton chop whiskers and a toupee, both colored the coffee-brown particular to the French.

"Mâitre Bernard," Meg said firmly, "*permittez-moi je voudrais-vous presente ma soeur, Sarah et mois. Je la regrette. . . .*"

"Vous *la regrette*!" Chef Jean Paul cried. "Je *la regrette! C'est une catastrophe!*" He bounded to the table, gestured dramatically at the ruined desserts, and began to cry. Large tears rolled down his face and into his whiskers. Quill was reminded of the Mock-Turtle in Lewis Carroll, and suppressed a giggle. The giggle didn't stay where it should have. She bit her lip hard, counted backwards from ten, and grabbed Linda Longstreet's arm, whispering, "Why don't we let them sort it out by themselves?"

"Do you really think so?"

"I really think so. Meg's great in a crisis like this. She empathizes."

"*Quelle dommage,*" Meg said to John Paul in a kindly tone. She dug into her tote and produced a Kleenex. "*Et vous, the mâitre!*" She patted the chef on the back.

Quill suspected that even Meg's French, which was excellent, wasn't up to the voluble harangue that followed this expression of sympathy. The institute, Quill gathered, had never appreciated the genius of him, Jean Paul, the master. She, Meg, had obviously not been informed of the specialities of the house, which had been prepared for her. But Linda, the manager. What a stupid! She tripped over her own boot laces, that one! She, Meg, a chef of the highest repute, although a woman (Quill mentally crossed her fingers at that one—but Meg merely continued to nod sympathetically) and a *petite* of the highest beauty (Meg smiled briefly) could *jamais jamais!* understand the indignities that he was forced to suffer daily. The power failed all the time. Linda forgot to pay people. He, himself, worked for a mere pittance. He would sell this place! For a sou! For less than half a sou!

"Can he?" asked Quill.

"Can he what?"

"Sell the Institute."

"He owns some stock," said Linda doubtfully, "and some holding company owns the rest. I suppose he'd have to, if the holding company sold out. Why? Do you understand all of that gibberish?"

"Some of it," said Quill. "Meg's more fluent. She's the one who spent a year in Paris."

"He'll start on me, next," said Linda gloomily. "He always does. What's he saying now?"

Quill turned her back on Jean Paul, who had started on Linda's ancestry in a villainous tirade. "He's just hollering," she said firmly. "I think we should make a diplomatic exit. Meg will bring him around."

They left quietly, shutting the door softly behind them. For a moment, Quill watched them through the glass. Jean Paul waved his arms frantically over his head, jabbed his finger three times into the air, and scowled ferociously. Meg nodded, shook her head in what appeared to be sorrowful agreement, then took a small pastry knife from the knife block and carefully cut a piece from a pale pile of soufflé.

"The Grand Marnier," said Linda, in a worshipful way.

Meg chewed the soufflé slowly, carefully. Jean Paul leaned forward in eager attention, a basset hound on point. She nodded, murmuring. Jean Paul broke into a weak smile that grew broader as Meg continued.

"What'd she say?" Linda asked.

"I think her first word was almond. Then she said 'have you ever tried . . . ' something something. I'm not good at lip reading."

Linda shrugged. "Chefs. Go figure. At least he's stopped crying. I hate it when they cry. Listen, how about some lunch?"

"I'd love it," said Quill.

"Good. I have a phone call to return. From Verger Taylor, if you can believe it! Anyway, we came through Le Nozze on our way up. You remember? I'll meet you there."

Quill followed her to the top of the stairs. "Do you have much to do with Verger Taylor?"

"Me? No. His wife—ex-wife, that is—is very interested in the Institute. Well, you know that, of course, because she's the one who got you here." She cast a harried look over her shoulder. Meg and Jean Paul were seated opposite one another, both nodding, both talking a mile a minute. "And thank goodness you are here, no matter what Mr. Taylor says. I haven't seen Jean Paul this relaxed for weeks."

"Linda, we had a rather unpleasant visit from Verger Taylor last night . . ."

Linda clutched her arm. "Hang on a second."

Jean Paul rose to his full height, grabbed a saucepan from the hanging brackets, and whacked it several times against the marble pastry top. He flung the pan across the room, gestured widely, and laughed. Meg smiled agreeably.

"See that?" Linda said proudly. "He's going to have a very good day." A pale smile crossed her face. "You just take any empty table at Le Nozze. The maître d' today is Greg. I think. I may have forgotten to post the schedule. I think I did forget to post the schedule. Well, someone will be there. I hope. Just tell him I'm joining you.''

''Okay. But Linda, I do want to talk to you about Taylor. How much of a threat is he . . .''

''And I want to talk to you about your lecture! Fundamentals of Innkeeping. The board of directors told me last week that I needed a few pointers. I mean, an institute isn't all that much like an inn, but Mrs. Goldwyn says that management is management.'' She tripped over a box of canning jars that had been left in the hallway corner, righted herself, and looked at her watch. ''My gosh! It's after twelve. I've got to return that phone call. See you in a few minutes. We'll talk then, I promise.'' She took off down the stairs at a run. Quill hoped she didn't fall down a rabbit hole.

Quill clattered down the stairs after her and entered Le Nozze from the STUDENTS ONLY door. It really was a very attractive restaurant, she thought. It had some of the qualities of the dining rooms in Provençal with dark wood wainscoting and terrazzo floors. The regency-style chairs were upholstered in a satiny dark green-, yellow-, and cream-striped fabric. But it had a nice, south Florida touch, too. Some really good pieces of sculptured glass—a dolphin, a miniature sloop, a narwhale—stood on the waist-high wooden room dividers.

Quill introduced herself to Bruce, the maître d' (he *knew* Greg was supposed to be on, but no one had posted a schedule), who bowed and seated her at a window overlooking the grounds. The only other occupied table was several feet away. Quill nodded to the two well-preserved ladies sitting over wine and opened the menu.

CHAPTER 4

Quill read the menu with professional interest. The dishes were varied, the prices quite reasonable. She'd try the wild mushrooms in pastry. It was a simple dish, and a good test of the saucier. She looked up for Bruce and blinked. Two ladies at the next table were watching her with unabashed interest. "That shade of Hey Sailor Red hair dye won't last in this Florida sunshine," said the widow with the metallic gold shoes and matching handbag. "Waste of money. Cheap looking, too."

"It's natural, Bea. And don't shout so. She'll hear you." The widow in the lavender, pink, and mauve silk jogging suit took a sip of her white wine, set the glass firmly on the dining table, and rolled her eyes at Quill.

Both of the ladies discussing her hair were over forty-five—how far over Quill couldn't tell. Plastic surgery, alpha-hydroxy treatments, and laser resurfacing tended to homogonize people's ages in Palm Beach. She did know they were widows: Both of them had wedding bands with Ritz-sized diamonds on their right ring fingers.

"I don't shout, Birdie," said Bea. "You've accused me of shouting ever since you got that damn miniaturized hearing aid and you're just showing off."

Quill mentally added twenty years to the ladies' ages.

"Pardon me, Bea?" asked Birdie sweetly. "You're mumbling again." She caught Quill's eye, smiled widely, and called out, "Are you here for the classes?"

Startled at being directly addressed, Quill bent forward. "Excuse me?"

"Margaret Quilliam's cooking classes," said Bea with satisfaction. "We've been waiting months to learn from her."

"Since mid-September, Bea," said Birdie. "Six weeks. We've been waiting six weeks, which is long enough, for goodness' sake. When you're our age, you never know if you've got another six weeks."

"Chef Quilliam's my sister."

"Your *sister*!" Bea waved her arms excitedly. The thick gold bracelets on her arms collided with a dull thud. Real gold, then. Quill decided that Bea must be wearing something in the aggregate of fifty thousand dollars around her neck and wrists and in her ears. "May we join you? We'd love to hear what it's like living with a famous chef."

Birdie, who was plump, wriggled out of her chair, pattered to Quill's table and sat down without waiting to hear her demurral through. Bea, rather more deliberately, gathered her gold-trimmed tote bag, gold-rimmed sunglasses and glass of wine. "You don't mind, do you? It's just that there's so little to do here! We're just dying for conversation other than our own."

"Of course not. Please." Quill indicated the empty space next to her with a generous wave of her arm.

Bea deposited her tote bag under the table and sat down. "Bea Gollinge," she said, "and this is my friend Birdie McIntyre. We're two-thirds of the Lunch Bunch."

"Two-thirds?"

"Selma Goldwyn isn't here." Bea leaned forward. "She had a little fix-me-up scheduled this morning."

"Face peel," Birdie said succinctly. "Upper lip."

"Absolutely refuses to touch the laser," Bea added. "Selma's always been a conservative."

"Which is ridiculous," said Birdie, "because the laser's so much safer. And who are you?"

Somewhat taken aback, Quill introduced herself.

"I demand to know what your secret is," Birdie said. "Tell!"

Quill had few secrets and sometimes thought herself the more boring for it.

"You're looking puzzled. She's looking puzzled, Bea."

"For staying so slim," Bea explained. "I mean—your sister. That marvelous, marvelous food. How can you eat it and not gain weight? Or do you turn it down?"

"I usually don't have time to sit and eat when Meg's in the kitchen. We have a small hotel in addition to our restaurant and that keeps me fairly busy."

"I should think so." Bea dived under the table, reemerged with her tote bag, and took a compact from it. The compact was covered with diamonds. Quill wondered if they were real. "My first husband was a restaurateur and it ate his *life*. He spent more time in the kitchen than with me. And had a lot more fun there, too. I don't know where we found the time to have three kids."

Quill murmured polite wonderment.

"And five grandchildren," said Bea. Her hand dived into the tote once more and reemerged with a fistful of photographs.

"Not *now*, Bea." Birdie took the pictures from her friend's hand and shoved them firmly back into the tote. "And your husband?"

"Oh, I'm not married."

"But engaged to be." Bea took her left hand. "Quarter caret. Nice. What's he in?"

"In? You mean what does he do? He used to be chief of detectives with the Manhattan homicide squad. He's a private investigator now. For a short time, he was the sheriff in Hemlock Falls. That's where Meg and I are from."

"A detective!" said Birdie. "How exciting. Does he look like Travis McGee?"

Quill smiled. "I think he's better-looking than Travis McGee."

"And he's with you now, dear?"

"He's coming Thursday, for a long weekend."

"I see Mrs. McIntyre and Mrs. Gollinge have been entertaining you." Linda Longstreet settled opposite Quill with a sigh. She was paler than ever, and she shivered in the chill of the air conditioning. "You've been introduced? Mrs. Gollinge and Mrs. McIntyre are on our board of directors, Quill."

"We've gotten most of her life history," said Bea. "And we'll get the rest if you give us half a chance. How are you, Linda? I see that Chef Quilliam must have arrived, since her sister's here in the restaurant."

"Oh, were you among the audience waiting this morning?" asked Quill. "I'm so sorry we missed the soufflés. I hadn't driven I-95 before, you see, and it was all my fault."

"You drove the freeway?" Bea said. "My dear, say no more. Say no more. What an awful experience for you. Bruce! Bring Ms. Quilliam some wine."

"I really think I should eat something first," said Quill.

"Nonsense," Bea said briskly. "Birdie, slice her some of our bread. No, no, you just sit there, my dear."

Birdie bounced up and over to her table, grabbed the bread, and bounced back again. Bruce came over with a chilled bottle wrapped in a napkin. Quill sat rather helplessly and watched. She nibbled at the bread, sipped at the wine, and decided to remain quiet.

Bea tapped her forefinger briskly on the tabletop. "And how are things going, Linda? Everything straightened out after that little contretemps with the plumbing this morning?"

"Well, the plumbing's fixed, but the electrical system's on the fritz again." She picked up the menu, set it down, tapped her fingers against the water glass, then signaled for the headwaiter.

"You don't look fine," said Birdie. "You look worried."

"Harassed," added Bea. "But then, you always looked harassed, Linda dear. You need to slow down. Is Chef Jean Paul throwing hissy fits again? Is that what's got you all in a fidget?" She twinkled at Quill. "Linda's the world's best customer for Maalox, aren't you, dear? I'm so glad I own stock in pharmaceuticals."

"Yes. I mean, no, Jean Paul's fine. I just checked. He and your sister"—she glanced nervously at Quill—"are getting along like a house afire. They're hanging the rabbit."

"The rabbit?" Quill frowned. "Oh. For the potted rabbit."

"Yes."

"Did she cry? Meg always cries when she has to hang the rabbit."

"They both cried," said Linda, "and Chef Jean Paul said a little prayer."

"Well, it's dead, isn't it?" asked Bea. "I mean, it's not as though she has to . . ." she made a sharp twisting motion with both hands.

"Humanely killed," said Linda absently. "And we are very careful where we buy our stock from. They're in nice, airy cages . . ."

"I," said Bea firmly, "am having vegetarian today. What about you, Birdie?"

"Absolutely."

Bruce, smooth and quiet, in the best tradition of head-waiters all over the world, appeared silently at Linda's elbow. She jerked her head up at him. "Oh. There you are. Would you take the orders, Greg?"

"Bruce," he corrected.

She rose to her feet, dropping her napkin. "I just . . . Quill, would you mind very much if Mrs. Gollinge and Mrs. McIntyre showed you around? I've just gotten some . . . I mean, I have quite a bit of work to do. And I've got to find Mrs. Taylor."

"You returned Mr. Taylor's call, didn't you?" said Quill. "Linda, I think I should tell you . . ."

"Dear Verger," Bea said. "How is he? I'm doing so nicely since we added the Taylor Towers to my portfolio."

Quill bit her lip. Whatever threats Verger Taylor had delivered to Linda over the phone, it was unlikely that she'd unburden herself in front of two members of the board of directors.

"You go right ahead, dear." Birdie patted her hand.

Linda, after further apologies interspersed with nervous flutters, almost ran out of the restaurant.

"Excitable," said Bea. "Of course, if she's talked with Verger today . . ."she shook her head.

"Terrible man." Birdie opened the menu. "I have simply got to lose another three pounds before the banquet, Bea. I'll never get into that gold lamé if I don't."

"Nobody can lose three pounds in four days," Bea said. "And I was thinking that you might want to go back to Saks and take a look at the lavender velvet, anyway."

"You're right, of course. But I wouldn't feel right gorging. Bruce, I'll have the salad Nicoise. And the *crème brûlée* for dessert." She frowned at Quill. "It's pudding, isn't it? And those little cups are so small. How many calories could there be in that little tiny cup?"

"Golly," said Quill, "I . . ."

"If you know, don't tell me."

"Mademoiselle?" Bruce asked, in a southwestern Texas accent.

"I'll have the mushrooms, please. And some iced tea."

He turned to Bea, who asked for a bowl of the seafood bisque, then gathered up the menus and bowed himself off. Quill waited until he was safely out of earshot and ventured, "Terrible man, Mrs. McIntyre? You mean Mr. Taylor?"

"Call me Birdie, dear. Everyone does. Everyone I like, I mean. Which does not include Verger Taylor. Does it, Bea?"

"Goodness, no. Dreadful man. Dreadful. I believe he'd sell his mother for a front-page headline. Good at making money, though."

"Very good." Birdie drained her wineglass. "You haven't touched your wine, dear."

Quill obediently took a sip. "The divorce seems to have been hard on Tiffany."

Birdie shrugged. "Young people today. That's all it is. Divorce, divorce, divorce. We didn't change husbands like that in our day, did we, Bea?"

"We did not."

"If we lost 'em, it was because they died."

"So neither of you are interested in her charity?"

"Excelsior?" Bea said. "Goodness me, no. That Dr. Bittern's a charmer though."

"Little too slick for my taste." Birdie sat up a little straighter. "Here's lunch."

Quill was quiet through Birdie's anchovies, the hard-cooked eggs, and the calamata olives. Her mushrooms were excellent, with just enough sherry in the sauce to pick up the flavor of the chanterelles. She sliced a Portobello in half and turned over several approaches in her mind. *Bea? Birdie? Are you two ladies rich enough to take on Verger Taylor?* Nope—too blunt. *Birdie—Bea. We had kind of an unpleasant scene at the Taylor condominium last night.* That was too tentative. It would be very easy for the widows to blink politely and move on to more pleasant topics. There was always the straightforward approach: *My sister and I are being blackmailed by a bleached-blonde shrew and a bully. And we want to go home.*

"My dear!" said Birdie, covering Quill's hand with hers. "Who is what?"

Quill, who hadn't realized she'd spoken aloud, looked up from her salad in some dismay and, with relief, summarized her predicament.

"Well!" said Birdie. "Isn't that just like Verger."

"Can you blame him, though?" asked Bea. "Not the burn-down-house part, Quill—there's no excuse for those kinds of threats—but Tiffany is doing her absolute best to embarrass him in front of his friends."

"All four hundred of his nearest and dearest," said Birdie dryly. "Remember when he opened that club on Beach Road?"

"And said that Henry Kissinger was going to be a charter member?" Bea thumped her fist on the table. "Ha!"

"An opportunist. No question about it."

Quill decided to have some wine after all. She swallowed the remainder of the wine in her glass and said, "We had no idea. None. About what we were getting into. We wouldn't have come if we'd realized."

"The problem is that a man like that is vulnerable, very vulnerable, to his ego. He sets himself up, then wails like a banshee when things don't go his way. He reminds me a great deal of my six-year-old grandson. Bratty. Very bratty."

"But he's a lot more dangerous than that six-year-old, Bea." Birdie's shrewd brown eyes flicked over Quill. "Tell me, dear. How is this inn of yours doing? Would it be a good investment for two old biddies like us?"

Quill blinked. She knew she shouldn't drink in the

middle of the day. As a matter of fact, she shouldn't drink at all. "I beg your pardon?"

"Why don't Bea and I buy out your mortgage ahead of Verger? That'll teach him a lesson."

"No. Thank you, but no. I didn't . . . I mean, I didn't burden you with this in order to ask you for money."

"That'd be a first," Bea muttered. "Get that message to my so-called friends, will you?"

Quill, conscience-stricken, had a brief glimpse of what it must be like to be elderly, widowed, and wealthy. She wished she'd insisted on seeing the pictures of Bea's family. It wouldn't have taken much time, and the old lady was obviously proud of them. "Meg talked to our family lawyer in Hemlock Falls this morning. He's a very good one, and he's taking steps with the bank to keep Mr. Taylor from pulling whatever strings he thinks he can pull. So thank you, both of you, for offering to help in a financial way. But we don't need that kind of help. At least, not yet."

"Don't be too grateful," said Bea a little cynically. "We'd insist on a substantial portion of the equity in your restaurant. Your sister's pretty well known, you know. And there's money to be made there, if it's handled right. You sure you don't want to reconsider our offer of help?"

"I'm sure," said Quill firmly. "What I want to know is how I can get past Verger's—prejudices, I guess. I mean, he seems to lump both Meg and me with Tiffany and her dread—I mean, her charitable work. I thought that Evan—his son—might be the way to approach him and get him to see that we're really innocent of any—well—malice. He seems to think we want to embarrass him, too."

"Evan," said Bea thoughtfully. "That's Cressida's boy, isn't it?"

"Cressida?" Quill asked.

"Verger's first wife. She's a Houghton. Was before

she married Verger and is again. She lives out on Hobe Sound. Good tennis player.''

''Better at bridge,'' said Birdie. ''Cressy's a whiz at bridge. Evan's a nice boy, but he is a boy.''

''You remember him when he was eight and played croquet with you at Cressy's, Birdie. He's all grown-up now. Went to Harvard.''

''Yale,'' said Quill.

''Whatever,'' said Bea dismissively. ''But he must be twenty-four, at least.''

''He's still wet behind the ears, Bea. I know what Quill should do. She should talk to Ernst.''

''Birdie! How clever of you.''

''Ernst?'' Quill asked.

''Ernst Kolsacker,'' Birdie said. ''Verger's business partner. The brains behind the whole Taylor empire, if you ask me. He's always been able to keep Verger from going too far over the line. That's it, Quill. I'll go give Ernst a call right this minute. You wait right here.''

''*You* wait right here, Birdie. Look!'' Bea pointed to the front entrance. ''My mother always warned me: Speak of the devil and he appears.''

Quill twisted around in her chair. The restaurant had filled up while they had been talking, and the noise level was high. The biggest racket was coming from Verger Taylor.

''Oh, my goodness.'' Quill felt a cowardly impulse to crawl under the table.

''Steady,'' Bea said. ''He's with Ernst. See? That short fellow there, with the wire-rimmed glasses and the golf hat. Looks like a little teddy bear. He's a dear, dear man.''

''Good friend of Arnie Palmer's, Ernst,'' Birdie murmured. ''Never could see golf, myself. Now polo, in my young days . . .''

''Forget your young days, Birdie. We're both long past them. Now what in goodness' name is Verger doing here?''

"Oh, yikes," Quill said. "It's Tiffany!"

The crowd in front of the cash register parted as for Moses. Tiffany's white-blonde hair was drawn up tightly over her ears and she sported a large black hat slanted over one elegant cheekbone. She wore a short black skirt and a black-and-white suit coat that flared at the hips and nipped at the waist.

"She looks like a pissed-off penguin," Bea muttered.

Verger gave Tiffany a mock salute, with two fingers to his forehead, then stuck a cigar between his teeth. A camera flash flared; both Verger and Tiffany swung toward it.

Tiffany began to breathe through her mouth. She yelled, "On the count of three, Verger. On the count of three. If you're not out of here, I'm calling the cops. This is harassment, you following me around like this. You hear that? Harassment. So out. Out. *Out!* Get out of my goddamned restaurant!"

His tone was mild. "This isn't your restaurant, Tiffany. This is my restaurant. I own the goddamn building, don't I?"

Tiffany's mouth dropped open. For a moment, Quill would have sworn that she was so shocked, she forgot she was in front of an audience. Her breath came back with a sound like a medicine ball hitting concrete. "You *bought* this place!"

"Yeah, I bought this place. About an hour ago. You think I'm going to let you make a horse's ass of me with this goddamn charity? In front of all my goddamn friends? You bet I bought this place."

"You don't have any goddamn friends."

Bea grabbed Quill's arm. "Oh, no! The sculpture! I donated that piece myself!"

The crystal narwhale flew past Verger's head. The dolphin followed the narwhale, glanced off Verger's shoulder, and crashed to the floor. He yelled "goddammit"—with what Quill felt was a remarkable lack of originality—and leaped for the safety of the half-wall in front of the cash register. The diners scattered like pigeons. Tiffany's shriek escalated to a yowl. Coffee cups, saucers, and wineglasses followed the crystal, shattering against the half-wall protecting the cash register in a fusillade of noise. It was like being trapped in a bowling alley. There was a muffled crash and clatter and another siren shriek from Tiffany, followed by a high-pitched marital squabble of Force 5 proportions.

"Good arm," said a blue-haired lady at the table adjacent to Quill's. "I've seen Tiffany on *Oprah*. She works out."

Her lunch companion frowned. "Too much muscle. I just don't like a woman with too much muscle. Now, that Debbie Reynolds? She's got a tape that tones without you bulking up so much."

Quill sighed and looked out the window. The sun shone yellow-gold in a deep blue sky. Waves broke amiably along the curving cheek of the beach. A group of black-beaked terns scuttled along the shore. Striated white clouds streaked the far horizon. She'd caught enough of the weather report that morning to know that there'd been six inches of snow at home last night with another five predicted for the afternoon.

The shouts in the restaurant died away.

"They're going," said Bea. Quill glanced at her. She smiled maternally. "See? Ernst's taken care of everything. I told you he was marvelous."

Quill turned her gaze unwillingly to the front of the dining room. The short man in the golf cap held both of Tiffany's hands in his. He spoke to her in a low, soothing murmur. Verger Taylor was gone. Everyone seated at the tables had resumed eating, drinking, or gossiping—most of them all at once.

Ernst Kolsacker released Tiffany's hands, gave her shoulder a comforting pat, and held the front door for her as she left.

"Quick, Bea," Birdie said, "He's going to leave, too. *Whoo-eee!* Ernst! *Ernst!* Over here." She waved energetically. All the people who'd been staring at the Taylors turned like grouper fish in an aquarium to stare at their table. Quill refolded the maroon napkin with an air of unconcern, cleared her throat, and scratched the back of her neck. If she were at home, she'd be sitting in that nice rocking chair in front of the fireplace in Meg's kitchen. The air would be filled with the scent of roast game hen. Myles would be rumbling cheerfully over the newspaper in the corner. She would not be wanting to crawl under the table.

Ernst rolled toward their table like a golf ball on a difficult lie—erratically, but with a purposeful forward movement. He stopped, shook hands with several people, patted the backs of others, restarted, and stopped again. He arrived, finally, and bent over Bea, his arm around her neck. He gave her a friendly shake. "Bea, you look younger every time I see you. Birdie, I like the new hairstyle."

Bea beamed. "Ernst, I'd like you to meet our young friend here, Sarah Quilliam. Quill? This is Ernst. Ernst Kolsacker. We've just been talking about you, Ernst. Sit down."

He sat. Up close, he appeared to be in his early sixties, with a broad nose, fleshy cheeks, and the omnipresent Florida tan. He was wearing a short-sleeved polo shirt. His hands and forearms were strong and muscular. A dedicated golfer, then; Quill had seen those same overdeveloped muscles in Tiffany Taylor.

"How do you do?" Quill asked politely.

"Not all that well," he admitted. "Sorry about that scene up front."

Bea nodded decisively. "That's what we wanted to talk with you about, Ernst. When is this ridiculous feud going to end?"

"You want my candid opinion?" He rocked back in his chair with a grin. "When one or both of them is dead."

CHAPTER 5

Quill turned over on her back, swam a few strokes, and floated, looking up at the sky. The Combers Beach Club pool was surrounded by a waist-high stone wall painted white. Palm trees fingered the sky. The air was soft. The sun was behind Quill, settling into the mansions of Palm Beach. She flipped over and watched the fading light through her eyelashes: The colors ranged through all the oranges and yellows, with a bit of mauve where the sky drifted into blue. The light fanned out like the tail of an orange peacock.

"Want to paint it?" Meg sat down and dangled her legs in the water, palms braced against the lip of the pool. The edging tile was Florida-teal and -pink.

"There you are. I can't believe you took a cab back here."

"I told you I wasn't going to ride with you again, and I meant it. I like subways. I like trains. I like airplanes. I *hate* traffic. And the way you drive in traffic turns my blood to ice."

Quill was feeling too relaxed to rise to this bait. "It's

because you're too impatient.'' She kicked out gently in the water.

''No sisterly advice today, please.'' Meg dived into the water, surfaced with a gleeful shout, and began to swim laps.

Quill held her breath, went under, and swam through the body-temperature water. The shimmering blue on top was deceptive; underneath, the water was blue-gray and faintly turgid. She exhaled and swam to the top. Meg reached the end of the pool, turned, and stroked back. She stopped in front of Quill and slicked back her hair with both hands. ''You have to admit this place is beautiful. You should be doing some sketching.''

''Nope. I don't want to paint it. It doesn't feel real. It's like a set for a movie, or an animated postcard. I can't take it all in.''

''Do you want to take a walk on the beach? It's hard to make the beach trivial if that's what your objection is.''

''Maybe later. Right now, I want to get some food.''

Meg looked faintly surprised. ''I'm hungry. I forgot to eat today.''

''It was because of the rabbit.''

''That poor rabbit. No, it wasn't the rabbit. That good old rabbit and its brothers are going to be the most delicious meal you've ever eaten in your life. That rabbit's going to get us the third star.'' She treaded water with a smile.

''You mean the banquet's still on?''

''Of course the banquet's still on. Why shouldn't it be?''

''You haven't heard? See, this is what happens when you disappear on me and take a cab. The price of cowardice. Verger Taylor's bought the building. Which means everything's off. I was going to call Myles and tell him we'd be coming home.''

Meg turned pink, then pale. She began to sink. Quill

grabbed her arm and pulled her to the side of the pool. "Meg? You okay?"

"The third star," said Meg. "This means goodbye to the third star." She pulled herself out of the pool.

Quill hung onto the concrete edge and kicked out gently, watching her. "There'll be other chances for the third star, Meg."

"When? *When!*" She stood up and danced up and down in her rage. "Oh, dammit, dammit, dammit!"

"Settle down, Meg. It's probably for the best. I mean, these people are lunatics. If this hadn't happened to interfere with the judging, something else would have. Guaranteed."

Meg buried her face in her hands and ground her teeth. Quill waited a few seconds, floating peacefully, and then asked, "Meg? Is being a two-star chef all that bad?"

"Yes." She straightened up. "Does Tiffany know this?"

"Yes. There was a humongous scene in Le Nozze."

"She hasn't called it off yet. I'll bet she's going to pull it off, Quill. She has to. She just has to. We need that third star."

"We don't need that third star. The inn's doing fine."

"I'm going in to check the answering machine. Maybe Tiffany's called with some news."

Quill sighed. Water got up her nose. She pulled herself out of the pool and grabbed her towel. She followed Meg back to the condo with her face buried in it. She was only peripherally aware of an obstacle and stepped aside, straight into a muscular, living surface. Wiping her face, she backed up.

"Sorry about that," said Evan Taylor. "I guess I should have called ahead."

"No problem." Quill, suddenly conscious of her bathing suit, wrapped the towel around her middle. "Did you come to see us?" Meg, who had raced inside the condo to check the machine, came out at the sound of voices. She looked at Quill and shook her head: no word.

"Yes, I came to see you." Evan smiled. He was really very attractive, Quill decided, with that dark hair falling over his forehead. "I'd like to say I braved all sorts of obstacles to get to see you, and I did."

"Lions and tigers and bears?" Quill suggested.

"Parental wrath, which can be quite tigerish, now that I think of it. No, the obstacles weren't physical. It wasn't even Florida traffic. Corrigan and I have a place on the third floor, right here. Tiffany probably mentioned that."

"In that case, you can go right back upstairs. Now's not a very good time," Quill said firmly. "Unless it's something quick?"

"Not really." He smiled that attractive grin again. "Tell you what. Why don't you let Corrigan and me take you both to dinner? Say, in about an hour?"

Quill shook her head. "Thanks, but no. We've already . . ."

"Don't tell me you've already eaten. I just heard you in the pool. You're both starving. So, what about dinner? On us. At Taboo. I'll tell you why I'm asking. Dad has an idea that maybe will save the week for Meg. It'll take some time to discuss it. And why not have a talk in a place where we all can relax?"

Quill looked at Meg, who shrugged. Taboo had a reputation for great surroundings and even better food.

"We'll pick you up in the Jag. It's an X-15." She looked blank. "A four-seater."

"Hey, how could we pass that up?" Meg asked sarcastically. "Okay, boys. We'll listen to what you have to say. But we'll go Dutch, as we say in New York. I'm not eating on your father."

"Eight o'clock, then. The dinner's on me, not Dad. And don't worry about reservations. They know me." He grasped Quill's arm briefly. His hand was warm and strong. He nodded to Meg and loped off across the lawn and up the stairs in the stack of buildings facing the pool.

''Arrogant little brats,'' Meg said tartly, marching inside. ''They know him at Taboo's, huh? I'll bet they know everyone in this place with more money than taste.''

Quill came in behind her and carefully closed the door. ''What the heck do you suppose that's all about?''

''I wouldn't trust Verger Taylor as far as I could throw a forty-gallon stock pot. So whatever it is, it's trouble.''

''Maybe we should cancel.'' Quill walked into her bathroom, draped the wet towel over the heated towel rack, and turned on the shower.

Meg trailed after her. ''Pass up a chance for a meal at Taboo? It was on my list of things to do this week anyway. If the food's lousy, I can complain and feel superior. If it's great, I can learn something.''

''You're looking too disingenuous for my taste, Meg. There are limits to what I'm willing to do to save this week for you. Striking a bargain with Verge the Scourge and his offspring is not among them.''

''Just don't worry about it, okay? What are you going to wear?''

''Something matronly. I think that kid's got ideas.''

''You're out of your tiny mind. He's ten years younger than you are and six years younger than I am—'' Meg stopped in midsentence. ''Which isn't all that much younger, come to think of it. Come *on,* Quill. Seduction as the price of getting my food in front of that judge from *L'Aperitif*? Phooey.''

''I,'' Meg said, firmly removing Corrigan Taylor's hand from her knee, ''am engaged to be married. So cut it out.'' She cocked her head and observed him through half-closed eyes. ''How old are you, anyway, kid?''

There was a brief silence—awkward on Corrigan's part, deliberate on Meg's. ''So,'' said Meg, after a sufficiently embarrassing period of time. ''What is it that your father wants us to do?''

"It's nothing much," Evan said. "Just two small favors. One for me and one for him. Let's talk about it after dinner, okay? We should enjoy the atmosphere here. Relax."

Meg snorted, sipped her Chardonnay, and said with a grimace, "Australian. Too young."

Quill took a sip of wine. She was ill at ease and wasn't sure why. It wasn't Taboo, which was pleasantly reminiscent of some of her favorite restaurants in New York. It was long and narrow, broken into a series of rooms by artfully placed dividers. Smoky mirrors lined the walls to give the illusion of greater space. The prevailing feel was one of chintz, masses of flowers, and carefully courteous service. Nor was it Meg's rudeness to Corrigan Taylor, who was wearing a striped blue shirt, blue blazer, white chinos, Gucci loafers without socks, and a blush. She was used to Meg. She was willing to bet that a lot of people who got involved with Verger Taylor and his crazy machinations felt ill at ease most of the time.

"Is your wine all right?" Evan Taylor slouched comfortably in the chair directly across from her. The maitress d' had greeted him with democratic familiarity when they'd come in. They'd been seated immediately, passing a long line of waiting customers.

"It's delicious." Quill set the glass on the table. It was the house red, a cabernet, and it was very good. Meg had been clear about wanting to sample Taboo's commercial menu, and not any private stock. "I'm a little uncomfortable because I'm not sure why Meg and I are here. And I dislike being put into a position where we may be pressured to do something contrary to the way we work. Your stepmother hired us, you know. We're here in Florida because she's paid for it. And it's pretty obvious that the family doesn't get along all that well with her."

"So your loyalties are divided." Quill hadn't actually

heard a sneer for a long time. She heard it now. "Quite the little Girl Scout."

Quill felt foolish. Her temper rose. "Loyalty isn't an issue. We have a professional obligation to fulfill and it's to your stepmother, not to you or your father. What is it exactly that you wanted to discuss?"

"I really would like to wait until after dinner. Just because it'll give you a chance to cool down. But I can tell you this now. You know that Dad's bought the Institute building."

Quill nodded.

"Well, he didn't buy the Institute itself."

"You mean the training program, the staff, the Institute name?"

"That's right."

"What does he want the building for, then? It's not much use to him if it isn't a cooking school. All those kitchens."

"We'll get to that." Smiling, disingenuous, Evan kept his eyes on hers.

The waiter, hovering, distributed menus. Quill opened hers with a slight frown and asked for the first entree she saw: the Taboo steak salad. Meg, after demanding separate checks, ordered two starters, a salad, and two entrees for herself, and the same number of items for Corrigan, who blushed more brightly than ever. She then asked to see the kitchens and marched off, Corrigan in tow.

"She's not going to eat all that?" Evan asked, startled. "They'll make half portions for her."

"She wants to see the presentation," Quill said. "And she's shameless about eating off of other people's plates. I'm just glad I escaped this time. Your poor brother's in for it, though." She looked directly at him. "Tell me. I'm getting very confused. Just why did your father go the trouble—and expense, because I'm sure a building in that location cost a ton of money—of buying that property? What does your father intend to do with it?"

Evan ignored this question. He had lost his careless slouch and was sitting upright, in apparent distress. "Forget the separate checks. I'm paying for dinner."

"If you insist on paying, Meg'll walk out," Quill said. "It's a point of honor with her to pay for meals at competitors' restaurants. Then she's free to criticize. I'd let her alone if I were you."

"This is nuts." He shifted in his chair, cleared his throat, and made an effort to hang on to his sophistication. "I mean—we invited you to dinner." He smiled, weakly, without his former confidence.

Quill felt some remorse. He was, after all, pretty young to be taking on business negotiations on behalf of his notorious father, and she supposed that she and Meg together could be a little intimidating. She laughed a little. "It's Meg's career, you know."

"She takes it pretty seriously."

"Of course she does." Quill swung back to the matter at hand. "So. You were about to tell me what Verger wants to do with this building. Is he going to try and buy the Institute programs? Hire the staff? Make it the Taylor Institute of the Culinary Arts?"

"Not exactly."

"Turn that gorgeous space into condos," Quill improvised, "or a garage, or a recycling center, or Taylor's Tire Kingdom? Have you noticed how imperial everybody gets in Florida? Tire Kingdom, Mattress Kingdom. And if they don't get imperial, they get galactic: Video World, Bath World, CD-Universe . . ." Quill, aware that she was babbling, pushed the wineglass to the center of the table. "What *is* it about Florida, anyway?"

"You don't want to paint scenes from the beach, then," Evan said.

"That wasn't a question." Quill was surprised. "No. I don't. My sister asked me the same thing. Why would you, of all . . ." Quill bit off her words. There was something about Evan—about his whole family—that inspired her to insult. She folded and refolded her napkin, feeling off center. Just how clever was Evan Taylor?

"Why would somebody like me have the sensitivity to understand why an artist of your caliber hates the state? Is that what you were about to say?"

"You can't hate a whole state," Quill said absently. Myles had said that. She missed him. "And I've been rude. I'm sorry."

"Sorry about what?" Meg arrived at the table, flushed and beaming. "Sorry about coming here? I was at first but I'm not now. Quill! You should see that stove. I want that stove. I lust after that stove. I'm in *love* with that stove."

"It's a pretty nice stove," Corrigan agreed. He looked stunned.

"Did Meg behave herself in the kitchen, Corrigan?"

"What? Oh. I guess. She asked the chef if he knew all the verses to 'Tennessee Birdwalk.' "

"Did he? Don't answer, I can tell by the way you look. They both sang it together."

"I like this place already," Meg said in satisfaction. "Now if the food has the same character as the chef, we're in business. You know, Quill, if this thing with Tiffany Taylor does get torpedoed, we should stay here a full week anyhow. We can toddle up and down Worth Avenue testing all the food. It'll be great."

"I can assure you that Tiffany's going ahead with the gourmet week," Evan said. "It may not look like it, but my father's indulged her in all kinds of idiot ideas. It's the charity crap that's not going to happen. The Excelsior. The Institute for Gold Diggers. Dad's sending that phony psychiatrist away."

"I knew he was a phony," Meg said in satisfaction. "What is he, an accountant? An osteopath?"

"He's a shrink, all right. An M.D. From Johns Hopkins, as a matter of fact."

"You're kidding." Meg, who clearly didn't care, nibbled a piece of bread.

Quill sighed. "You know, I feel kind of sorry for your

stepmother, Evan. I mean—it's a silly sort of charity, I grant you that. But she's committed to it. Neither Meg nor I would have come here if we weren't certain of that. I know your father thinks she's doing it just to embarrass him, but . . ."

"Don't you?"

Quill considered. "I think there's some of that. But I don't think it's all of that. And my goodness, he's big enough to shrug off a little criticism, isn't he?"

"He dumped her, you know." Meg looked critically at the plate of ceviche the waiter set before her and picked up a fork. "I don't think anybody should underestimate the wrath of a dumped ex-wife. Think of all the things she could be doing instead of this little banquet and these little therapy sessions. In front of the cameras of all the major television stations." She chuckled, ate a forkful of the ceviche, and nodded. "Excellent. Very, very excellent. I like this, Quill." She put the plate aside, selected a clean fork, and took a portion of Corrigan's pâté off his plate. "Now this—no. We make a better pâté. Too much pepper. The sorrel's wrong for the liver. And someone in the kitchen went nuts with the onion." She handed the fork to Corrigan, who held it with a bewildered expression, then began to eat the pâté himself. "As I said, just think of all the mischief she could be doing instead of this little charity. She could be suing him in court for all kinds of stuff . . ."

"She is," said Evan. "She is suing him over my grandmother's house in Cannes."

"Or she could be going on those talk shows and talking about their sex life."

"She's booked on *Oprah* next month."

"Or trying to wreck his credit or something."

"Wreck his credit?" Corrigan asked with alarm.

"Well, that'd be the way to get to a real-estate mogul, wouldn't it? The point is, I think that if everybody ignored everybody else, stuff would quiet down and the whole family would get off the front pages of the newspapers.'' She gave Evan a sharp glance. ''If that's what you want.''

''That's what I want,'' said Evan. ''You have no idea how hard it is to have a life while all this crap is going on.''

Impulsively, Quill put her hand on his. ''It must be awful.''

''It is, rather.'' He turned his palm up and curled his fingers around Quill's wrist. She tugged free, broke off a piece of roll from the bread basket, buttered it, then set it on her salad plate. Evan picked it up and ate it, smiling. ''I was hoping you could help make it less awful.''

''Madame's steak salad.'' The waiter, carrying a loaded tray, set Quill's dinner in front of her, Evan's salmon in front of him, then several entrees each in front of Meg and Corrigan. He placed a half-dozen clean forks at Meg's right hand. ''Enjoy the meal, Mâitre Quilliam.''

Meg grinned, pleased to be recognized. Quill regarded her salad in dismay. It was large. Beautifully presented, but large. The steak had been char-grilled, chilled, and cut into thin strips. She counted three kinds of lettuce—radicchio, Boston, and butter—and two types of sweet pepper. The vinaigrette smelled wonderful: a hint of garlic, balsalmic vinegar, and spicy mustard. She wished she and Meg were sitting alone, so that she could enjoy it. She raised her eyebrows at Evan. ''I don't see any way that we can help you and your brother, Evan. I'm sorry.''

''Oh, but you can.''

''How? We can't go home, if that's what you want, because we've accepted this project. If Tiffany cancels it, that's fine. But . . .''

''Oh, no. I don't want you to go home. Far from it. I want you and Meg to stay here and do your best for the Institute.''

''You do?''

"Of course I do. The thought of Tiffany pitching another screaming fit in front of the cameras gives me the cold chills. I think I've brought Dad around to letting her go ahead with the plans this week—not the therapy crap of course—that's too much even for Dad. But the food stuff's no problem. Meg's classes, your lecture. He's even agreed to let the banquet go on as long as Bittern doesn't give a speech. It's good that a Taylor, even an ex-Taylor, is sponsoring something this classy."

"What about Dr. Bob and his 'woman's reach must exceed her grasp or what's a heaven for' psychology?" Meg asked. "What's going to happen to him?"

"We're taking care of that," Evan said.

There was a brief silence. Quill took another sip of wine and considered the large flower arrangement on the bronze pedestal behind Evan's chair. She liked the trumpet lilies.

Evan, who had regained his sophisticated air, said, "So don't worry about Dr. Bob. Everything on the food end is going to be fine. As long as you do one little thing for my father and one little thing for me."

Quill gave an exasperated *tcha!*

He held his hand up. "Don't turn me down before I even bring it up. I want you to let my mother join Meg's cooking classes."

"Your mother?" Quill said.

"Cressy," said Corrigan, suddenly. "Cressida Houghton. She and my father divorced quite a while ago."

"I know that. And of course I know who Cressida Houghton is. Everyone in the Western hemisphere knows who Cressida Houghton is." Quill ate quietly for a moment, then said, "I don't understand."

"Mother's a fan of yours, Meg." Meg's eyebrows rose in rude skepticism but Corrigan persevered, "Well, not a fan, precisely, but she'd love to take your courses. Tiffany told her that the classes were filled, and that you absolutely refused to have more than six people at a time in your cooking courses . . ."

"That's true," Meg said. "Six is the maximum number of people I can teach in one session."

"We told her we'd met you," Evan added. "Actually, Cory did, and she put it to us like that." He snapped his fingers. "Wants to join the class, and can't because it's full."

"Sorry," said Meg.

"Meg, for heaven's sake," Quill said. "There might not be any classes if you don't let his mother join. I thought you wanted to compete for that rating more than anything." And besides, although she didn't want to say it aloud, who in the world would turn down the chance to meet Cressida Houghton?

"Look, Meg." Evan leaned forward, forgetting about his food and his wine in his earnestness. "Have you ever met Cressy?"

"No." Meg hesitated. "I've heard about her, of course. Who hasn't? She's as famous as Mrs. Kennedy was."

Quill nodded. Cressida Houghton had been the youngest of the Babe Paley crowd, the elegant, distant women that Truman Capote had written about in his ill-fated book, *Answered Prayers*. She was an intensely private woman, appearing only to promote her charitable interest in the homeless.

"Then you have no idea what calm she can bring, what good she can do. You give her half a chance and she can keep both Tiffany and Dad from embarrassing the family. You don't know her."

"What she's like?" Quill asked.

Corrigan interrupted his brother. "She's wonderful. Calm, beautiful—she's just great. She's not like Tiffany at all."

Evan agreed, although in a more temperate tone. "Or Mariel, for that matter. Mariel's worse than Tif."

"Mariel?" Quill asked.

''Dad's new bimbo,'' Evan said. ''She's nineteen. An up and coming rock star. Or so she claims. I can understand why you'd turn somebody like that down as a student. She shaves her head and lives on brown rice. But my mother appreciates fine food.''

''Hm,'' said Meg, who was weakening.

Corrigan pressed forward. ''It's not too much to ask, is it? That she be there to keep the peace? That's all we wanted from you. Really.''

Meg shook her head in a way that meant she was on the fence. She made one last stab at maintaining her class size. ''Guys, I'm sorry, but the rule about six students is fixed. It's sacred. I just can't.'' She picked up a lobster claw with one hand, looked at it, and set it down again. ''Quill, what do you think?''

''Why don't we go talk to her?''

''Talk to her?''

''Yes. See if what Evan and Corrigan have said is tr—'' Quill stopped and attempted a retreat. ''Look how late it's getting!''

''You mean see if we're lying?'' said Corrigan. ''We don't lie. We don't have to.''

Quill considered this statement and decided it was one of the most arrogant she'd ever heard. She wanted to shake herself, to rid herself of the feeling she and Meg were involved in some complicated game whose master plan was known only by somebody else.

''We think you're up to something,'' said Meg. ''We just don't know what the heck it is. And that's a good idea, Quill. If by some wild chance these guys are right, and Cressida Houghton can keep the lid on any blowups, I'd be crazy to stick to my six student rule. So, yeah. If we can meet her, and she's not going to send either Tiffany or Taylor himself into fits . . .''

Corrigan shook his head. ''No way. They both respect her. She's already talked to Tif about televising this therapy crap.''

''So Tiffany is dropping the Excelsior racket voluntarily?'' Meg asked. ''Not because your father is blackmailing her?''

Evan hesitated. ''As far as I know.''

''You know, Meg,'' Quill said, ''it makes sense. Tiffany can get a lot more mileage out of Cressida Houghton's sponsorship of this—what are you calling it now, Evan, the Gourmet Week?—than an ersatz phobia institute. And I can't see Cressida Houghton involved in such a thing.''

''That's right.'' Evan nodded. ''Mother won't talk to the press. Never has and never will. And think about what you know of her relationship with Dad. Post-divorce, that is.''

Quill said, ''It's all been very good. Verger was quoted as saying she was the greatest lady he'd ever met.''

''And even Tif respects her,'' said Evan. ''She's scared of her but she respects her. I remember one Christmas, when we were little, just after Mother divorced Dad, Tiffany showed up at the house in Hobe Sound—well, never mind. Anyhow, take it from me, Tif behaves as good as gold when Mom's around. Think of it. You won't have to worry about anyone throwing pots and pans or pitching screaming fits on the kitchen floor. The week will go like silk.''

Meg raised one finger in admonition. ''If, and I say *if* what you're telling me is true, then I say okay.''

''Really?'' For the first time that evening, Quill felt that Evan's response was a genuine one. ''You mean it?''

''Sure,'' Meg said. ''Why not?''

Evan rose halfway from his chair. ''Let's go right now. She lives out near Hobe Sound. That's a twenty-minute drive from here. We can be there by ten.''

''Now?'' Meg said in alarm. ''It's too late to call on your mother now. Besides, we haven't finished eating.''

''Tomorrow, then.''

''Tomorrow's Tuesday,'' Meg said. ''I have to be at

the institute early. I've got my first class at ten o'clock. We're hanging the rabbit for the students. For heaven's sake, we'd welcome your mother. I'll let Linda Longstreet know that she'll be there."

"And Tiffany," Quill murmured.

"We'll take care of Tiffany," Corrigan said.

Meg sighed happily. "That's that, then. Now for goodness' sake let me finish this squab. It's getting cold." She deftly severed a wing, sliced off a piece of breast meat, and nibbled delicately. "Now that we've heard the easy part—the favor to you—what's the favor your father wants?"

Even grinned—not the ain't-I-a-cute-preppy-stud grin that had both repelled and attracted Quill, but a full-scale, malicious you're-going-to-love-this smirk. "Let's start with what he's planning for the institute. Hamburger U."

Meg inhaled sharply, coughed, sipped at water, and gasped. "I beg your pardon?"

"Not Hamburger U, actually. It's more like Poultry High. Poultry. Chicken," he said, impatient at Quill's bewildered look. "Fried chicken, to be exact. He's just bought up the Southern Fried fast-food chain. He's going to turn the institute into a training center for the franchises."

"Wow," said Meg. "Those great kitchens. Those marble counters. Those incredible stoves. All turned over to fried chicken?"

"And fried potatoes. And fried pies. And fried cauliflower, broccoli, and mushrooms. When that chain says Southern Fried, they mean it," Quill said. "I think they'd deep fry Kleenex if they thought it would sell. Evan, does this mean everyone at the institute will be fired?"

"I'm afraid so."

"Does the staff know yet? Does Chef Jean Paul know?"

"No. Which brings me to the second favor I have to

ask. Dad thought you might attend the management meeting tomorrow morning. It's a monthly thing, apparently.''

''Me?'' Quill said. ''Why?''

''To let them down gently.''

''Me tell them about the Southern Fried people? Me *fire* them? Why me, for heaven's sake!''

''Because you have a nice way about you. Because you have a reputation for fairness. And mostly because you'll be leaving town at the end of this week.''

''Forget it, Evan. I might as well stick my head in one of the gas ovens.''

''Sorry, Quill. That's part of the bargain. It was Ernst's idea, actually. Or maybe it was Frank Carmichael's—he's our lawyer. To have you take the heat. You know Dad—he can be, well, abrasive. Ernst thought you'd provide less of a target than one of us. Or even one of the PR hacks we've got on staff. You can see the strategy here. Keep things calm, quiet, nonconfrontational.''

''She'll do it,'' Meg said.

''I will *not* do it!'' Quill sat up straight, spread her napkin carefully over her lap, and began to eat the Taboo steak salad. It was delicious. ''Never,'' Quill said, swallowing an exceptionally tender piece of filet, ''in this life.''

CHAPTER 6

''A hurricane's coming,'' said Meg, appearing at Quill's bedroom door.

Quill struggled out of sleep. She'd been dreaming. A giant chicken wearing gold-trimmed sandals had been chasing her down the beach. It had Verger Taylor's head. She opened her eyes. Bright sun flooded through the bedroom in a reddish gold wave. ''What time is it?''

''Seven. We're due at the Institute in an hour. My class starts at ten and I have a lot of stuff to prepare. Did you hear what I said?''

''A hurricane's coming. No kidding. And I'm starting it by agreeing to go to that management meeting. I can't believe you talked me into going. When Chef J. P. finds out about Verger Taylor's plans for Southern Fried, there's going to be floods of tears, a tornado of hot air, a hu-u-uge blowout. When . . .''

''Stop,'' Meg ordered. ''I'm serious.''

Quill sat up and rubbed her face with both hands. ''You mean a real hurricane?''

''Come and watch the weather channel if you don't believe me.''

''Meg! You're watching the weather channel? Everyone here watches the weather channel. It's so they can call people up at home in the Northeast and gloat. That is so . . . so . . . Florida. Next thing you know you'll be wearing pink and teal jogging suits.''

''Just shut up and come out to the kitchen.''

Quill reached for her robe and found she didn't need it because it was too warm—almost sultry. She looked out the window. The sky was spectacular. The orange and yellow light on the eastern horizon was deepened in places to a fiery red. Now that, she thought, was something to paint. She stood watching the colors for a moment, jumped at Meg's shriek, scrubbed at her face with both hands to wake herself up, and went in search of her sister.

She was sitting on the high stool in front of the microwave. The small TV overhead featured two smiling blonde people—one male, one female.

''They're chirping,'' Quill said glumly. ''I hate chirpy TV people at seven in the morning.''

''Hush.''

Quill poured herself a cup of coffee and leaned against the counter. The two TV anchors smiled into the camera.

''As you know, Doug,'' the woman said, ''hurricanes are formed from high-velocity winds blowing around the low pressure center known as the eye.''

''That's right, Kell,'' Doug responded affably. ''The strength of a hurricane is rated from one to five. The mildest, category one, has winds of at least seventy-five miles per hour. The strongest—and rarest—is category five. These winds can exceed one hundred and fifty-five miles per hour—and on rare occasion, winds of over one hundred and eighty miles per hour.

Kelly swiveled in her chair with a beaming smile. The camera followed her like a dog after a treat. ''And it's a category five that may be headed our way, folks. Right, Doug?''

"Right, Kelly. If tropical storm Helen turns into Hurricane Helen, she may be headed straight for West Palm Beach. Within the eye of the storm, which can be as much as fifteen miles in diameter, the winds stop and the clouds lift. But the seas remain violent."

Kelly and Doug went on to inform Quill that the strongest hurricane to hit the western hemisphere in the twentieth century was Hurricane Gilbert, which had winds gusting up to 218 miles per hour. Agnes, Gilbert's baby sister, created three billion dollars' worth of damage and 134 deaths. Quill reached up and shut off the television when Kelly started on the destructive prowess of Andrew, Gilbert's younger, meaner brother.

"Did you hear the talk about the swells?" Meg demanded. She flung her arm in the direction of the ocean, sparkling peacefully outside their door. "Twenty-five foot swells coming up this channel? Over that teeny, inadequate little pile of rocks they call a seawall? Through the French doors and into this oak-floored living room? Quill, *what about that third star!* I can't believe this. First Verger Taylor and his nutty family try to wreck things, and now nature."

"They said it *may* be headed here, Meg. Not for certain. And you know what the media's like. Remember Whitewater."

"Whitewater? What the heck's Whitewater got to do with becoming flotsam and jetsam?"

"Think about it."

The phone rang.

"We should go home," Meg said. "Or at the very least move inland." The musical burr of the telephone continued, and she picked the receiver up with an exasperated "What?" She scowled.

Quill, glad for the diversion, asked, "Who is it?"

Meg gestured at her to shut up. "Hey. Yes. I'm not coming back. No. I was just telling Quill . . . she seems unimpressed. And she's probably right. As usual. Here. *You* talk to her." She thrust the receiver at Quill. "It's home. I'm getting dressed and going on to the Institute. My cab's due in twenty minutes."

"Meg, I'll be happy to drive you . . ."

"No way. Here." She shoved the phone into Quill's hand and marched off to get dressed.

"Don't leave before you talk to me, Meg! I want to go over what I'm going to say at this meeting. Can you think of *anything* good to say about the Southern Fried people?"

"They're not wasteful! They don't change the deep fat oftener than once a week."

Quill shuddered. She put the receiver to her ear. A familiar foghorn voice barked into it. She felt a pang of homesickness. "Doreen!"

"That you, Quill?"

"It's me. How's everything at home?"

"All right, I guess. If you don't count that blonde sniffin' around Sher'f McHale."

Quill considered several replies to this. Doreen had several strong prejudices, which included a fixed belief that no single woman should travel more than fifty miles from home unaccompanied by armed guards. This supported a determination to see Quill and Myles married as soon as possible.

She fell for Doreen's bait. "What blonde?"

"Some divorcée what's been making up to the sheriff. Been here a couple of days, I guess. Stay on with that Nadine Peterson till the baby comes. Don't look like she's goin' to be movin' on soon, 'less you two get back here where you belong."

"Myles isn't the sheriff anymore, Doreen. Davy Kiddermeister's the sheriff. And we'll be home as soon as we've finished up here."

"Huh. Thought you'd say that."

"Then why did you bring it up? Myles isn't the type to chase blondes." She weakened. "How old is she?"

"The blonde? 'Bout your age, I guess. Younger maybe. So I guess I'd better bring him along with me."

"Who? Myles? Along where?"

"If you ain't coming home with this hurricane coming . . ."

"Doreen, I saw the weather map. The thing's a hundred miles off the coast of South America and *may* be headed this way. And if you listen through all the baloney the television's blabbering, it isn't even a hurricane yet. It's a tropical storm. So where are you going?"

"Got tickets to the Palm Beach airport, don't we?"

"Do you? I mean, you do? What about Andy? I thought he was coming with Myles."

"Ayuh. For Thursday. Unless we can't land because the hurricane took out the runway."

"If the hurricane comes, it won't be until the weekend. You're kidding, aren't you? You're coming to Florida with Myles?"

"I don't kid," said Doreen with some indignation. "Stoke's goin' to some newspaper convention in Rochester for a few days and John don't need me here, he says, so yeah, we got tickets. You tell Meg Doc Bishop is sorry, but Nadine's 'bout due and he may have to do a C-section. You got a pencil?"

"Well, yes, but . . ."

"We're coming in on Delta." She gave Quill the flight number and arrival time and then rang off at length, alluding darkly to the probable total of the long-distance charges for the call, the iffy state of the bank balance since Meg and Quill were off gallivanting and the inn was closed, and the outrageous state of American debt in general.

Quill hung up. The *beep* of an impatient taxi sounded. Meg called, " 'Bye." The front door slammed shut and Quill was left alone. "Hey!" she shouted. No answer. "Darn it!"

She went into the bathroom to shower and change. If Myles were here now, she could practice her approach to the hapless innocents at the Institute. *You're not fired, you've been downsized.* No. *Right-sized.* No. Face it—

they were all going to be fired to make way for the chicken people. They were about to be deep fried. And Myles's advice would be to stay out of it. Completely.

"Well," she said aloud to the absent Meg. "Here's another fine mess you've got us in." She had a couple of alternatives; she could call Myles, exchange affectionate greetings, and diddle away another twenty minutes when she'd see him Thursday anyway. And he'd know something was up from the tone of her voice. Or, she could check the third bedroom on behalf of Doreen—except the daily maid service—silent, (as far as Quill could see—invisible) changed the sheets and towels daily, whether anyone had used them or not. Or she could get dressed and go to meet her own personal hurricane at the Florida Institute for Fire Food monthly management meeting.

The traffic. She brightened. If she took I-95, she might miss the meeting altogether.

"You're early," said Linda Longstreet, sounding delighted. "Mr. Taylor said you were going to join us this morning." Her delight was brief; she looked pale and as though she needed a good night's sleep.

"Traffic was great," said Quill glumly. "It said on the radio that a tractor trailer accident closed six westbound lanes outside of Miami. Everyone else is stuck up there."

They were in one of the institute's classrooms. Logically, Quill knew that it was impossible for all sides of a rectangular building to face the sea, but this room—as did all the others she'd seen—had a splendid view of the ocean. The walls were painted a pale raspberry. The floor was made of dark mahogany, slightly sticky in the way such floors were. A set of daguerreotypes of Parisian cafes were arranged on one wall. The air was scented with garlic, burnt sugar, and baking bread. Quill much preferred that to the odors of fried chicken.

It was very cold.

A banquet-sized table—at least eleven feet long—occupied the center of the room. Twelve chairs were pulled up to it, four on each long side and two at each end. A yellow pad and pencil had been placed in front of each chair.

"They'll all start coming in a few minutes," Linda said. "Sit anywhere you like."

"Who comes to these meetings?"

"Well, Chef Jean Paul, of course. He's the director. And each of the heads of the five other kitchens: desserts, entrees, breads, and so on. And me. And the board of directors, those of them that are here. This month we've got two of the five: Mrs. Gollinge, and Mrs. McIntyre."

The lights flickered and went out. "Oh, no," Linda wailed. "Not now, dammit. Please not now, with the board of directors here!"

The lights went back on.

"Birdie and Bea," Quill said.

"The Merry Widows," Linda said with a smile. "Plus Selma, of course, although she won't be here today. We're very lucky in our board."

"Eleven," said Quill. "That's eleven people. Who's the twelfth?"

"I assumed that Mâitre Quilliam would be with you."

"Meg? I don't think so. She's in the middle of a class with the student chefs."

"That's right. I should have known that, because Chef Bruce, the *manàge à gare*, was quite put out that he would miss seeing Meg teach. The others, I'm afraid, took the high road—you know how chefs can be—what could a rival teach you—and a woman! They're all frantic, of course, over the competition. Now, I wonder." She frowned. "Mr. Taylor said two guests would be here, I'm sure of it."

The door to the classroom swung open and Bea and Birdie marched in. Bea's track suit this morning was white and gold, with silver metal stars scattered across the breast of the jacket. Birdie wore a Chanel suit in a vibrant pink tweed with black velvet collar and cuffs. She had a long strand of pearls draped around her neck, and her eyeglasses hung from a lapis lazuli chain that reached the last button on the jacket. Quill began to get an inkling about the high level of the air conditioning all over southern Florida: How else could you wear expensive outfits in the heat?

"It's Quill!" Birdie said with warm pleasure. "How are you, dear?"

"I'm fine, thanks."

"Mrs. Gollinge, Mrs. McIntyre. Please sit down." Linda fluttered around them like a distressed bobwhite. "I was sorry to hear that Mrs. Goldwyn is indisposed. Is she feeling better?"

"Eyelashes," said Birdie. "She's getting them dyed this morning. And of course, with that face peel she had yesterday, she won't be fit to be seen for at least ten days, so as far as I'm concerned, she should have waited."

"Which means she'll miss the cooking courses," Bea sighed. "Poor Selma! But we're ready to roll. We've signed up for Meg's classes, did we tell you?"

"Yes, you did," Quill said.

"There are twelve chairs here, Birdie," Bea said. "Are you and your sister going to join us, Quill?"

"I don't think that Meg is. I don't know who the twelfth is for."

"My two favorite widows!" Verger Taylor boomed. He walked into the classroom with an air both expectant and threatening. Ernst Kolsacker and a large man in a pin-striped suit were with him. The unknown man was well barbered, with a clean-shaven pink face, and a full head of recently clipped white hair. The suit must have been miserably hot in any temperature higher than sixty-five degrees. He was chewing gum.

Ernst was in his golf shirt and chinos. He gave Quill

an impish smile. Both he and the suited man ranged themselves against the side of the wall.

"Verger?" Bea put her gold-trimmed glasses to her eyes, then let them fall again. "And Franklin. Quill? You've already met Ernst. This is Franklin Carmichael, Verger's lawyer." Her face closed in displeasure. "Frank? Are you chewing gum?"

He blushed. "Sorry. It's that nicotine gum. I'm trying to quit smoking." Both Verger and Franklin Carmichael seemed taken aback by this attack, which may, Quill thought to herself, have been Bea's intention. Ernst gave her a large wink. Quill bit back a snort of laughter and sat down.

"Spit it out at once, please." Franklin took the gum from his mouth and wrapped it in his handkerchief. Bea rounded on Taylor. "I didn't expect to see you here, Verger. What's going on? Is it true? I heard that you've bought the buildings here. You're a damn fool if you have. The electrical system's all screwed up. Why didn't you let Linda know you were coming? You should have been on the agenda."

Verger's bluster returned in full force. "I always like a little surprise. Keeps the troops on their toes." He winked at Quill. She blushed furiously. She held onto her temper; if he wanted to sit and watch how she handled this mess, fine. Just fine. He shook hands vigorously with Bea and gave Birdie a hug. "Linda? Where the hell are the kitchen chefs? And where the hell's the coffee?"

Linda gave a squeak, knocked over one of the chairs, and rushed out.

"I've got exactly ten minutes for this meeting, and then I'm outta here. Have to meet the Concorde. I'd tell you who's coming in on it, but I'm sworn to keep the old lips closed. Linda?" He looked around, instantly angry. "Where the hell did she get to?"

"I think she went to find the chefs, Verger," Birdie said dryly. "None of us expected to find you here this morning, or Miss Quilliam either, for that matter. What's going on?"

"You're goddamn late," Verger snarled as Linda ushered a group of white-hatted men into the classroom. "When I call a goddamn meeting, it's to start on time."

"Verger?" Birdie demanded. "You didn't call this meeting. It's the monthly meeting of the board of directors. Technically, you're our guest. Franklin, can't you teach him some better manners?"

Carmichael smiled genially. But Quill noticed he wasn't as cool as he appeared; he reached into his pocket, took out a silver foil packet, put another piece of nicotine gum in his mouth, and chewed it nervously.

"You chefs all here?" Verger demanded. "Vegetables, desserts, *manage a* whatever the hell it is? Yeah? Okay. Sit down, all of you. This is only gonna take a minute, and then Miss Fancy Pants Quilliam here is going to answer any questions you got Linda, I thought I told you to get coffee. And some goddamn something to eat. All right? Now. I want everyone to sit the hell down. You." He jerked his thumb at Chef Jean Paul, who had seated himself at the head of the table. "That's my chair. Beat it." He swung his head toward Linda Longstreet, who was looking pale, frightened, and determined. "Hel-lo? Hello? I thought I asked for coffee."

"I'd like to be here, Mr. Taylor, for whatever it is that you're going to say to us."

"I'll get the coffee," Quill volunteered. Once she was out of this room, she decided, she was going to get into the Mercedes and drive straight back to the condo. I-95 was infinitely preferable to this.

"Linda will call for coffee," said Birdie. "She certainly doesn't have to fetch it herself. I'm sure that the students in the pastry kitchen can spare a few minutes to bring it over." Linda nodded timidly and went to the wall phone near the door. "We will all sit down now. Verger? What is it you have to tell us?"

Verger walked to the head of the table with impressive slowness. The five kitchen chefs sat stiffly in their chairs. Chef Jean Paul pulled mournfully on his mustache. Quill sank back into her seat, between Birdie and Bea. Verger thrust his chair aside and, standing, grasped the edge of the table with both hands. ''*The Wall Street Journal* will announce today that Taylor Incorporated has acquired the property at one Sea View Drive in Palm Beach County, formerly known as the Florida Institute for Fine Food. As of next week, I want you all out of here.'' He glared at Linda. ''Especially you, cookie. You I want out of here today. The way you maintain this place, I'm amazed it hasn't fallen around my ears.''

The assembled group looked at him like frozen rabbits. Franklin snapped his gum, apparently in mild distress. The sound was profoundly irritating. There was a small, dismayed gasp—from Linda Longstreet, Quill thought—but no more reaction than that. Of course, it wouldn't have come as a surprise; the altercation between Tiffany and Verger at Le Nozze had hit the six o'clock news; since then, the town had been rife with rumor.

''I'm calling a press conference later in the day to go into the specifics.'' He grinned. Quill told herself his teeth were *not* pointed; it was merely an illusion of the light. ''But if anyone here in this room objects, I want to tell you this. A lot of people have tried to take me down before.'' He lowered his head, thrust out his jaw, and repeated in a stagy rumble, ''Yes, they've tried to kill me.'' There was a kind of swell around the table as if some mammoth Moby-Dick were about to rise from beneath an ominously still ocean.

''You don't mean that, Verger,'' Birdie said.

Taylor raised his eyebrows in exaggerated surprise. ''You don't believe it. Sure. I can read you. Don't think I can't. You think I would have come as far as I have if I couldn't read you all like a book? *Hunh!*'' He made a sound that managed to be expressive of contempt, lofty amusement, and menace all at once. "Yep-per," he said cockily. "They tried to beat me. Bankrupt me. Run me out of town. Me! I don't take this kind of bullshit lightly, ladies and gentlemen. Not from the press, not from my so-called colleagues in banking. Not from the goddamned Supreme Court of the United States of America. Not from . . ." He rolled his eye upward. "Anyone."

"Do get to the point, Verger," Birdie said tartly. "What are you planning on doing with these buildings?

"Miss Quilliam'll tell you that. I just wanted you to know—you don't like it—you can lump it. I just wanted you to know."

"Verg?" Ernst Kolsacker looked at his watch. "The helicopter's on its way. The freeway's backed up again, and you'll miss the Concorde if you don't fly to the airport." He looked mildly exasperated. "I told you Miss Quilliam had agreed to take care of this."

"You wanna see something done right, you do it yourself, Ernst." His eyes swept the room in a menacing way. "You all got what I just said. You listen to this broadie here and take it like troopers. Quill? You stay here and take care of any questions. 'Kay? All right?" He turned to Franklin Carmichael and said "Frank? We got all this covered?" Franklin jumped, slapped his hand against his breast pocket, found it empty of a cigarette pack, and pulled out another piece of nicotine gum from his pants pocket. He popped the foil packet, tossed the small square into his mouth, and began to chew.

Verger clapped his hand heavily on Franklin's shoulder. "Good man!" He thrust his thumb up in triumphant farewell. He turned and went through the door, Franklin Carmichael in his wake like an obedient tug. Ernst Kolsacker stood aside and closed it softly after them. He then pulled up the chair Taylor had dragged away from the table and sat down. There was a brief hesitation, then a babble of noise broke out.

Linda's face was pale. "He's going to evict us."

Quill nodded, tremendously relieved not to have to actually say it.

"He dares?" Chef Jean Paul rose to his feet with a shriek. "This pig. This swine! This *vache stupide* has bought my kitchens! And he does not want me to cook? *Quel imbecile*!" He shot a nervous glance at Ernst and hastily sat down.

"What in the world for!" Linda wailed. "Why? Why? We knew about the sale of the building, of course. Everyone did after that scene in *Le Nozze*. But to fire us all? Why, what in the name of goodness is he going to do with all the equipment?"

They all looked at her. Quill rubbed the back of her neck. She coughed slightly. Ernst Kolsacker was looking at her with a slight smile. She sent him an appealing glance and the smile broadened. Not for the first time since she had come to Florida, Quill felt she was a pawn in some lunatic chess game. She got to her feet. "I want to assure you that Mr. Taylor—" she began. She cleared her throat. "Mr. Taylor has apparently purchased just the institute's buildings. Not," she said hastily, "the program or anything like that. The Florida Institute for Fine Food is still a . . . a . . . viable entity." Two of the kitchen chefs eased back into their seats. Heartened, Quill continued, "You don't exist because of this building. This building exists because of you." Without realizing it, she held up her hand for silence. It seemed to work. The outbreak of noise quieted. "I've been thinking about it. You clearly have a wonderful place here, with loyal staff and dedicated students, and why can't your board of directors find another facility—maybe even nicer than this one—where you can all run the program in peace?" She sat down, slightly breathless.

"Do you know how much a facility like this costs, Miss Quilliam?" asked Birdie coolly. "It's a nice idea, but really, dear. This is a four-or five-million-dollar plant at least."

"But it's profitable, Birdie." Bea looked alert. "And I must say, it would be nice to have a little more control over things."

"But what is he going to do with this building?" shouted the *manage a gare.*

"Well, um . . ." Quill looked again at Ernst Kolsacker. He shook his head sympathetically. "He's going to bring the Southern Fried people in. In sort of a training center."

"Fried food!" shrieked the salad chef. "Fast fried *food*?"

"I will *not* give up my kitchen to such. Me? *Non!*" roared Chef Jean Paul. "I will kill this son of a sea cock. This bastard. This *canaille.*"

"You don't think, Birdie and Bea, that we could find another building for everyone?" Quill said. "I mean, it's profitable, surely?" She raised her eyebrows at Linda Longstreet.

"Profitable," said Linda. "Well." She twisted a piece of tissue her hands and bit her lip. "On a month-to-month basis it's profitable, yes. But overall . . ."

"What does that mean?" Quill asked in a nonconfrontational way.

Birdie's eye sharpened. "Yes, Linda. Tell us now, if you please. When we convene every month, we look at cash flow, receivables, and that sort of thing. But come to think if it, we haven't seen a balance sheet all year—have we, Bea?"

"No, we haven't, Birdie. Tell us, dear—just what is the outstanding debt?"

Linda told them. There was a glum silence.

"It was pledged against the equity in the building, of course," said Linda.

Ernst gave a snort.

"But the Institute doesn't own the building, does it?" asked Quill. "I'm a little confused here."

"The building was mortgaged through Florida First," said Linda.

"Verger's bank," said Bea, in an aside to Quill.

"And Florida First pledged the loans the Institute itself took out against the equity in the building."

"Pledged?" Quill frowned. "You mean that the loan to your institute was secured against the equity in the building?"

"No. I'm afraid not. There was an assumption that if we needed money, there'd be enough equity to cover our debt, so it was really just a handshake deal." She turned to the stunned onlookers. "The man at the bank said it would be fine. And not to worry about it."

"But is that legal?" Quill asked. She looked at Ernst. His face was an impassive mask. After a moment he said, "Yes. It's legal."

"How can undisclosed debt be legal?" Quill demanded.

Ernst smiled. "Oh, I think you'll find it's disclosed, all right. Nobody's tried to hide anything. When we bought the building, there were no legal liabilities attached—other than the balance of the mortgage, which Taylor Inc. paid off, of course."

"So we're all out of a job?" Linda asked steadily. "Is that what this means?"

"Verger would like you all to stay on until the end of the week."

"Not me," Linda said bitterly. "He fired me right now." To everyone's intense discomfort, Linda burst into tears.

"Everyone else," Ernst continued, "is to stay on. We have two famous guests with us—Chef Quilliam and her sister, who's a well-known artist—and we wouldn't want any bad publicity to interfere with events going on this week. Isn't that right, Miss Quilliam?"

"*She,*" Chef Jean Paul blurted, red-faced, "she is interested only in the saving of Chef Meg. For the star, you understand. I say *pah!* and *pah!* again to this." He spat impressively on the floor.

"This means you'll stay the week?" Ernst said.

"For what? For what do I stay this week? I walk out on this week."

"For a decent severance package. I can talk Verger into that much."

Chef Jean Paul spat on the floor once more, then said, "I demand a month, me. And for my friends, two weeks."

"Hey!" Chef Brian leaped to his feet. "How come you get a month's worth of pay and we get two weeks?"

"Because I am the master, you scum!"

Ernst spread his hands in a gesture of conciliation. "Tell you what, guys. Come up here and we'll talk it over."

The six chefs clustered around Ernst like cabbage flies on new peas.

Quill was shaken. "I wish," she murmured to Bea, "I'd never heard of Tiffany Taylor, that'd I'd never accepted this project, that I'd never heard of Palm Beach, and that Florida didn't exist."

Bea patted her hand in a sympathetic way and said briskly, "Well dear, you did, and it does. What are you going to do now?"

"Find Meg, I suppose, and carry on."

"Good girl." She raised her voice. "Ernst!"

"Yes, Bea."

"You can tell Verger from me that this move may be a profitable one, but it is heartless, heartless. These are my friends—Chef Jean Paul, Chef Brian, Linda, and the rest. Taylor has summarily put them out of a job and like many such tactics in the business world, I disapprove. I highly disapprove."

Impulsively Quill applauded.

Linda Longstreet looked at Bea with damp eyes. "Does this mean that you and Mrs. Goldwyn and Mrs. McIntyre will help us find a new building?"

"I doubt it, Ms. Longstreet. We'd do far better to take that investment and buy a few more shares of Taylor

Incorporated. Ernst? Will you see to that? Quill? You look . . ." She paused and regarded Quill quizzically. "A little dismayed. This is how you keep wealth, my dear. By hanging tough. Sentiment should never enter into it, or so my dearest Charles always told me. Birdie!"

"Yes, Bea."

She nodded majestically. "We are going in search of Chef Meg. I have always wanted to learn how to jug a hare."

CHAPTER 7

"This rabbit," Meg said to the assembled students, "is not a rabbit but an American hare, which means that the meat is all white. As you can see, it weighs around . . ." She stopped, pursed her lips, and placed the soft limp body on the scale. "Eleven pounds, two ounces." She looked up sternly. She was wearing her toque and her dress-whites trousers and tunic. There were seven students standing around the butcher block table in the center of the chacuterie kitchen. They were all wearing white jackets and the starched white berets that distinguished the cooking students from the chefs. One of them stood apart from the others: a tall, slim woman with a calm, beautiful face. Her hair was a silvery gray and she was graceful, attentive, quiet. Quill was reminded of the scene from Galsworthy's *Indian Summer of a Forsyte*, with the beautiful Irene coming across the grass: the spirit of beauty in a twentieth century kitchen in Palm Beach. Two things to paint here, then: the sky over the sea before a hurricane and Cressida Houghton. Tiffany Taylor stood closest to her, a neon light next to a glowing candle. There were lines around Tiffany's mouth that Quill hadn't noticed before.

"Test the age of the hare by turning the claws sideways," Meg said, demonstrating. "The claws should not crack. If they do, the hare is old. The ears should be soft, bend easily, and the animal itself should have a short body and long legs." She set the hare aside and reached to the overhead beam, where four animals hung pathetically by their hind legs. "These hares have been hanging for twenty-four hours. They can hang for as long as four days, but if the hind legs are not stiff when you take them down, throw the animal out. You're risking tularemia. Sometimes called rabbit fever, this is a bacterially based flu."

"My goodness," said Bea. "That poor bunny looks so innocent, Birdie."

"It's a hare, Bea, not a bunny." Birdie intercepted a glare from Meg. "Now hush."

"You know a chef by her knives," Meg said. She held up a long, thin boning knife, its edge honed to a dangerous sharpness. "We will prepare this hare for marinating." She drew on a pair of rubber gloves and began to dress the hare. The lights flickered off and then on again. Meg held the knife up for a moment, cursed fluently, then set to, once it appeared the power was going to remain on. She sliced the skin of the front and hind legs away from the joint; tied the hind feet together with kitchen string and peeled the skin off the hind legs, body, and forelegs. "Just like turning a glove inside out," she said cheerfully.

Quill turned away to inspect the kitchen; Meg's next step was to sever the head, remove the intestines, and wash the carcass with vinegar water. One of the women standing at the table looked a little green, but she steadied herself and managed to look attentive as Meg carefully sliced around the heart and the liver.

Cressida Houghton, seeming to glide rather than walk,

came to Quill as she was looking critically at a sixty-gallon stock pot. "I'm Cressida Houghton," she said, extending a slender hand.

Quill couldn't think of a thing to say. *Of course you are!* would seem too hearty. *Oh really?* seemed impertinent. "I'm Sarah Quilliam."

"I have two of your iris sketches. They're wonderful."

Quill blushed, unable to respond to praise of her work, as usual.

"The essentials of a marinade," Meg said loudly, "are that of any basic stock: celery, carrots, onions, bay leaf, parsley, vinegar, and water. The choice of your curing agent—vinegar—is critical to the success of the dish."

"Your sister . . . marvelous," said Cressida Houghton. "I must get back. But the boys and I would love it if you would come out to my house for dinner this evening. Say at seven-thirty for drinks? Then dinner? And perhaps a few hands of bridge?"

White Queen to King Four? Quill sighed. This game was getting murkier and murkier. "We'd love to," she said. "Thanks."

"It's the first place off your left as you come over our little bridge into Hobe Sound. Number four."

She drifted back to the butcher block table. Everyone in Cressida's orbit—except, Quill noted with a sudden stab of fondness, Meg herself—was so aware of her presence that their attention was almost tangible. Tiffany, with a discontented pout, signaled to Quill with one finger. Quill held up a hand in response and slipped out the door. She would wait until Meg's class was over to let Tiffany know how things stood.

With more than half an hour until Meg's class broke for lunch, Quill was somewhat at loose ends. There wasn't time enough to take the Mercedes out for a little run (the speedometer went to two-twenty, and Quill had been dying to find a quiet road and discovered how the car handled at high speeds), and it was too much time to sit and do nothing, unless she had something to read. She recalled that the institute had a small library of cookbooks next to the administrative offices, and she decided to look up old recipes for potted rabbit. Meg was always interested in new ingredients for her marinades—although the one with which she hoped to earn the third star seemed unsurpassable to Quill. Even she didn't know the basic curing ingredient, but she had a hunch it was very old brandy, from a comment John had made about the liquor bills in the past few months.

The library was on the ground floor of the Institute, past what Linda Longstreet had called the Food Gallery. Quill went down the stairs and through the archway to this area and stopped in mild astonishment. The room was square and lined with glass display cases, much like the ones at the British Museum in London. The cases were filled with food art. One shelf was devoted to creations from spun sugar—cottages, flowers, even zoo animals. The case next to that was hung with brush paintings out of cocoa. Several large montages of seashells and driftwood were on the walls unoccupied by display cases. Quill put her hand out and touched one: spun sugar, dyed with food coloring and air-hardened. The work was clearly that of students. Quill viewed all this with bemusement. She had to bring Myles to see it. The displays were the sort of thing you had to see yourself. Like Snake World and Reptile Kingdom along the Florida Turnpike. She passed up and down in front of the exhibits for some time.

"See that," said a voice from behind the wall. "You can *see that*, can't you?" In a fit of manners, Quill was about to turn away when she heard, "Verger. You heard me. I think he's on to the whole thing. Why else would he have bought this place? He could have put up a chicken palace six times larger than this at half the cost."

Linda Longstreet. No longer in tears, but sounding very angry.

Quill flattened herself against the wall adjacent to the door to the administrative office. Linda's office was on the other side of the wall containing the sugared seashell exhibit. Quill peered around the archway to the corridor. Linda's office door was closed. From this position, Quill couldn't hear a thing. She walked softly back to the point where she'd first heard Linda's voice. By some trick of construction (or, Quill thought, misconstruction) her voice was clearer than ever. She was weeping. There was a soft murmur of a reply, then Linda sobbed, "I'd like to kill him. Just kill him! And you would, too, I know it!" The second voice again, in cadences of agreement. And behind Quill, in the hall leading to the stairs, the shuffling of feet. Meg's class must be out. Quill stepped back in apparent contemplation of a particularly vibrantly colored blue bird, then turned and smiled as the students from Meg's class in potted hare came flooding through the gallery on the way to Le Nozze. After the morning session, Meg was scheduled to create a working lunch for the students in the Le Nozze kitchens. They clattered through the hallway past Linda's door. Quill followed them; as she passed Linda's office the door opened, and Dr. Bob Bittern, head of Excelsior, came into the hall. He saw Quill, stopped, and folded his hands reprovingly. "Ms. Quilliam. May I speak to you a moment?"

Quill felt herself blush. He couldn't have known she was eavesdropping. He took her arm and drew her back through the gallery.

"I would like to ask you to speak to Mr. Taylor on behalf of Ms. Longstreet."

"Me?"

"She's in quite a bad state. Quite."

Quill wondered if this was a psychiatric diagnosis: "quite a bad state."

"She is in desperate need of employment?" His voice

rose at the end of the sentence, as though he were asking a question. "And if she is not reassured that she has a place in this new business, I cannot answer for what she may do next. She is a qualified accountant, you know."

The lights in the gallery flickered off. For a moment, Quill and Dr. Bittern were in almost total darkness. Except for the gleam of his white hair, Quill couldn't see a thing. She imagined Meg's curses floating through the air, the refrigerated units losing power. She didn't like Verger Taylor's business methods, but she had to agree that Linda was not a particularly efficient manager. "There isn't a thing I can do, Dr. Bittern. And I'd like to find my way out to the light. I need to speak to my sister."

"Come this way." His hand was soft on her bare arm. He drew her through the hall and out into the sunlit expanse of the area next to the stairs. The darkness behind them winked into light. "There we are. Light is restored. Now it would be quite neat, would it not, if you could restore some light to Ms. Longstreet."

"I'd love to help," Quill said, "but I honestly don't know what I could do. I'm not even sure how I've gotten into this position . . ." She trailed off. He looked at her attentively and didn't respond. It was an extremely effective tactic—before she realized it, Quill blurted, "I don't even want to be here. I don't know why Verger Taylor asked me to tell all those people they were going to lose their jobs. I mean, he came in and did it himself, anyway, didn't he? So it's clear he doesn't think any better of me than he does anyone else. I don't have any influence with him at all, really. I don't want to have any influence. I'm very, very sorry for Linda . . ."

"She is in a desperate way," he repeated.

"Surely there must be some other accounting jobs she can find, Dr. Bittern. Perhaps if we called an employment agency, a job would turn up. Accounting skills are some of the best to have. All businesses need bookkeepers."

He looked at her gravely. "You haven't spent much time here, in this state, that is clear. Linda could find a job, that is true. But it would pay—if she were lucky—a little above minimum wage. She doesn't have a degree, you see, only experience. She has two children and a great many bills to pay. The economy of this state is most peculiar. While jobs are plentiful, they are jobs at low wages. A great many of our senior citizens—myself among them—prefer to work part time. This keeps the competitive salary rate low. And yet, the cost of living here is quite high, again as a result of you northerners. Linda can't afford grocery money—much less housing for her family—on what she could earn at a bookkeeping job here in Palm Beach County."

"I'll speak to Mr. Taylor," said Quill reluctantly. "Although . . ."

"Speak to that son of a bitch," Tiffany snarled, coming down the stairs. "Why in the hell would you speak to that son of a bitch?" She reached the foot of the stairs and stretched out her hands to the psychiatrist. "Dr. Bob! Dr. *Bob*," she wailed. "He's wrecked everything. I knew it. I just knew it."

"He only has the power you give him," Dr. Bittern said, with what Quill thought was a remarkable lack of sense. Verger Taylor seemed to have more power than the nine justices of the Supreme Court put together. "Excelsior will survive. I have a small building for sale right off of the main boulevard on Singer Island. There is a marvelous view of the ocean, and the quiet will be perfect for our clients."

"How in the world am I going to afford that?" Tiffany demanded. She'd shed her protective apron. Her outfit today consisted of yet another tightly fitted jacket, flared at the hips, and a short skirt. The predominant colors were black and yellow. Like a giant, discontented bee, she walked agitatedly around Quill, then into the Food Gallery. She walked along the walls, tapping restlessly at the glass enclosed exhibits with her sharp red nails. Dr. Bittern followed her—and, as if drawn by a psychic magnet, Quill followed them both. "You don't understand. I've got to abandon my precious Excelsior altogether. Verger's cut off all the funding. All of it."

Dr. Bittern's precise diction dropped away. "What do you mean? Your settlement is more than enough to carry the costs of running the Excelsior."

Tiffany's bright blue eyes avoided his. "There's this little villa in Cannes. Right next to the center of the village. I must have it, Dr. Bob. You understand, don't you? The sea air, the breezes, the vitality of the film festival in March of every year. This will be far, far better for my frame of mind than the clinic." She stopped in front of a butter sculpture of a cow. "You understand, darling Dr. Bob."

"So he's bribed you, too," Dr. Bittern snapped. The lights flickered for a second time that day, once, twice, and then out. Quill could hear his harsh breathing in the dark. He said, "Someone, at some time, is going to give that bastard his just desserts."

A shadow darkened the archway leading to the stairs. Quill heard the snap of gum. "You folks okay in here?" Franklin Carmichael stood aside and beckoned them back toward the light. "Come on out. I'm afraid that this particular outage is permanent. Verger sent me back here to see if I could straighten things out. It's not precisely within my duties as his attorney . . . but, there you are."

"Mr. Carmichael?" Quill said. "Dr. Bittern and I were both wondering if you could see your way clear to help Linda keep her job."

Franklin took out his gum, folded it carefully in the little foil packet from which he'd originally taken it, and sighed. "Look, Dr. Bittern, Miss Quilliam. Come to the window here." He beckoned with one finger. Quill and the psychiatrist went to the foot of the stairs leading to the second floor. A large window looked out over the parking lot. "See that truck there? That fellow's delivering three gross of paper napkins; several hundred boxes of plastic knives, forks, and spoons; and a couple gross of plastic cups. To a gourmet facility. The picnic supply company's owned by Mrs. Longstreet's cousin. Now, see that electric truck pulling out of the driveway? That's her brother, Curtis. He's the one who's been doing the electrical work on the building up until now. If you check the food stores and the inventory, you'll find a lot of items this institute wouldn't use in a million years. If you check the bills for electrical repair, you'll find a lot of money going out and very little work to show for it. Are you getting the picture here?''

''But do you know for sure that Linda's intent is criminal?'' Quill protested. ''I mean, I do the inventory ordering for my sister, and you'd be amazed at the weird things you have to have on hand.''

''Two gross of canning jars?''

''Well, maybe, yes. That's a lot of jars, but . . .''

''Two hundred and eighty-eight, to be precise. Priced at four dollars each. And how many classes in canning? None. Zero. Zip. As Chef Jean Paul so elegantly put it when I questioned him—zis is not ze Betty Crock. And what about one gross of Doritos? Three cartons of Miracle Whip? Skippy peanut butter, Rice Krispies Treats, Stove Top stuffing . . . I don't need to go on, do I? And what have we got to show for forty thousand dollars' worth of electrician's bills this year? As you see . . .'' He waved one hand at the dark room behind them. ''She's been earning a lot more than her salary here, Miss Quilliam. Give Linda Longstreet her job back? I don't think so. At least Verger isn't going to prosecute. I talked him out of that.''

''Next stop, drinks and bridge with Cressida Houghton,'' Meg said. She tossed her tote in the corner of the leather couch in the condo's living room and the Bloomingdale's shopping bag after that. She sat down with a sigh. ''What a day. I tell you, Quill. Everything seemed to be going well this morning. Do you know who was in my class?'' She grinned. ''Not only Cressida—she asked me to call her Cressida, by the way—but that actress, Ellen Kale? It was hard to recognize her without all her makeup and stuff. She says she hates being recognized on the street. Those two, plus a couple of women whose net worth could buy a small African country. You know who else came in, after you left? Ernst Kolsacker and Franklin Carmichael. No kidding. Turns out they're avid amateurs. And Ernst was a *hoot.*''

''Until the lights went out.''

''Yep. It's going to last a couple of days—so its *phhhtt* to the cooking classes. But the banquet's still on. This is a great vacation, Quill. Can you believe we had time to go shopping?'' She poked at the Bloomingdale's bag with her toe. ''What a place Florida is, Quill. I mean, the weather's fantastic. Just fantastic. But did you see those bumper stickers in the parking lot at the mall?''

''The one that said, 'When I get old and sick I'm going to move up north and drive real slow'? Yeah.''

''Or how's about my favorite: 'Florida. We love it. You leave it.' ''

Quill went to the French doors and opened them to the sea breezes. ''There's a lot of hostility here.''

''I'll say. I wanted to disguise myself as a native. Lie and tell people in a cracker accent that I was born in Okeechobee. And they shoot tourists in Miami.''

''I didn't mean that sort of hostility. I meant all the hostility toward Verger Taylor.''

''That's nothing new. I think the guy thrives on it.''

''Do you know how many people want to get rid of him?''

''Well, Tiffany, for one.''

''And Dr. Bittern. And poor Chef Jean Paul. And I overheard Linda Longstreet threatening his life.''

''Linda Longstreet? She couldn't threaten a moth with a flyswatter.''

"I'm not so sure." Quill curled up in the chair across from her sister. She pulled reflectively at her lip.

Meg lowered her head, raised her eyebrows, and said, "No."

"No, what?"

"I recognize that lip-pulling. It's your investigative detective mode. No corpses. We left all the corpses behind in Hemlock Falls. This stuff is just nice nasty group dynamics."

"I'm not so sure, Meg. If anyone's ever ripe for murder, it's Verger Taylor."

"You said Myles and Doreen are coming in Thursday morning, right?"

"Yes. And I'm sorry Andy's not going to make it. But why did you bring that up now? We've got a nice little murder shaping up here, Meg. I can feel it."

"When Myles and Doreen show up, you'll be too busy to think up reasons why someone is going to murder Verger Taylor."

Quill regarded her curiously. "You aren't sorry that Andy's not coming with Doreen and Myles?"

"Well, I miss him, of course. But I'm worried about the marinade. And you know what happens just before I have to cook big. I get a bit worked up."

"And you have to cook really, really big this time." Quill smiled. "How's the marinade going?"

"I'll know tomorrow."

"Did you bring the stuff back here with you?"

"Of course not! I'll just have to take a flashlight into the Institute. It's a good thing they have all those windows. The hares are hanging in the bread closet, because that's the airiest, driest place, and the marinade's in there, too. To tell the truth, I'm a little worried. The climate's different here, Quill. The air pressure and everything. That affects cooking. You can't tell me it doesn't. I'm afraid it's going to throw the timing off. What do you think?"

"I think that odd clock in the kitchen says a quarter

past five and that we should get ready to visit Cressida Houghton."

"How long does it take to get there?"

"An hour. And I'm going to wear that new lime-green cotton dress I bought this afternoon."

"Does it take an hour by cab?" Meg asked suspiciously.

"No, Meg. By borrowed Mercedes. I looked it up on the map."

"The last time you looked a destination up on a map you turned a ten-minute drive into a marathon. I think we ought to talk to Luis and his handy-dandy computer. Either that or leave at least an hour early. It'd be horrible to be late to Cressida Houghton's house."

"Look. I'll show you. We take PGA Boulevard to highway One-A, highway One-A for ten miles to Hobe Sound, and then a right over the bridge. Verger Taylor lives east of the bridge, Cressida lives west. So we take a right. How simple can you get?"

"Don't you tell me about simple. You'll drive us into a canal. There's a directory of the residents of this condo around here somewhere, isn't there?"

"Yeah. By the phone. Why?"

"I vote we ride in with Evan and Corrigan. They live here. Let's call them and go with them."

"No," said Quill firmly. "N. O. No. I'm not getting any more involved with the Taylor family than we are already."

"Okay," said Meg. "You've got one more chance. Hobe Sound in an hour, or I never ride with you again. And just in case, we leave at six."

"We'll be really, really early."

"Then we'll drive around and look at the view."

"This isn't Hobe Sound," said Meg some time later. "That sign says Jupiter Beach."

"Jupiter Beach is near Hobe Sound," Quill said with a confidence she was far from feeling.

Meg picked up the map and eyed it. ''It's at least six miles in the wrong direction. Turn here.''

Quill peered through the Mercedes windshield. ''That road says 'private.' ''

''They aren't going to arrest you if you turn around. Which is what you need to do if we aren't going to be later than late at Cressida's.''

''We still have plenty of time. It's just past six-thirty.''

''Thanks to me.''

''And stop calling her Cressida,'' Quill said irritably.

''She asked me to call her Cressida! Quill, dammit, look out.''

The left bumper of the Mercedes struck a solidly built mailbox. Quill craned her neck over the side of the convertible and pursed her lips.

''Well?'' Meg demanded. ''How is it?''

''It's a mailbox. Not a very nice one, I'm afraid. The pedestal is one of those jockeys in a red-and-white outfit that used to be black and are now painted white. It's dented slightly. Thank goodness I didn't hit those gold lions. That would have been a real mess.''

''I don't mean the mailbox, Quill. I meant this super-duper expensive car lent to us by the charming and charitably inclined Tiffany Taylor. How much does this thing retail for?''

Quill thought a moment. ''Sixty or seventy thousand.''

''Fine. Just fine. So if you figure that left front bumper is what—one twentieth the value of this thing—we're looking at a thousand dollars worth of damage. Easy.''

''Fifteen hundred.'' Quill said. ''Your math sucks. It always did.''

The blare of a car horn made both of them jump. Quill turned around in her seat, groaned audibly, and put the Mercedes in park.

''What is it?'' Meg asked. ''More important, who is it? The cops?''

''Turn around and look for yourself,'' Quill hissed.

''I'm not turning around. I have nothing to do with this. I was the one who wanted to take a cab, remember?''

''What the hell you two broadies doin' here?''

''Hello, Mr. Taylor,'' Quill said.

Meg turned around. Verger Taylor was coming through the rear door of a large silver Cadillac. His chauffeur was a blur behind the tinted windshield.

''Sorry,'' said Quill. She eyed the mailbox, which had been knocked askew. The little jockey underneath it had a woebegone expression on its concrete face. The name on the box—in gold letters—said V. Taylor. ''This is your driveway?''

''Yeah. What the hell happened?''

''We took a wrong turn. Sorry. We're were looking for Ms.—I mean Miss—Cressida,'' Quill said lamely. ''We had no idea this was your driveway.''

''Would that have saved my fuckin' mailbox?'' he chuckled. ''Women. Who says they can drive? You want Cressy's, you want to continue down that beach road for three miles. She's on the beach side.'' His face softened, and for a moment, Quill thought, he looked quite appealing. ''You can see her place from here, at night.''

''Is there a green light on the dock?'' Meg cracked. Then, at his frown of incomprehension, ''Never mind. Sorry about the mailbox.''

''Don't worry about it. Wouldn't expect less from you women drivers.''

Quill gave him a thin-lipped smile, got into the convertible, and turned the ignition on. She pulled ahead, let the Cadillac drive by, and reversed into the street.

''How come you didn't give him the 'driving skills are not gender specific' speech?'' Meg asked.

''Because it's kind of sad, don't you think?''

''What?''

''The way he looked when he mentioned Cressida's name. He still loves her, I think.''

Meg snorted. "Love and Verger Taylor. Right. Okay. I know where we are. Take the long way around and we'll be there at just past seven."

The drive to Cressida's home on Hobe Sound was an extraordinarily lovely one. The sun was setting in a gentle haze. The warmth of the air was a blessing. The two-lane road to Hobe Sound was tree-lined, heavily shrubbed, and very quiet. An occasional car passed them, going at a leisurely pace. All of the cars were police cruisers. The glimpses of the ocean among the heavy vegetation were infrequent, even though it was no more than five hundred yards away. The beach was rocky, the swells thick and slow. Quill liked what she could see of the houses; most of them were low, resting quietly on the dunes like huge, somnolent sea birds. No obvious opulence, just serenity and an appreciation of the land itself.

"There's the turn on the bridge," Meg said. "We're coming in backwards from the directions, so the house should be just ahead, on the right. Yes. There it is, Quill, see? The number four on the blue-painted board and the name: Tern House."

Quill pulled onto a white concrete driveway lined with oleander, bougainvillea, and the white fire of tropical ginger. The way was twisty, and the little car handled the curves with quiet assurance. The house appeared slowly, first a flash of gray between two southern pines, then a long length of gray driftwood siding, and finally a circular drive. Quill parked the car a short way from the entrance. The driveway was well-worn cobblestone.

The front door opened as they approached and a maid in dove-gray greeted them with a polite smile. "Miss Houghton is very glad you made it on time," she said. They followed her into a short hall, paved with flagstones. "Would you like to freshen up?" asked the maid. "There is a toilet over here."

"Thanks, but no," Quill said. "We're fine."

It was dim in the twilight, and Cressida Houghton

appeared from the depths of the house like a wistful ghost. "Come in. It's so nice to have you here at Tern House. We're out on the lanai, if you'd like to come with me."

They passed through the living room. The floors were wide-board mahogany, well polished. The furniture was old and comfortable. Quill saw two of her paintings—*Iris studies*—over a low chest on the wall facing the screened porch. Cressida stopped in front of them and touched each with one slender finger. "I bring them down with me when I come here after Christmas," she said. "Otherwise they are displayed in my little apartment in New York. Such color, Quill. They're wonderful. Well. The boys are out here."

Evan and Corrigan both got to their feet as they came out onto the porch. Evan's hair was tousled; he wore a white turtleneck sweater against the faint chill in the air. His eyes, very blue, met Quill's. She felt that shock of sexual recognition that bears no explaining—unconnected to loyalties, pledges, commitments. Disconcerted, she glanced past him, over his shoulder, to the view beyond the porch. The ocean spread before them, a huge, hushed presence just beyond the screens. "Hurricane weather," Evan said with a smile. He took Quill's hand and held it.

The look Cressida Houghton gave her was poisonous. She didn't move—or didn't seem to. But her face was a mask. Her eyes—the famous silvery eyes—were as cold as the nitrogen room at the Qwik Freeze plant back in Hemlock Falls.

Quill had the unsettling feeling that her throat had closed up, forbidding her to speak above a murmur, damping her reactions, slowing her down like a mouse in front of a very bright light. It was the proximity to this very famous, too-perceptive, very furious woman—an icon of grace and gracious living for people the world over. An icon that seemed to want Quill's blood to water the roses out front.

Meg broke the strained silence. She suddenly shook herself like a puppy and said, "What a great view! How's about a walk on the beach?"

"What wonderful idea," Cressida said. "Perhaps after dinner. Please, sit down and tell Anna what you would like to drink before dinner. It's "just fish", I'm afraid."

Quill accepted a chilled glass of Vouvray. Meg, with a slight wink in Quill's direction, asked for Coke, which, to her somewhat shamefaced embarrassment, was duly brought in a Baccarat water tumbler, poured over shaved ice.

The dinner was "just fish." But it was simply, elegantly cooked, with a touch of fresh tarragon, green peppercorns, and slices of orange. The table was set with hand-dyed linens from Provençal and a basket of daisies, larkspur, and winter roses. The service was whisper-quiet, and Quill had to suppress the urge to sit bolt upright and shout "chocolate!" like the guy who'd yelled "fire!" in the old Smothers Brothers song.

Conversation was minimal. Evan looked frequently at Quill. At some point—Quill later recalled it was sometime between the fish course and the salad that ended the meal—he asked Meg if she'd sung to the chefs at the Institute that day. Meg looked at him blankly, opened her mouth, and closed it again. Quill introduced one topic of conversation: art, only to have her hostess murmur "wonderful, wonderful" in response to each comment she made. She tried politics—and was met with the gentle comment that he (the current president) had been a great friend of the family for a long while—and they never discussed him. Never.

Cressida, with a slightly disdainful eye on her guests, brought up the activities of Allen on the polo field, Tracy on the tennis court, and David and his sailing—none of whom were known to Quill or Meg. Finally, when Quill heard herself murmuring "wonderful, wonderful, wonderful," like Lawrence Welk after a sex-change operation, she gave up and ate as circumspectly as she could.

In the British tradtion, which Quill would have found pretentious anywhere else, Cressida led the ladies away for a short time after dinner, and Meg joined Quill in the bathroom. Quill liked the bathroom a lot. Like the rest of the house it was old, unpretentious, and there wasn't a Water Pik in sight. The walls were paneled with white pine, reminding her of the pleasant Nantucket beach cottages she and Meg had spent time in as girls.

"I can't stand it," Meg hissed at her, closing the door. "I want to play the banjo or something."

"Chocolate!" Quill said, in a subdued yell. "Chocolate! Chocolate! Chocolate!"

"Why'd you yell 'fire' when you fell into the chocolate," Meg sang. "Why'd you yell 'fire' when you fell into the choooc-late?"

"Because who would have come if I'd yelled 'chocolate!' Oh, dear." Quill looked in the tiny mirror, ran her fingers through her hair, sighed, and gave up. The humidity made it curl like bedsprings. "Hands down, this is the most awful dinner party I've ever been to."

"Quill, there's no conversation."

"I know there's no conversation. The thing is, Meg, we don't know anyone this woman knows except Verger Taylor. And other than talking about other people, I don't think Miss Houghton has much to say. About anything. Except her boys. Did you see how she looked at me when Evan grabbed my hand?"

"I sure did. Yikes." Meg stood beside her and they both looked into the mirror. Meg's eyes, clear and candid gray, met Quill's greenish-hazel ones. "What do we do now?"

"Bridge, I guess," said Quill. "And I haven't played for months."

"I haven't played for years," Meg complained. "You're the one that started the tournaments at the inn. You know what? There's five of us. And you can't play bridge with five people. So I'll sit out. I'll go for a walk on the beach."

"Coward," Quill said. "I'm the one Cressida Houghton wants to make into mincemeat. Why the heck did she invite us if she resents us?"

When Meg and Quill rejoined their hostess, she rose and gracefully introduced an elderly gentleman, impeccably groomed, apparently the David of the yachting stories. David was, Cressida said, an old and dear neighbor and would make up a fourth. The boys, she said, with a slight emphasis in her tone, were going out to meet some friends closer to their own age.

Two thoughts struck Quill at once. The first—that Cressida Houghton thought she and Meg were cradle robbers, that she had encouraged Evan's attention—hit her with the force of the so-far nonexistent hurricane. The second, that she'd forced Cressida Houghton, famed for her *politesse*, into overtly rude behavior, made her want to crawl under the worn chintz couch and stay there. She, Quill, had managed to offend the second or third most famous woman in America. Was that why she and Meg had been invited here? To let the gold-digger twins discover that the Taylor boys weren't up for grabs? Quill started to giggle. It was the kind of giggle that, once suppressed, surfaced harder than ever. She sat down with a pink face and bitten lower lip.

Cressida looked at her with no expression at all. "Shall we sit in the game room? Everything's set up in there. I'm afraid the boys and I have been playing three-handed bridge in there since five." She smiled gently. "But the cards are all warmed up."

To Quill's relief, the game room was brightly lit. It was the dimness in the rest of the house, she decided, that had put her so off-balance. A card table with a battered green felt cover had been drawn up before a cold fireplace. Quill sat in the scorekeeper's position, noting idly that East/West had been badly set by North/South three rubbers in a row in the three-handed game that afternoon. One of the games had been a grand slam: seven no-trump, doubled. Ouch.

"If you wouldn't mind," Cressida said, "David and I will play North/South. I had the worst luck this afternoon."

"I can see that," said Meg irrepressibly.

Meg and Quill were down by a thousand points when the dove-gray maid appeared at the game room door with the portable phone on a tray. Cressida took the call. She said "yes," "no," and "I see." For a long moment, she remained perfectly still. Then, "Please call the police. I'll send Mr. Hawthorne." She set the phone back on the tray for the waiting maid and sat relaxed until she'd gone out of the room. "You might as well know this. It's going to be in the newspapers tomorrow morning." She sighed. "And the television news, too, I expect. The boys took their two friends over to their father's home. I think they were planning a visit to Au Bar." A slight grimace flitted across the perfect face. "At any rate, there's a great deal of blood in Verger's study. And Verger himself has disappeared."

CHAPTER 8

"I knew it. I just knew it." Quill put the Mercedes in reverse and eased down the driveway. "Didn't I tell you that someone was going to get Verger Taylor?"

"There's no body," Meg pointed out. She leaned back in the seat. "What an evening."

"It was awful. Did you pick up the message I did?"

"That we were harpies after the gold-dust twins? Yeah." Meg stared up at the sky. There was a frosty nimbus around the moon. The air was heavy. They drove in silence for some moments. Meg said, "What do you suppose she's doing now?"

"Cressida? Calling a platoon of lawyers, I expect. She couldn't be as unconcerned as she appeared. Evan and Corrigan found the body . . ."

"There wasn't a body," Meg said.

"Or the blood, rather, and you can bet that the media will be on this like a flock of pigeons after bread crumbs in Central Park. They always are."

"How much blood do you suppose there was?"

"Meg!" She reached the road, stopped, and put the car in drive.

"I mean, was the place awash with it? Was it human blood? Was it little drops that might come if you'd cut yourself and driven to the emergency room?"

Quill didn't answer for a moment. She pulled onto the road and drove in silence, then said, "There was a security guard, surely."

"Was there?" They looked at each other. Meg raised her eyebrows. "You know, we're coming up on his house in a moment. Let's go find out."

"We can't interfere in a police investigation."

"Quill, wc'vc investigated how many murderers?"

"Four," said Quill glumly. "And a dozen corpses."

"And we've never worried about interfering in a police investigation before."

"Myles was in charge of almost all of those cases, Meg. I hardly think that the police here in Florida are going to welcome the services of two amateur detectives." She slowed. They were approaching Verger Taylor's mansion. The two gold lions shone brightly in the glare of the Mercedes's headlights.

"There's no one there!" Meg said in surprise.

"We were closer to the house than the Palm Beach County police," Quill pointed out. "They haven't had time to get here yet."

"Pull in," Meg said.

"Are you sure?"

"My investigative instincts have been roused. Let's just see what's going on."

Although there was absolutely no traffic, Quill signaled a left-hand turn and pulled past Verger Taylor's elaborate gates. The drive to the house was broad and straight. The front of the mansion was illuminated likc the Christmas tree in Rockefeller Plaza.

"There's that little Jaguar of Evan's," Quill said. She came to a stop. They both got out and went to the front door. It was twice Quill's height, perhaps more, and made of heavily carved wood. A lion's head door knocker was placed squarely in the center. Quill hesitated a moment, then rapped the knocker sharply against the brass plate. The door opened almost immediately.

"Quill!" Evan said. He was pale. His hair stuck up in little tufts around his head.

"We wondered if there was anything we could do for you," Meg said. She pushed Quill firmly over the threshold and into the foyer. They had both seen photographs of Verger Taylor's home, but the reality was overwhelming. The foyer was lined entirely in pink marble: floor, ceiling, and walls. Three enormous flower arrangements had been placed on pedestals with gold cherubs as the bases.

Meg looked up at Evan. "We thought we could drop your two friends off at their home. Get them out of the way of the police."

Behind them, through the open door, the wail of a police siren was abruptly cut off as a cruiser swept up the drive to the door. Two uniformed policemen scrambled out of the vehicle and approached the foyer at a run. A second cruiser came to a halt behind the first. Two more uniformed policemen spilled out of it. One took off at a run around the west wing of the house; the other, gun drawn, proceeded at a more deliberate pace around the east end.

Meg pushed Quill through the other end of the foyer into a living room which, at a glance, was the size of a basketball court. This, too, was entirely lined in pink marble. The fourth wall of the room was a series of ornately framed sliding glass doors, overlooking the darkness and, Quill presumed, the beach. The glass door at the farthest end of the wall had been smashed in. Glass littered the floor.

Corrigan and two young girls were huddled on a large, navy blue brocaded sofa in front of the fireplace. The cherub motif had been continued here in the supports for the black marble mantel. Both girls were blonde, thin, and tanned. They were wearing tight spandex dresses that stopped well above the knee. The one in red was smoking nervously. The girl in black huddled in the shelter of Corrigan's arm.

"Hey, guys," Meg said. "What's going on?"

Corrigan automatically rose to his feet. The girl in black whimpered and curled into a tight ball on the sofa. Accompanied by Evan, the two uniformed police jogged past them to a half-open door set in the west side of the room. The room beyond was dimly lit. Meg and Quill followed Evan.

This room had been a study, although, Quill thought, it looked more like the office of a Renaissance pope than that of the fourth largest real estate mogul in America. The room had a domed ceiling painted with scenes of the Annunciation. Bookshelves soared into the reaches of the dome on both sides of the room. Most of them were locked behind grilled doors set into the shelving.

A desk, which was at least six feet long, occupied the center of the room. A laptop computer lay shattered on the floor. The screen was cracked, but the monitor glowed eerily. A ten-line telephone had been tossed—or had fallen—next to it. The receiver was off.

There wasn't all that much blood. A small pool was next to the phone, and the handset had streaks of red on it. Quill narrowly avoided stepping in several splashes at the door. The younger of the two policeman—the one with a crew cut and wire-rimmed glasses—glanced at Meg. He barked, "Remain outside this area, please." The cellular phone at his belt beeped. He took it, flicked open the top and began to speak rapidly into it, his voice low and confidential. Meg moved into the shadow cast by a large statue in the Greek style—a copy, Quill thought—of the Mercury in the Louvre.

Quill backed out of the office. She stepped carefully on the marble floor, watching for splashes of blood. There was a small but discernible trail of red linking the office door to the smashed glass at the beachfront side of the living room.

The glass had exploded inward. The shards sprayed out from the door in a parabola, which clearly demonstrated that at least two powerful blows from a heavy object had been struck from the outside. Remnants of shattered glass clung to the door frame. The most damage seemed to have occurred about four feet from the ground. Quill wished she had a tape measure.

A powerful flashlight swept the area immediately outside the door and a voice ordered Quill away. She backed up. One of the policemen outside yelled, "Ange! We got a body! Not Taylor, do you read? Not Taylor. Seems to be security."

The girl in red screamed. The policeman with the crew cut came out of the study and said calmly, "You're not on the radio, Kyle. I don't read you, I hear you just fine." His gaze swept over Quill—sharp, appraising, indifferent. "Out of the way, miss. Confine yourself to the fireplace area."

The policeman outside called for an ambulance. Quill went to Corrigan and sat down in the chair directly across from him. He had half-risen at the policeman's shout about the discovery of the body, then sat back when he'd heard it wasn't his father. He looked bewildered. Out of the corner of her eye, Quill saw Meg slip across the living room into the east part of the house. She spoke gently to Corrigan, who jumped nonetheless at the sound of her voice. "Did your dad have a large security force, Corrigan?"

"What? No. No. It was twenty-four hours a day, but it was just the one guard. He doubled as a chauffeur. I mean, there was a whole group of them, but only one at a time." He bit nervously at his thumbnail. "What do you think happened? Do you think my father's dead?"

The girl in black started to cry, not, Quill judged, from grief, but from sheer nervous tension. The one in red stubbed out her cigarette, lit another, and jiggled her left leg up and down.

"Just the one guard, Corrigan? Surely somebody like your dad had better protection than that."

"Well, sure. The whole place is wired for security." He pointed upwards. "Cameras all over the place. The guard didn't even have to patrol, just watch the video monitors."

"When did you four come to pick up Mr. Taylor?"

"About nine-thirty. Ev and I went down to get Shirl and Beth just after dinner, and we came straight here."

Quill addressed both girls. "How far away do you guys live?"

"Shirl's here for the weekend, at Beth's house," Corrigan said.

"Is your house here, Beth?"

"I live in Juno," the blonde in black said sullenly. "Why the fuck do you want to know, anyway?"

"Officer!" The shout came from the part of the house where Meg had gone. Quill jumped to her feet.

"Officer!"

"That's Meg!" Quill said.

"She must be in the kitchen," Corrigan said. "What the hell?"

Quill ran ahead of the others to the east wing archway, skidding on the floor in her high-heeled shoes. "Meg? Meg!"

"Down there," Corrigan said from behind her. "Take a right. The kitchen's beyond the solarium."

Two policemen ran past Quill, their guns drawn, Ange in the lead. "You civilians stay back," he ordered.

"That's my sister," Quill said, and then immediately felt silly. She dropped back behind the cops and followed them into the kitchen. Verger Taylor's baroque tastes hadn't stopped with his pink-marble living room. This area was almost exclusively black granite and cherrywood. At first glance, there appeared to be no appliances at all, just a huge granite-topped island in the center of the floor. Meg was standing at it, her arm around a cowering, terrified maid.

"Maria was locked in the pantry," she said.

"You let her out?" Ange demanded.

"Of course I let her out. She was kicking her heels against the door, poor thing."

"She was tied up?"

"With clothes line and duct tape," Meg said. She pointed to the detritus on the floor. "It's all right there."

"You," said Ange sternly. "Don't leave. I'm giving myself a good hard think about arresting you for interfering with evidence." He scowled. "Step away from the witness, ma'am."

Meg saluted smartly. "Yes, *sir*, officer, sir."

Quill gave an exasperated *tcha!* and pulled Meg aside. She looked for an appropriately secure place to yell at her sister and found one in the maid's room. It was just off the kitchen, next to what Quill realized was a set of triple ovens concealed by cherry paneling. She shoved Meg into the room. It was small, with a neatly made twin bed, wicker chest, a print of the Scared Heart on the wall, and a small television set. Quill closed the door firmly and sat down on the bed. Meg prowled restlessly around the room. "Good idea, Meg, pissing off the police."

A look familiar to Quill—mulish in the extreme—spread over Meg's face.

"You know why it's not a good idea to piss off the police? Because if you get arrested, you can't present your potted rabbit at the banquet on Friday. And goodbye third star."

Meg's face cleared. "You've got a point."

"Of course I've got a point. Now what did that poor maid tell you before you called us in?"

"I called you in right away," Meg said indignantly.

"I know you, Meg. You grabbed the chance to question her, didn't you? What'd she say?"

"That she didn't know anything was happening until she heard the glass door smash."

"Did she know what time that was?"

"About six-thirty."

"Good Lord. That's just after we met him. This must have happened just after we left."

"I know. It's horrible."

"Is she sure about the time?"

"How should I know? Anyhow, she ran to the living room, thinking maybe a seagull had hit the door or something."

"A seagull?"

"She said it's happened before. And she said the security alarm hadn't gone off. The whole place is wired, Quill. The robbers must have disconnected it somehow."

"You're making a highly speculative assumption that they were robbers, Meg."

"No, I'm not. I'll tell you why in a minute. Anyhow, Maria said she thought a seagull came through the glass."

"Meg, there's no way a seagull could smash those thermal pane doors. Not even a three-hundred-pound seagull."

"I'm just telling you what she said. Will you shut up and listen? She ran to the archway leading onto that womb with a view . . ."

"Pretty funny, Quilliam."

"All that pink marble, Quilliam. Ugh! Anyhow, she saw two men struggling with Verger Taylor. Burglars, she said."

"Did she recognize them?"

"Of course she didn't! What self-respecting burglar would burgle with his bare face hanging out? Both of them had those arctic masks on their faces. You know, the woolly thing you wear to keep the cold out when you ski."

"How were they dressed?"

"I couldn't get that out of her. She screamed, ran back to the kitchen, and hid in the closet."

"She didn't call 911?"

"She was too scared."

"Oh, dear."

"Anyhow, she hid in the closet and said the burglars came looking for her."

"How did she know that?"

"Because they were calling, 'come out, *señorita*, come out. We will not harm you if you come out.' Devils, she said."

"Were they hollering in Spanish?"

"They must have been. Her English isn't very good. Anyway, they flung open the door of the closet, found her, blindfolded her, tied her up, and left her for dead. She says. But as far as I can tell, they didn't mean to harm her at all. She was tied up pretty tightly, but she could breathe. And she wasn't beaten or anything. Then one burglar came back."

"Came back?"

"That's what she said. She was lying there, scared out of her wits, crying, and praying when she heard this devil come back. 'This devil, snapping like the flames of hell.' That's her words."

"This was all in Spanish, Meg?"

"Yes. What of it?"

"Your Spanish sucks, that's what of it."

The door to the bedroom flew open. Ange the policeman stood there. His face was red. He called over his shoulder, "Here they are!" and stepped back. "Out." He motioned with one hand. The other was on his pistol. "Out now. The sergeant wants a word with you two."

He shepherded them back to the living room. As huge as it was, it had become crowded. An ambulance team waited with a stretcher. Five or six forensic technicians were crawling around the floor, vacuuming, taking pictures, and otherwise gathering evidence. Two men in dark three-piece suits conferred by the fireplace with Evan and Corrigan. A policewoman sat with Shirl and Beth. The intact door next to the shattered one where the robbers had entered was open, and a man and a woman in plain clothes were headed towards it.

"Sarge!" Ange called out. "Here they are."

The woman looked over her shoulder and snapped, "Hold 'em."

Ange gestured sternly at a pair of Louis Quinze chairs on either side of an occasional table. An ormolu clock ticked away in the center of the table, and Quill noted the time: eleven-fifteen.

She and Meg both sat down. Ange took up what Quill thought of as the guard-dog stance: feet braced apart, hands on his position belt, a stern and unforgiving look on his face.

"Ange?" she said chattily. "Are you from around here?"

"New Jersey, ma'am."

"Is crime more interesting here or in New Jersey?"

Meg rolled her eyes. Ange didn't respond at all. Quill tried again. "Been on the force long?"

"Two years, ma'am."

"So you've had some experience," Meg cracked. "Mostly traffic though, right? Don't even bother asking him stuff, Quill. He doesn't know a thing."

A tinge of red crept over Ange's cheeks. Quill looked at Meg, bemused at her rudeness. Meg dropped the merest wink and Quill murmured, "Oh, of course." Then, with indignation, she said, "What a mean thing to say, Meg. Officer . . ." She darted a glance at his uniform. His last name had more consonants than syllables. "That is, Ange knows what's been going on here. Don't you, Ange?"

"Seen this before, ma'am."

"Where, on that dumb TV show *Cops*?" Meg snorted. "Hah."

Ange's gaze drifted downward. Meg was wearing a gauzy white cotton dress that she'd picked up in Bloomingdale's that afternoon. Despite her tough-guy diction, she looked a lot younger than thirty. "Home invasion, miss."

Quill, a little huffy that she'd been 'ma'amed' and Meg had been 'missed,' said with more force than she'd intended, "Home invasion? You mean armed thugs breaking into people's homes and taking their valuables? That's ridiculous!"

"Oh?" Officer Ange, despite his youth, had an unexpected depth of shrewdness. "You two know any different, you'd better let the sergeant know."

"Know what?" The female detective's companion, the one who had gone out the door to, presumably, examine the body of the security guard, approached with a frown. "Your names?" he snapped. He was of medium height, with very broad shoulders and a big chest. His hair was fair—mixed heavily with gray and thinning on top. His nose dominated a thin, tanned face. Quill liked his looks.

"Sarah Quilliam. This is my sister, Meg."

The set of his shoulders shifted a little. "Sarah Quilliam? You involved in that business with Hedrick Conway up in Hemlock Falls?"

"Why, yes. I was."

"Hm. It's all right, Corporal. I'll take it from here."

Ange straightened and put his hands behind his back. "Sir?"

"I said it's all right. I know them. Or of them, at least." Quill, who had the sudden, undeniably thrilling thought that news of her exploits as a solver of crime had gotten as far as Miami, smiled brilliantly. "Nosy," the detective added, "but harmless."

"If you say so, sir."

"Those two bimbos of the Taylor boys will need an escort home. Why don't you take them and report back here in half an hour. No more than that."

"Yes, sir." Ange marched off. Quill noticed that the tips of his ears were red.

The detective shoved both hands in the pockets of his sport coat, balanced on the balls of his feet, and said unexpectedly, "How's Myles?"

''Myles?'' Quill blinked at him. ''Oh, my goodness! You must be Jerry. Myles's friend from his days in New York.''

''Hear he's fallen into a pretty lucrative line of work.''

''Yes. He's an investigator for a company that handles corporate crime. He spends a lot of time overseas.''

His eyes went to the ring on her left hand.

''And yes, we're getting around to that. At some point.''

''Good to hear it. Thought things were kind of rocky there for a while.''

''Oh?'' Quill's voice was cool.

''We thought we might get him on the force in Miami a while back. Just before he took that investigator's job. Didn't say much, Myles. Never does. But I gathered that if you two were really going to get married, he wasn't interested in moving down here. So.'' His tone shifted. ''You two know anything about this?''

''We might,'' said Quill. ''Actually, um . . . Jerry . . . I'd been expecting that something was going to happen to Verger Taylor.''

''You had, huh?''

Quill ignored Meg's warning glare. ''In the past few days, I've heard no less than two significant threats against Verger Taylor's life.''

''No kidding?''

Quill, a little uncertain at the sarcasm in his voice, nodded.

''You realize that keeping track of people who want to murder Verger Taylor is a full-time job? The list's pretty long. In the past month we've had''—he paused, drew a small notebook from the breast pocket of his jacket, and flipped through the pages—''three significant death threats against him.''

''Three?'' said Quill.

''Significant?'' Meg asked. ''What do you mean by significant?''

"Threatening letters, phone calls, that sort of thing. Taylor's attorney, Frank Carmichael, turns them over to us pretty routinely."

"Corporal whosis, that is, Ange."

"Wisc. Just like it's spelled."

"Yes. Him. That is, he. Said that all the evidence pointed to a home invasion."

"That's right. It's a typical M.O. for this part of Palm Beach County. The perpetrators scope out the victim's home beforehand, posing as television repairmen or electricians, then pick a night when there's not a lot of activity. They don't care in particular if anyone's home or not. They disable any alarm systems, shoot whomever's in their way, and take off with what they can steal. In this case, it was a bag with twenty thousand dollars cash, a lot of small silver and jade. The contents of the safe in Taylor's office."

"Twenty thousand in cash?" Quill was stunned.

"The boys say keeping that amount of money on hand was typical of him. It's not all that unusual around here."

"Couldn't have it been premeditated murder? Planned to look like a home invasion?"

"Anything's possible," Jerry said agreeably. "But I'll tell you one thing about police work, if Myles hasn't told you already—the simplest explanation is usually the best. We checked the security log, and two telephone repairmen checked in to the mansion three days ago. One of our guys just contacted the phone company—and no such team was sent out. The security guard was shot through the head, execution style, and all the indications are that Taylor's been shot, too."

"Do you have any suspects yet?" Meg asked.

"A home invasion is usually staged by young kids without anything to lose. Except their lives. Most of them don't care about that. Half the time around these parts, the homeowner's armed and blows at least one of them away. The other half of the time, they shoot to kill, but the victim survives to put them in jail. Seems to me if one of Taylor's business victims want to blow him off, they'd choose a much less risky way. But then, you tell me."

"Where's his body?" Meg demanded. "If this was a home invasion, where's Verger's body?"

"Now, that's a good question. I don't know." He grinned.

Quill, who had been feeling a little intimidated, couldn't help but grin back.

"I know you two have been involved in a number of cases. Myles tells me you're actually pretty sharp at solving crimes. So, you have any ideas? I'll listen."

"Where do you think the body is?" asked Meg. "If the types of criminals that stage home invasions just leave the bodies, where is Verger Taylor?"

Jerry nodded. "Now that, Miss Quilliam, is the best question anyone's asked all night. There's one possible explanation. And if it's true . . ."

"Jer!" Jerry's woman partner, a pleasant-featured, heavyset woman in her fifties, waved at him urgently from across the room. "We got it. We got the call."

"Oh, my goodness," Quill said. "Kidnapping. Of course!" She and Meg sprang up after Jerry and trailed behind him to the living room telephone. Evan, his face tight, was listening intently on the telephone. A wire was attached to the head of the phone by the same kind of rubber suckers that used to tip Meg's play arrows when she was six. The wire ran to a recorder that was spinning slowly. Evan held the receiver away from his ear, so that the police officers nearby could hear the conversation. The kidnapper's voice was heavily distorted. And from the look on Jerry's face, Quill knew that they were either unprepared or technically unable to trace the call.

"But is my father all right?" Evan said. He was sweating. It seemed hard for him to get his lips under control.

"Waaann hunnnnert t'ouusaanndd . . ." the voice

hissed. "Leeffttt onnnn theee noooommmbbber nine buoy oonnn the chhhannnell. Byyyy tenn-thhhirty tommorroowww."

Evan's look at Detective Fairchild was desperate. "One hundred thousand dollars," he repeated, "left on the number nine buoy in the Port of Palm Beach Channel at ten-thirty tomorrow night."

"Nnoooo pollisss. No ppollllosss. Orrr . . ."

A sudden scream, agony-filled, clearly male, blared from the receiver. Evan dropped it with a shout. There was a *click* and then the dial tone droned implacably.

"Did you hear him, Detective?" Evan's voice was high and uncontrolled. He stopped, put his hands over his face, and took several deep breaths. When he took his hands away, his face was pale, but calmer. "You didn't hear it all. He said that if we didn't get that money there, tomorrow night, without police involvement, they'll send Dad back to us. Piece by piece." He shuddered.

There was a clatter and thump. Quill turned. Corrigan had fainted.

"Cor!" Evan leaped for his brother. The two medics stepped over the stretcher and knelt by him. "Don't touch him! Leave him alone!" Evan shoved one medic aside and snarled at the other to move. He cradled Corrigan's head in one hand and slapped him lightly, swiftly across the cheeks with the other. "Cory," he said. "Cory!"

"Good God," Meg said, "this is terrible."

Quill went quietly to Evan's side. She knelt next to him and touched him on the shoulder. "Evan? Evan." The boy turned to her with dilated eyes, not seeming to see her at first, free hand raised, the other still fiercely clutching his brother's head. Quill closed her hand over his. "Here. He's just fainted. Let him down. Gently. That's it. Let me take him. You see how his eyelids are fluttering open? The shock's just been too much for him." She looked around. "Anyone have any smelling salts, or whatever it's called?"

"Ammonia carbonate," said one of the medics. He was a slight man, with a pencil-thin mustache and sympathetic brown eyes. He pulled an ampule from his breast pocket, broke it, and waved it under Corrigan's nose. The boy coughed and his eyelids opened and closed. The color began to seep back into his face and he sat up. Evan grabbed him by the shoulders and shook him. "Cor! *Cor!* It's me. Evan! Wake up. Wake up!"

Corrigan held up his hand and nodded. He sat up, then shakily got to his feet. Quill, still on her knees, thought she had never seen anyone look so pale.

"Dad?" Corrigan said.

"Dad's going to be all right, Cor." Evan, fiercely determined, hugged him. "We're going to get him back. We're going to get the money."

"How?" asked Corrigan simply. "We don't have any. Where are we going to get it? Where are we going to get a hundred thousand dollars?"

"We'll get it, Cor."

"But it's all Dad's! And that will take time! And they said no police! How are we going to get Dad out of this mess without involving the police?"

For the first time since Quill had met him, Evan showed some of his father's behavior. He snapped his fingers. "Hawthorne. Hawthorne!"

There had been two men in three-piece suits conferring with Evan and Corrigan just before Meg had found Maria in the closet. The older of them wound his way through the crowd of policemen, medics, and technicians surrounding Evan and his brother. "Yes, Evan."

"I want my brother and myself out of here. Right now."

"Okay. Who exactly is in charge here?"

"Jerry Fairchild," Evan said. "Fairchild?"

"Right here, Mr. Taylor."

"Clear this room. My brother and I want to talk with

you alone." His gaze swept over Quill; he didn't see her. "Everyone out of here. Now."

It was another forty minutes before Meg and Quill were allowed to leave. The police ushered them—accompanied by Maria—back into the kitchen. A detailed statement about their activities was taken from them. They gave their current address and the address in Hemlock Falls. Ange, who'd returned from taking Shirl and Beth back to Beth's home, volunteered to see them to their car and follow them out the gate.

"It's sweet of you, Ange," Meg said flippantly. "But we can manage to drive home alone." She looked critically at Quill. "Although if I look as bad as she does, I can see why you're concerned."

"It's not that, miss. It's the crowd outside the gates. We can prevent the media from coming onto a crime scene, but you're going to be mobbed once you leave here."

"Oh, my God," Meg said in disgust. "You might give us an escort at that, Ange. Just to Beach Road. We can take it from there. But you'd better alert the medics." She grinned. "I'm so flipped out by all of this that I'm going to break a solemn vow and let my sister drive."

CHAPTER 9

Quill sat in a lounge chair overlooking the Atlantic and sipped orange juice. It was late, after ten o'clock in the morning. The sun was high overhead. The French doors were open to the breezes, and she could hear Meg clattering away in the kitchen. There was a brief hiatus, the patter of her bare feet, and then she came out onto the terrace. "Try this." She held out a quarter-cup of dark, strong-smelling liquid.

"No," Quill said. She folded her legs under her and started at the horizon. The clouds looked iffy. News about the weather had been supplanted by the disappearance/kidnapping of Verger Taylor and (less interesting from the media's points of view) the murder of the security guard. Although the tropical storm had been officially upgraded to a grade one hurricane, it was languishing somewhere off the coast of Puerto Rico and was not supposed to pose a threat, except in the minds of the weather anchors, who'd been vainly trying to scrape up a little bit of pleasurable terror all morning with possibilities of doom, death, and destruction.

"There'll be rain later in the day, though," Quill said aloud.

"What? The so-called hurricane? I told you," Meg said with splendid inaccuracy, "that it wasn't going to show up here. Now, taste this. Quill! Come on! Please? Just a teeny, tiny taste."

"Meg, for heaven's sake. This is the third marinade recipe I've tried for you this morning and I hate it! It's horrible having all this strong stuff before I'm even awake."

"Just tell me what you think. I added something really different."

Quill groaned, carefully took the stainless steel cup, and sipped. "Rum," she said. "You added rum."

"What do you think?"

"Actually, I like it better than the brandy. Besides, it's less expensive."

"You do? Like it better than the brandy?"

"I really doubt, with all this upset about the kidnapping and with the Institute closed for electrical repairs, that Tiffany's going ahead with the banquet. I don't know why you're fiddling with the marinade, anyhow. You can't get to the rabbits until tomorrow morning and even then, they're already marinating—oh, forget it."

"You're right, of course. I'm giving up the whole idea. The third star would look better on a gravestone, under these circumstances." Meg tossed the remainder of the marinade over the terrace railing. It landed on a pair of peach double hibiscus and turned them an unpleasant brown.

"Now look what you've done," Quill scolded, mildly. She gave Meg's hand an affectionate squeeze. She knew how much the possibility of being rated had meant to her.

Meg perched on the edge of the tiled table. Tiffany—or, as Quill suspected, Tiffany's decorator—had done a wonderful job on the terrace. The furniture was wrought iron. The tables had tiled tops in deep jewel tones. The one Meg sat on was a cross between sky blue and cobalt. Quill had seen the color on a pair of Fu dogs at an exhibit at the Guggenheim, but nowhere else. She rubbed her hand absently on the tabletop and sighed.

"What's the matter, Quill? Did Myles holler at you last night?"

"Don't be an idiot," Quill said crossly. "Myles never hollers, as you so gracefully put it. He did make a suggestion that we keep our noses out of Jerry Fairchild's investigation, but that was it."

"It's a terrible thing," Meg said soberly. "Kidnapping. Who do you suppose is behind it? Terrorists? Why would terrorists want to kidnap a real estate mogul? A hundred thousand dollars isn't much these days—it's enough to maybe make a little bomb and bomb, say, a place like Scranton, Pennsylvania, or Topeka. But not much more than that. Why not real money?"

Quill pulled at her lower lip. "That's it. That's part of it. It's been bothering me. That ransom is a pittance these days."

"I think it's proof of these home invaders' amateur status."

Quill shook her head decisively. "I don't believe it. I don't believe it was a home invasion. I think this was murder, and I think it was someone we know who kidnapped Verger Taylor. This whole home invasion thing is too stagy, Meg. Too coincidental."

"You could be right. But you know what? Myles is righter. It's none of our business. I think we should call Tiffany, thank her for a perfectly awful experience, and go home."

Quill raised her head. "Is that the doorbell? Who do you suppose could have gotten past that media crowd posted at the gates? Luis was pretty good about keeping them out." Quill walked down the hall to the front door. Before she could get to it, the door pushed open and Tiffany appeared. "Hi," Quill said, surprised. "Meg and I were just going to give you a call."

"Sorry," she said. "Had to use my key. I was simply pursued."

Quill looked over her shoulder. She could see the front gates from where she was standing. There were two vans from the local television stations, a crowd of cars with camerapeople sitting on the hoods and roofs, and a gaggle of reporters just standing around. One or two of them looked Tiffany's way, but the others kept their attention in the direction of the second stack of buildings where Evan and Corrigan had their apartment. Pursued, my foot.

Tiffany shook her hair out dramatically—today's color was a bright gold—and put her hand to her head. "Jackals," she said. "The press. Could I have a cup of coffee?"

"Sure. Come in. Meg and I were just sitting on the terrace. Go on out and I'll bring you the coffee there. Black?"

"Yes." She patted her slim midriff. She was wearing a scarlet pant suit, bare feet with fashionable slides, and huge acid-green earrings. Her eyes seemed very blue. As she walked across the living room to the porch, the slides squeaked against her instep.

Quill set three cups on a tray and sliced coffee cake. When Meg was nervous, she tended to bake rather than cook, and she'd been up early that morning. She'd made the sour-cream coffee cake, a strudel, and brioche dough was rising in the corner of the kitchen by the television set. Quill put the kettle on the boiler, poured it through the carafe of coffee, and carried the whole arrangement out on the porch.

"The coffee takes a while to drip through," she said, setting the tray on the largest table. "Tiffany, these tiles are absolutely marvelous. Where did you find these colors?"

"How can you *think* of tiles at a time like this?"

"Oh." Quill took a moment to regroup. She ignored Meg's sarcastic grin. She'd been wondering what to say to Verger's ex-wife about the kidnapping. *I'm so sorry* didn't seem quite appropriate when the day before she would have been glad to see Verger cut up into little bits and fed to the fish. It was clear now that the sympathy accorded to widows would be welcomed. "I'm so sorry," she said inadequately. "This must be terrible for you."

"It is. It is. Poor Verger," she said intensely, "poor, poor Verger." She took a slice of cake from the tray, nibbled a corner off it, and put it back. "Cressida said I shouldn't talk to the press at all," she said with a pout. Then, "I think that's wise, of course."

"Very," Quill agreed. It was becoming clearer that Tiffany, with attention switched to her missing ex-husband, the Institute closed, and no one much interested in her vitriol now that genuine tragedy was in the making, had nowhere else to go but here.

"We're sorry about the banquet," Meg said, courteously. "A lot of planning went into it."

"The banquet? No. Oh, no. I don't think that would be wise at all, to cancel the banquet. Do you? I mean . . . I would think poor Verger would have wanted it to go on."

"I shouldn't think poor Verger would want anything of the sort," Meg said tartly.

"It's still on," Tiffany said defiantly. "And Ernst assures me that the building will be open tomorrow, just as soon as the whatchamacallit boxes are all replaced. So I expect to see both of you there bright and early tomorrow morning. We've had to cancel Quill's lecture on innkeeping, which is okay because the only person who signed up is Linda Longstreet and she's history. And of course, the Le Nozze kitchens will be tied up with the banquet, so we've had to cancel your cooking courses, Meg. But I promised the students we'll have it next week."

"We're going home," Meg said, "as soon as the Syracuse airport opens."

"Nonsense. In the middle of all this excitement? And of course, Dr. Bob's therapy sessions are on, too." She sighed happily. "It's going to be a nice, full couple of weeks. And I think that the media people will be very interested in the therapy group. Very interested."

"So everything's the way it was before the murder?"

Tiffany's eyes got wide. "So he's dead? How do you know?"

"The security guard's dead," Quill said. "And that makes it murder. Whether Verger is alive or not."

Meg jiggled her foot impatiently. "It's going to be a circus, Tiffany. Please reconsider."

"Everything's set," Tiffany said firmly. "The press releases are out. My secretary in New York faxed them this morning. The banquet's on, the Excelsior therapy sessions are on, and I've rescheduled your cooking classes for next week. Besides, I haven't even gotten to the best part yet. You'll drop all this talk of going home when I show you what I've brought you."

"What if Verger comes back?" Meg asked.

"He'll be far too interested in letting everyone know about his experience to worry about my little old Excelsior. Trust me on this one. Now, how would you two like to help me solve the murder of that little person? The security guard? Might be good for a laugh, wouldn't you think?"

"How would we like to help you solve the murder?" Meg echoed. "Not a lot, I have to say."

"The early news had some clips of the crimes you and Quill helped solve up in Hemlock Falls. Bernie Waters from *Hot Tip* thinks you already may be working on the crime. Are you?"

Quill carefully avoided looking at Meg. "I did have a couple of questions. About who would want to harm Verger."

Tiffany snorted. "Everyone who met the son of a bitch," she said in quite the old way. Then, sorrowfully, "I mean, Verger's a successful businessman. And there are many people jealous of him. Many. But the police are saying that it's one of those gangs that does home invasions.'' For a moment, real fear shone in her eyes. ''I think it's terrible. Just terrible that you can't even be safe in your own home.''

''It's either one or the other, isn't it?'' Quill said firmly.

''Either . . . what?''

''Either a home invasion or a kidnapping, but not both. It doesn't make sense that a gang breaking into a house, ready to shoot anyone who gets in their way, carefully ties up the maid and puts in her in the closet, and on impulse kidnaps Verger Taylor and sets up an elaborate method of getting a pitifully small ransom for him.''

''Elaborate?'' Meg said with raised eyebrows. ''Leaving the mon—'' She stopped. Before they had left the Taylor mansion last night, Jerry had warned them not to leak any information about the money drop. They were the only outsiders, other than the family lawyers, who knew of the purposed method of delivery. ''Well, just leaving the money, wherever the kidnappers ask them to leave it.''

''You know what the demands are?'' Tiffany dropped her discontented, diffident manner and leaned forward in excitement. ''I knew it! I just knew you were working on the case. Tell. Oh, do tell!''

Meg offered Tiffany a cup of coffee. She took it and leaned back. ''When you see what I brought for you, you'll help me solve the kidnapping, won't you? If I just had something to tell those press pe—well, never mind. So you both think Verger's kidnapping was planned beforehand, is that it?''

Somewhat taken aback at this evidence of intelligence, Quill said, ''Yes.''

Tiffany set the coffee carefully on the table. She brushed idly at her trousers. ''In these sorts of things, how do you go about solving the crime? I mean, you guys don't have a crime lab with you, do you? You can't do scientific evidence and things like that. So how do you do it?''

Quill sighed. ''You're talking as if we go looking for crimes to solve, Tiffany. And we don't. So far, all the cases we've investigated have been right in front of our noses.''

''Like this one,'' Tiffany said. ''So how would you go about solving this one?''

''Well, we talk to people. Sooner or later with every crime, a pattern emerges. And you get the outline of the pattern by retracing the victim's steps, talking to everyone who knew the victim, fitting the pieces together.''

''Look.'' Tiffany wiped one finger delicately along her lower lip. Then she pulled carefully at a piece of mascara on her eyelash. ''If I told you girls something—strictly in confidence, you know—well, you know this Detective Fairchild pretty well, don't you?''

''Close as houses,'' Meg lied. ''But, Tiffany, there's a bare possibility that Verger is alive, that this is a kidnapping, and if you know something important, you'd better tell the police right now.''

''It's not what I know. It's what I've got.''

''What you've got?'' Quill asked. ''You don't have a ransom note, do you?''

''Nope. I've got this.'' She was carrying a crocodile envelope purse. She opened the snap, careful of her long red nails, and withdrew a little black leather book. ''Verger's appointment book. It has all his meetings in it. And some other stuff, too.''

''His appointment book?'' Quill reached for it. Tiffany held it out of reach, like a little kid refusing to let another little kid play with a desirable toy. ''How did you get it?''

''I saw him yesterday, you know. He arranged to sign the house in Cannes over to me . . .''

''In return for dropping the Excelsior charity,'' Meg said.

''Oh, he would have come around to my way of thinking. Poor Verger. Always so thoughtful. Anyway. He got a phone call while we were yell—I mean talking, and he turned his back to me, because he didn't want me to know who he was on the phone with, like I didn't know it was that little teenaged tramp Mariel, so I reached over and took the book. Just to look. And then when he turned around, he started screaming at me, and in all the confusion, I just forgot to put it back.'' She waggled the book in the air. ''So. Would this help?''

''It might help get you arrested,'' Meg said dryly. ''You said Verger keeps all his appointments in there?''

''Every single one. And what do you mean, arrest me?''

''My guess is,'' Quill said, ''that Jerry's looking at everyone who knew where Verger was going to be that day. The most important tool a kidnapper would have is knowledge beforehand of a victim's schedule.''

Tiffany, Quill noted, wore a lot of blusher. She went pale, and orangey-tan swathes of color stood out starkly from her temples to her cheekbones. ''So the police would think that I, *I might have done this?*''

''If I were a policeman, I would,'' Meg said sunnily. ''As a matter of fact, I'm wondering right now. Where were you all day yesterday, Tiffany?''

''Jail is horrible,'' Tiffany said. ''Have you seen movies about what happens to women in jail?''

''Do you have any kind of alibi at all?'' Meg asked.

''I was at the Golden Door Spa all afternoon. It was my day for a facial, my manicure, my seaweed bath, and my hair. I was there from three until way after ten o'clock. And there are dozens of witnesses. Dozens.''

''Then you may be okay,'' Meg said. ''Unless there was an opportunity for you to slip out for an hour or so.''

''Stark naked and wrapped with seaweed mud? You've got to be kidding!''

''Of course,'' Meg said. ''This book really should be

turned over to the police, Tiffany. Why don't I call Jerry right . . ."

"No! No. No. No." She was breathing quickly, and her eyes were bright with panic. "Couldn't you two do it? Couldn't you tell Jerry that Verger left the appointment book at the board meeting yesterday and you picked it up to give back to him?"

"No. Jerry'd start to suspect us." Meg looked sorry, but not truly sorry.

"You could explain to him, then, that I just took it. I just took it because Verger puts everything in there. And I was . . . I wanted to find out what he was doing with that twit, Mariel. That's all."

Quill suspected that it wasn't that at all. And she also thought she knew why Verger, who must have missed his appointment book immediately and known who'd taken it, hadn't protested. Verger and Tiffany were very careful to keep each other aware of where each of them would be. Just as one or the other was always careful to let the press know where they would be. How could they stage the famous confrontations if they didn't? "Good," said Quill. "If you give it to us, we can see Jerry gets it with a full and complete explanation."

"You could maybe say that one of you found it somewhere and picked it up for safekeeping," said Tiffany.

"No, we couldn't say that. But the book is critical, Tiffany. Whoever snatched Verger from his house last night knew he'd be home and knew the only staff on Tuesday nights were the security guard and Maria. Does Verger keep a very complete record of his appointments?"

"Very," Tiffany said. "You have no idea. If you don't have to mention my name to Detective Fairchild you won't, will you?"

"We'll do our best to keep you out of it," Quill promised. "But I don't think it will be possible."

"Hm," said Tiffany. "Arrested. My God. And Verger told me my spa days were a stupid expense. Just goes to show you, doesn't it? Well, toodle, girls." She got up, feet squelching with that annoying sound, and turned before she reached the French doors. "By the way. When all this is over? I want that appointment book back, if at all possible. The tabloids would pay a pretty stiff price for it. 'Kay?"

"The tabloids?" asked Meg.

Quill, thinking hard, didn't respond. She waited until she heard the click of the front door closing, then said, "Did you notice that Tiffany was wearing those slides with bare feet?"

"You mean her shoes? Yes, but so what?"

"That crackling devil Maria talked about. Close your eyes. Pretend you're tied up in a closet, blindfolded, scared to death. You hear one of the kidnappers come back. Snap-snap. Snap-snap. Bare feet in slides, Meg?"

Meg, who had leaned back and closed her eyes, opened them with a thoughtful expression. "Slides like Linda Longstreet was wearing? Thin, Quill, very thin."

"She's got a motive. According to Carmichael, she's been taking rake-offs from the deliveries. She's got a lot of big strong cousins with vans. All that nervousness makes sense if she's involved with criminal activity."

"So we want to check her out." She waved her hand grandly. "Make a note, Watson."

"*You* make the note. You're Watson."

"Okay, I will." Meg jotted down *L.L. interview?* on the notepad with an amiable expression. "Anything else for right now?"

"You know, at first I thought Tiffany might be the one behind all this."

"So did I," Meg agreed. "But did you notice that spa alibi? Pretty good."

"I noticed." She hesitated. "You don't think that Verger staged this thing himself, do you?"

"Why in the name of goodness should he?"

"Anything's possible. Well, let's take a look at what his day was like." She opened the address book at random. ''Oh, my!'' She closed the book with a gasp, then promptly opened it again.

''What?'' Meg demanded.

Quill started to laugh. ''He's—er—rating his women!''

''You're kidding! Let me see that!'' Quill held it out of reach. Meg got out of her chair, leaned over Quill's shoulder, and shrieked at what she saw.

''It's a separate section from the appointments.'' Quill gasped, still laughing. ''Oh, my. Oh, my. Tiffany was a three-star but he's crossed it out! Oh, ugh!''

Meg shook her head in disgust. ''What a jerk.'' She refilled her coffee cup and sat down again. Quill continued to read, shaking her head. ''Good grief, this guy got around. And he didn't even code the names, Meg. I mean, Tiffany's right, the tabloids would pay a—'' She bit off her words abruptly.

''What?'' Meg demanded. ''What?''

Quill closed the appointment book slowly. ''Linda Longstreet. She's in here. She is—was—one of Verger's women.''

CHAPTER 10

Luis shook his head. "You don't go down Australian Avenue." He leaned one elbow in a friendly way on the driver's side of the Mercedes.

Quill squinted at him in the sunlight. "Your computer printout says all three addresses are right off Australian," she pointed out. "How do we get to addresses off Australian without going down Australian? Longstreet Catering, Longstreet Hauling and Trucking, and poor Linda Longstreet herself."

"It's a very bad section."

"You mean it's a poor section?" Meg asked. "We haven't seen any poor sections since we came to Palm Beach. What we've seen are a lot of drop-dead gorgeous homes and some terrific landscaping. Even the regular-people type sections, the middle class, have drop-dead gorgeous homes and terrific landscaping, on a much smaller scale, of course."

"You do not know how West Palm Beach came into being? I will tell you. Then you will know not to go down Australian Avenue. This man who built Palm Beach . . ."

"Mr. Flagler," said Meg. "His name's all over the island. The Combers are off Flagler Drive, there used to be a Flagler Hotel, there's a Flagler Inn . . ."

"Please." Luis held up his hand. "This man built the Royal Poinciana Hotel."

"There's a lot of Royal Poinciana's, too," Meg said merrily. "There's Royal Poinciana Drive, there's . . ."

"Shut up, Meg," Quill said. "Go on, Luis."

"Almost a hundred years ago, this man used the sons and daughters of slaves from Georgia, South Carolina, and Mississippi to build this hotel. The biggest, grandest hotel in the world. All this—" Luis swept his hand in a grand gesture. "This was jungle. Tropical jungles. Snakes, alligators, all these terrible things, the sons and daughters of slaves fight to build this hotel. So, the hotel is built. It is beautiful. But this man thinks, these black people are not so beautiful. I will get them off my island. So. They have built shacks, these Americans around the hotel, and one day this man invites them all to a festival. To thank them, he says, for a job well done. And while all are at this festival, he and his men burn their homes. These workers, they watch the flames and all they own"—he spiraled a finger skyward—"gone.

" 'Too bad,' says this man. 'Too, too bad. But I have land for you. Very cheap. Across the Flagler bridge. I will take you there.' "

"Australian?" Meg said.

"The same. These workers, if they are black, if they are African-American, the sons and grandsons of slaves? They must carry a pass to get over the bridge. A worker's pass. And they are not allowed anywhere on this island except for the boss's home."

"Johnson's Civil Rights act took care of that," Meg said.

"Since nineteen sixty-five, it has not been true. Before that, it was true. I found out by browsing the Net." Luis backed away from the Mercedes. "So you are warned."

"Not to go down Australian because it's a ghetto?"

Meg said. "It's the middle of the day. And I've never heard of the Australian Avenue ghetto in all the stuff I read and heard about Palm Beach. Phooey."

Meg directed Quill off the Flagler Bridge, down Broadway to Blue Heron Boulevard and then to Australian. The transition from monied homes with beautifully treed lots was abrupt. Not, Quill realized, because the residential districts were poor and ill-kept, but because the zoning boards had clearly fallen prey to business interests. Broadway was filled with decaying, boarded-up buildings with signs faded from the Florida heat and humidity. Earl's Gas Station and Fran's Upholstery and similarly named small businesses would run for entire city blocks. Then the homes, smaller and smaller, but neatly kept, with fenced yards and late model cars in the driveway, would appear for a short stretch, to be replaced by dead and dying commercial property, then reappear again.

The faces of the people on the street were like those of the people in Hemlock Falls—working people, middle-class people. The only difference was the color of their skin.

Traffic in this area was modest, and Quill relaxed behind the wheel. Whoever had laid out West Palm Beach had done a neat, sensible job. It was a grid pattern, with numbered streets running east-west and avenues and boulevards running north-south. The Longstreets lived within a few blocks of one another. Meg, who was navigating, directed Quill to Linda's house first.

The house, like the others around it, was neat and clean. The small yard was enclosed by a chain-link fence. The house itself was concrete blocks covered with stucco and a red tile roof, architecture ubiquitous to south Florida. Next door, outside a small stucco house painted aquamarine blue, an elderly black man hoed his garden. He stopped and leaned on his hoe when the Mercedes came to a halt at the curb.

A nondescript tan dog lay under the shade of an orange tree in Linda's yard, and when Meg and Quill approached the gate, got up, tongue lolling in the heat, head down, tail wagging. Quill reached over the fence and patted its head.

"It doesn't look like anyone's home," Quill said.

"You lookin' for Miz Longstreet?" the elderly man called. "She'd be at her brother's today. Two blocks over."

"Thanks," Quill said.

Longstreet Catering was housed in a small, cheap Morton building with aluminum sides and a low pitched roof. A house trailer sat in front. Children's toys were scattered around the steps. Two plastic, webbed lounge chairs had been placed near a small, inflatable pool. One was occupied by a large, bare-chested man in his early thirties. He had a beer can in one hand, a cigarette in the other. A small, tow-headed boy played in the plastic pool. He was naked, probably about three years old, and he splashed merrily in the sunshine.

The occupant of the second lawn chair was Linda Longstreet.

"You have any idea at all how to approach this with her?" Meg asked in a low voice. "Do you suppose that's her husband? Or her boyfriend? How do we talk about her affair with Taylor in front of him?"

"It wasn't an affair," Quill said. "He—um—encountered her twice, once in the patisserie kitchen and once in the bread closet."

Meg sighed. Quill pulled the car up to the curb. Linda jumped up from the chair, raised her hand, shading her eyes. She was wearing a blue-checked, short-sleeved shirt and a pair of cutoffs. Her feet were bare. She was visibly relaxed when Meg and Quill got out of the car.

"Welcome," she said as they walked up. "Isn't that Mrs. Taylor's car? For a moment, I thought it was her, but it's you come to call. Isn't it awful about Mr. Taylor? We heard about it on the news. We saw you on the news, too. All about how you both are really detectives from New York? And not cooks at all."

"I'm a cook," Meg said indignantly.

"I'm an innkeeper." Quill added. "We're not genuine detectives, you know. Amateurs."

"It's just a thrill to meet you," Linda said. "Just a thrill."

Quill, who wanted to point out that she had met them before, said, "May we talk to you a moment?"

"Me? Sure. This man here? My brother, Curtis. Curtis. This is Margaret and Sarah Quilliam. You both want to sit down?" She turned to her brother. "Curtis, you bring folding chairs from the back. And can I get you ice tea? A Coke?"

Quill was forcibly reminded that if you peeled away the resort and vacation atmosphere, Florida was a Southern state, and this was Southern-style hospitality. Curtis brought two rusting lawn chairs from behind the trailer and opened them onto the lawn with a grunt. Quill pulled her chair a little closer to Meg's and sat down. Meg went over to the plastic pool and knelt down in front of the little boy, who stopped splashing and regarded her with an unsmiling, direct blue gaze.

"You sure I can't get you ice tea?"

It was hot. Quill was thirsty. Southern ice tea was always heavily sugared. Besides, Nero Wolfe had a strict rule about breaking bread (and, Quill assumed by extension, drinking tea iced or otherwise) with potential murderers. Quill reflected that here, on home ground, Linda was more relaxed, less jittery. If she had something to drink with her, she might relax even more. Even the way she spoke—while as rushed and disconnected as her speech at her offices—was less defensive. Less servile. And she certainly didn't appear to be guilty of anything—either overbilling or kidnapping.

"I'd love some," Quill said.

Linda darted up the steps to the trailer, knocking over a scraggy pot of geraniums as she went. Curtis settled back into his lawn chair, drained his beer, and burped. He crumpled the beer can with one hand and threw it on the grass.

"And whose little boy are you?" Meg asked the child.

"Curtis," Curtis called. "C'mere."

Curtis (Junior?) stuck his thumb in his mouth and regarded his father balefully.

"C'mere, I told you."

Curtis shook his head.

"You want me to come and get you?"

Curtis took his thumb from his mouth, grinned, and then yelled, "Yaaahhh!"

"I'm comin' to get you," Curtis Senior threatened genially.

Curtis the younger squealed. His father got up from his lawn chair with another grunt, walked heavily to the pool, his stomach jiggling, and picked up the little boy. "Time for his nap," he said to the air over Quill's head. He carried his son up the steps, standing well aside as Linda came out the door with a metal tray, a pitcher, and three glasses. "You don't spill that, Lin," he warned. He went into the trailer, banging the screen door shut behind him.

Linda set the tray on the grass and poured the tea. Meg came back from the pool and sat next to Quill. "So," Linda said. "You both were right there, last night? In the mansion? I've heard it's plain beautiful."

"It's out of the ordinary," Quill said carefully. "Linda—we came across some information that we'd like to check. Do you mind if we talk about it a bit?"

"Well," she said, with some return of her old manner, "I can't say that I'm all that sorry he's been kidnapped. If you'll excuse me for being rude. He was a bad man. Now, I hope nothing awful's happened to him, but honestly, it doesn't bother me a bit if he's scared a little somewhere. But I guess I'll help if I can."

"The—ah—first little problem is one of the inventory. Franklin Carmichael implied that—''

The sound of Curtis Junior's giggle floated through the air. Quill heard his father chuckle in response.

''He's a great kid,'' Linda said proudly. ''I'm sorry, you were saying?''

''Carmichael thought there were discrepancies in the inventory. That you and your brother conspired to fill the shelves at the institute with overpriced, unnecessary goods.''

''You found out about that?'' Linda's eyes filled with tears. The effect on Quill was sudden and unsettling. ''We had permission. Mr. Taylor gave us permission.''

''I don't understand,'' Quill said gently.

''You okay out here, Lin?'' Curtis came out of the trailer. ''Hey. You crying or what? You two upsetting my sister?''

Quill took a deep breath. ''It's about the inventory at the institute, Mr. Longstreet.''

''So?'' His eyes darkened. ''Oh. I get it. That son-um-bitch disappears and now he's gonna try to get back those payments? You tell him he can stuff it.''

''I can't tell him anything, Mr. Longstreet,'' Quill said quietly. ''Verger Taylor's either been kidnapped, murdered, or both.''

''Far as I'm concerned, that bastard's better off at the bottom of the Okeechobee. You two get out of here. You, Lin. Get in the house.''

''I'm all right, Curtis.'' Linda pulled the tail of her shirt out of her shorts and wiped her eyes. ''I knew it was all going to come out anyway.'' Tears fell faster down her face.

''All what?'' Quill asked.

Meg nudged her with her toe. ''Linda, can I sort of summarize what I think happened?'' Linda nodded miserably. ''Verger Taylor forced you, didn't he?''

''Not forced,'' said Linda. ''It was my fault. I should know what men are like. I do know what men are like.

Things just got kind of out of hand and, you know, you just sort of give up.''

Quill found it hard to breathe. She clenched her hands and dug her fingernails into her palms.

''I told Curtis. He said, you can't fight the big bosses. But he wanted me to quit my job. Couldn't afford to quit. The pay was great. So Curtis went to talk to him. Mr. Taylor, I mean. He was going to punch him out.'' Linda smiled through her tears. ''Anyhow, Mr. Taylor said he was sorry. Mistook the matter, which he very well could have, I mean, he and that Mrs. Taylor fight like cats and dogs in public. Who knows what rich people like that do in their bedrooms? So he could have mistaken the matter. So he joked about it, really. Said to Curtis, looks like I have to pay a fine. Say, twenty thousand dollars. But he didn't want to embarrass me, so he said, you just take it out of inventory over the next year. I know the auditors. I'll fix it. Then, Mr. Carmichael found out about the inventory overcharges, and Mr. Taylor hadn't fixed things at all. I couldn't tell Mr. Carmichael it was an honest deal. That Mr. Taylor wanted to keep my name out of it, because he was sorry that he mistook me. So I lost my job after all.'' The tears came again, in a flood.

Meg, her face tight with rage, put her hand on Linda's arm. ''Keep your name out of it?'' she said, her voice shaking. ''That bastard was keeping his own nose clean and set—''

Quill, her voice sharp, said, ''Leave it, Meg.'' She rose from the lawn chair and shook Curtis's hand. ''I doubt very much you'll hear any more of this, Mr. Longstreet. I'm sorry to have troubled you both. Linda? You take care of yourself.'' She wished she could tell her. She wished she could say, *It's not your fault. You should have had Taylor arrested. You should . . .*

You should have been born rich.

CHAPTER 11

They drove back to the Combers Beach Club in silence and sat on the porch again. Quill drank iced tea without sugar and leafed through Taylor's appointment book.

"Turn to the week before he disappeared," Meg said.

Quill turned to the start of the book for the January entries. It appeared as though Verger's aggression, when not directed toward helpless female employees, was directed toward his career. His days were filled with appointments, usually beginning at seven in the morning and ending well after midnight. Daily meetings had been scheduled through February; the frequency of appointments dropped off in March, but he'd scheduled himself well into the fourth quarter of the year. "Look at all the society entries. He's rated those with exclamation points. The yachting meet with the Lantanas has four, the Red Cross Ball has one, then three more were added in a different color ink because the First Lady's apparently coming. For God's sake, Meg, he even penciled in his appearance at our condo the night we got here! Look: 'eight forty-five, C. E.'—that must be Corrigan and

Evan—'at C.B.C.'—Comber Beach Club."

"What about yesterday?" Meg, still pale, had said only one thing on the drive home from the interview with Linda Longstreet: that she hoped Verger Taylor was dead, and preferably had died slowly.

" 'Board meeting at institute'—he was there, lucky me. 'Concorde and D.' Who's D? 'Kill Murex' scheduled for three P.M. Who or what is Murex?"

"A company, I think," said Meg. "Wait a second. Let me get the *Palm Beach Post*. It's got the stock listings."

"Since when do you read the stock listings? Is that in between snatches of the weather channel? You're becoming a true Floridian, Meg. Next you'll be getting one of those icky little dogs."

"No, stupid. If Murex is a publicly traded company, it'll be in there. That's all. As a matter of fact—we've got the last three days of the *Post*, don't we?"

"In the wicker basket in the den," Quill said. "Bring a paper and pencil when you come back, will you? I want to write this stuff down. Then we should give Jerry a call and turn the book over to him."

Tuesday had been a fairly light day for Verger. There'd been a lunch meeting with "D," apparently from the Concorde, then "D" had returned to the airport and Verger had executed Murex at three. There was a short meeting with E. K.—which was easy, Ernst Kolsacker—then nothing until nine P.M., which was noted "C. and E., Au Bar."

"Well, he didn't make that date," Quill mused aloud.

Meg brought the business sections of the newspaper out on the terrace, her cheeks pink. "Now this is interesting, Quill. Murex was trading at six and a quarter on Monday, and jumped to eight and three quarters on Tuesday."

"There's reasons for Verger making his pile of money," Quill said. "How come we can't make money like that?"

"Because we don't play the market. Now, look at today's paper. Murex is down ninety percent. That's a lot. That's very unusual. That's something the SEC would look at."

"So we check that out." Quill started to scribble notes on the pad of paper Meg had brought. "I wonder how far back we should go with this?"

Meg didn't answer.

"Meg, I asked you . . ." She looked up. "What's the matter?"

"Look at this." She thrust yesterday's paper at Quill.

"It's the section on bridge?"

"Look at the account of the tournament at the Palm Beach Polo Club yesterday."

"Oh, ugh, Meg. I like bridge, but reading scores is boring."

"Not this one. Read it."

COUPLE SET TOURNAMENT RECORD

In an excitedly fought series of rubbers at the Palm Beach Polo Club today, Luellen Barstow and Frank Barstow of Fairhaven, Connecticut, set local yachtsman David Young and his partner three thousand points. Playing North/South, the Barstows scored a doubled no trump *grand* slam for a record two thousand six hundred points in the third rubber, setting East/West.

Quill stopped reading. She set the paper on the table, slowly. "The bridge scores in Cressida Houghton's game room."

"Copied right from that reproduction of the score." Meg's face was grim. "So the boys would have an alibi."

"Oh, my God." Quill shivered in the warmth. "No. Meg. It's not possible."

"Sure, it's possible. Remember the Menendez brothers."

"There's got to be another explanation." Quill took a couple of deep breaths. "For one thing—and it's the most obvious—we were *there* when the call from the kidnappers came through. And even if those boys are good actors, Meg, there was no question that both of them were in shock."

"Easy enough to have an accomplice. Maybe it was even Cressida Houghton herself."

"No." Quill shook her head decisively. "This can't be. Other than the fact that Verger was—is?—a bottom line sort of bozo, why would the boys want to have him kidnapped?"

"Corrigan said it himself—they don't have any money. So far, they're the only offspring, right?"

"Right."

"And Verger was going to marry a third time—to a nineteen-year-old, who is presumably fertile."

"But, Meg, there is no way that those two were pretending shock last night. No way."

"I agree with you. Maybe they had an accomplice and the accomplice screwed up."

"If they had an accomplice, they wouldn't need an alibi, would they? The accomplice could have done the whole thing. Or two accomplices, since the maid saw two men in arctic masks struggling with Taylor."

Meg looked cross. "Okay. No accomplice. The boys shoot Verger, staging the murder to look like a home invasion. Their sainted mother, the one and only Cressida Houghton, gives them an alibi that no jury in America is going to question . . ."

"It seems pretty thin to me," Quill objected.

"Yeah. And so was O. J. Simpson's. Justice is this country is frequently for those who can buy it, Quill."

"I hardly think . . ."

"That's what you're doing. Hardly thinking. They've got an alibi from Cressida. And of course, the rest of the evening, there's us."

"Okay. Let's assume this is possible. Possible, not probable, that Evan and Corrigan kidnapped and/or murdered their father and somehow both of them have enough acting ability to convince us that their grief is genuine. Let's say they even taped and recorded the kidnapper's call, so they'd get it while the police were there. Verger Taylor's worth a lot more than a hundred thousand dollars. Why the piker's fee for the kidnapping? If Taylor's alive and it's a real kidnapping, why not ask for ten times that much? His estate can certainly afford it. And if he's dead—why ask for a hundred thousand dollars at all? Why not just let the body be discovered?"

"You've raised some good questions," Meg admitted.

"Good questions? It's an entire bloody defense. And the only evidence you have to convict is the score to a bridge game."

"What are the odds on two doubled no trump grand slams being played within fifteen miles of each other on exactly the same day?"

"Very small," Quill admitted.

"I'd say they're nonexistent."

"Which is actually a point in Cressida's favor, Meg. I mean, why take such a risk?"

"You can bet there won't be any grand masters on the jury. Besides, she may have been in a panic, and let's face it, Quill. She's beautiful, and cultivated, and the closest thing America's got to aristocracy, but she's not a rocket scientist."

"That's true." Quill leaned back in the lounge chair and sighed heavily. "Okay. So I suppose we call Jerry, give him the appointment book, and make a statement about the bridge scores. He's going to think we're nuts."

"He won't think we're nuts." Meg bit worriedly at a

fingernail. "He'll follow up. If he didn't know Myles, yeah, he might think we're nuts and drop it, and then we could go home in good conscience. Or reasonably good conscience. But he won't, Quill. And what if we're wrong?"

"We've been wrong before. Maybe we're wrong now. Actually, I'm with Myles on this one. I don't really want to get involved. To tell you the truth, these types of people scare me to death."

"That's the biggest problem, isn't it?" Meg said quietly. "If we are wrong, one word, just one word from Cressida Houghton could destroy the inn. Permanently. We'd never get any business, not the type that can afford our prices."

"We can't ignore this."

"No. We can't." She sat straight up with a yelp of excitement and said, "What we can do is witness the money drop."

This appealed to Quill, who, like Ratty, loved messing about in boats. "And see who picks the money up? Okay," she said thoughtfully. "We conceal ourselves near the number nine buoy as what, fishermen or something?"

"Sure. That little boat of Luis's is out there all the time. So are half a dozen other people. It'd look abnormal if no one was out night fishing."

"So we're fishing and fishing and Evan and Corrigan come out, tie the waterproof bag to the buoy, and then what?"

Meg shrugged. "Who knows? I don't think there's going to be a pick-up. I think Evan and Corrigan are going to fake it."

"And if we're wrong? And this is a real kidnapping?"

"My best guess is that the pick-up will be a diver. It'd be too easy for the police to pick up a boat and follow whoever's in it back to shore. *If* there's a pick-up."

''And if there is a pick-up, we let it happen, right? No funny stuff with trying to capture whomever it is.''

''Of course not. I don't like Verger Taylor any more than anyone else, but if this is a real kidnapping, I'm not going to be responsible for his extremities being carved off and sent through the mail. Ugh.'' Meg shuddered. ''Gross. So, let's go rent a boat.''

''We're going to need more than a boat, Meg. We're going to need a disguise, a pair of infrared binoculars so we can watch what happens at a safe distance, and some fishing gear. But first, let's talk to Luis.''

CHAPTER 12

"I'll just bet there are policemen all over this complex," Meg said. She was wearing an old straw hat over a long black wig, a battered pair of espadrilles, and a baggy cotton shirt, all borrowed from Luis on the pretext of a scavenger hunt. She'd rolled the bottoms up on Quill's second-best pair of khakis and rubbed them liberally with dirt. Quill had tucked her hair under a cheap navy captain's hat. She was sweltering in a gray sweatshirt and jeans. She'd picked up dark tan makeup at the same shop in which Meg had purchased the wig and covered her face and hands. Both of them had gotten costumed too early. They were waiting for nightfall, seated on the leather couch, looking out at the ocean.

"I'm turning the air conditioning on," Quill said. "I can't stand this." She got up and closed the French doors, then set the wall thermostat on cold.

"I hate air conditioning," Meg complained. "I feel like Spam in a Tupperware container in air conditioning."

"Tough." Quill tugged at her hair and wound one

strand around her finger. "The ocean looks quiet, at least." Heavy, oily swells had been coming in all day. She walked to the doors and peered out, scanning the horizon anxiously. "Do those look like cumulonimbus clouds to you?"

"Like what?"

"Cumulonimbus clouds. It's what shows up just before a hurricane. 'Dark, heavy-looking clouds rising like mountains high into the atmosphere, often showing an anvil-shaped veil of false cirrus clouds at the top.' "

"You've been watching the weather channel."

"While you were in the shower. How come you took a shower before the fishing trip?"

Meg, who was scrabbling through a bright-red tackle box (also borrowed from Luis), held up a spoon-shaped lure. "Why not? Hey, do you think we might catch anything?"

"Not with that. Luis said there's mainly mullet in the bay. You need a net for mullet. Check those clouds out, Meg."

"No. We're going maybe a quarter mile off the channel into the bay. We've got a nice little motor on that boat and a pair of nice little oars in case the motor fails. We'll have plenty of time to come back to shore if the wind comes up. If bad weather's coming, I don't want to know about it."

"There is a rain forecast for later on. It's the edge of Hurricane Helen."

"Shut up." She dumped the infrared binoculars they'd purchased at the tackle shop out of the shopping bag. "Do you suppose these things work?"

"If they don't we'll have spent a whole bunch of time on the water for nothing. We won't be able to see a thing in the dark. They upgraded Hurricane Helen to a three. That's winds of . . ."

"Shut up!" Meg stored the binoculars next to the lure, closed the tackle box with a snap, and picked up the pair of rods. (They'd been rented from Luis for ten bucks each. He hadn't believed Quill when she swore she wouldn't drop it over the side. Meg had made Quill pay him—if he hadn't seen her drive, she'd said, they would have gotten the rods for free.) She crossed to the French doors and peered over Quill's shoulder. "Those are plain old cumulus clouds. They've shown up like that every afternoon we've been here."

"There's been a hurricane forecast every afternoon we've been here."

"Let's go fishing."

She went to the front door, opened it, and Quill followed her out.

Luis was waiting for them at the kiosk. Meg broke into a flood of voluble, cheerful Spanish, for the benefit of anyone who might be watching.

"*Cara Luis! Buenas tardes! Comme ca va!*"

"That's French, you dufus," Quill muttered. "It's *como 'sta.*"

Quill could almost feel Jerry Fairchild's furious eyes boring into her back. Her disguise wouldn't have fooled Myles for a minute. She wasn't entirely sure where Jerry and his people had concealed themselves—but she knew they must be all over the complex. She was just as sure that he didn't dare come out and stop the two of them from going out in the boat. The risk to Verger Taylor—if he was still alive—was too great.

Luis—used, perhaps, to the vagaries of the rich—blinked several times at the way they looked, but offered no comment. He hadn't wondered at their interest in the number nine buoy, either, just printed out a channel locater map on his PC. He led them past the pool and down to the breakwater, where his little boat lay gently bobbing in the swells.

"Sixteen feet," he said proudly. "Belonged to my grandfather."

"She's beautiful," Quill said. The name of the craft

was printed neatly on the gunwale: The *Verity*. ''Did he name her?''

Luis nodded. ''He was an *avacato*. In Cuba. Pre-Castro. Batista, you understand. He did not survive. What are you fishing for?''

''Mullet,'' said Meg. ''We want mullet. Have you got a mullet net?''

Luis pointed to a pile of green cord folded under the seat in the center of the boat. He seemed slightly reassured when Quill expertly started the little thirty-five horse motor after she hopped into the boat, and waved them genially off the shore.

The *Verity* took the heavy swells with ease. Quill kept her right hand on the tiller and her left on the throttle. There were three other boats on the water near the number nine and number twelve buoys out in the channel. Quill had seen two of them several times before: the twenty-two-foot Chris-Craft had a solo occupant, a grizzled old man who spat tobacco over the side with stolid regularity; the eighteen-foot Welbilt carried a honeymoon couple who spent a lot of time horizontal under the gunwales. The third was an Osprey day sailer Quill hadn't seen before. She was willing to bet that the Palm Beach County police didn't use blonde, teenaged girls in brief bikinis as undercover agents. Although anything was possible.

She opened the throttle and increased her speed, looking back to the shore. The waves slapped smartly against the bow, and the breeze was cool. From the rapidity with which Luis's figure dwindled in size, she figured she was going about thirty miles an hour.

''Slow down!'' Meg shrieked. ''I want to fish!''

Quill throttled back and looked for a good spot to cut the motor and drift. She look for the dimpled ripples in the water that meant a school of mullet was swimming by. The swells were deeper out here. The boat rose steeply, then slid down the far side of the rising water with an eerie slowness. There was an absence of pelicans.

Quill cut the throttle out and then drifted for a moment. The silence was not complete. From their vantage point—about halfway to the number nine buoy—they could see all the way down the beach. The high-rise condominiums and village mansions on Ocean Boulevard were distant, but noise carried over the water: radios, the shriek and chatter of a party, the thrum of traffic. To her right—or starboard, Quill thought—was the long, pleasant beach of Singer Island with its hotels. Ahead lay the Atlantic. They really were at sea, at the edge of the Atlantic, and beyond that—"Algeria!" Quill shouted. "Whoop! You want to head due east?"

"I want to fish!"

Quill looked over the side. The water changed beyond here to a deep, navy blue. If they drifted farther out, it'd be too deep for mullet. She debated about casting the anchor; it would slow their drift and the wind out here was quite brisk. She shaded her eyes against the sun and scanned the water. No evidence of mullet yet. The old man in the Chris-Craft was about three hundred yards to port. He spat once over the side, gave Quill a malevolent look, and opened his throttle. The boat shot away in a curve of spray.

"Follow that guy, Quill."

"Why?"

"Because every time I've seen him bring his boat in, it's been full of fish. He's obviously a pro."

The Chris-Craft slowed, throttled down, and stopped. Quill, squinting against the light despite her sunglasses, saw him cast his net from the boat with an efficient snap of the wrists. The net floated in an arc, then settled into the water. Leaning over the side, the old man pulled, heaved, and brought up a net full of fish.

"Yes!" Meg shouted.

Quill pulled the rope start with an sharp tug and, at a sedate pace, edged to about a hundred yards from the

Chris-Craft. She throttled down. They were in the middle of a vast school of mullet, racing out to sea. Their silver backs flashed in the water; one or two leaped out of the water in small, swiftly executed arcs.

"They're like little robot soldiers," Meg said. "They all look exactly the same."

Quill touched her hat to the old fisherman, who gazed back at them expressionlessly and shouted, "Hope you don't plan on settling here."

Splat! Another gob of tobacco hit the water.

"The guys are out bowling," Quill improvised. "Told them we'd have a nice fish fry for them when they got back!"

No answer. He probably couldn't hear her. Although his steady stare was a little unnerving. He undoubtedly didn't want to share the mullet.

Quill dropped anchor. It was deep here and she failed to hit bottom. The weight would slow the boat, though, and give them a chance to cast the net.

"Okay," she said to Meg.

"Okay what?"

"Okay, we're ready to fish."

Meg bent over and dubiously regarded the net.

"Well?" said Quill. "We're being watched, Meg, I can tell you that right now. And it's not just the old geezer there, either. Jerry and his team undoubtedly have high-powered telescopes or whatever trained all over this coast. Besides, you've been nagging me to fish for the past twenty minutes. So fish."

The pilot of the Chris-Craft threw his net a second time, with what seemed to Quill to be an insultingly easy flick of his wrist. He drew it up full, swung the net into the boat, then deftly emptied most of the net into a large bucket. He disentangled the fish that had failed to escape the net, refolded the net deftly over his right arm, and cast it out again.

"It looks easy," Meg said.

Her first cast was actually quite respectable, although

the sinkers attached to the net collided with the bulwark and the net failed to spread. The second cast was worse. The third was worse than that, and when the man in the Chris-Craft spat loudly and with obvious contempt, her face turned pink. The fourth cast netted three very small mullet, which Quill insisted on throwing back.

Luis had provided them with a good-sized bucket and Quill, who'd been wondering how they were going to pass the long hours until ten o'clock, figured that they might not have enough time to display a respectable catch if they happened to be accosted by annoyed and affronted policemen.

The dark came quickly, as it always did this far south, and as it came, the wind rose. The clouds in the west flared briefly in a last, martial show of red, and full darkness followed. Lights came on over the water. A large yacht sailed by, portside lights blinking frantically, then a small and efficient-looking sloop. A large fishing charter roared by, temporarily sending the mullet in frantic disarray. The man in the Chris-Craft, too far away to hail, turned on his running lights and shone his spotlight into the water.

Meg had netted several pounds of mullet, which flopped in the bucket until she filled it with sea water. The wind buffeted the little boat with increasingly harder gusts. Finally, Quill pulled up anchor and set the throttle on low.

By nine-thirty, everyone had left the water but the Chris-Craft. Quill was worried. It was becoming increasingly harder to keep the *Verity* steady. Meg had to bail out the bottom more than once. They'd both strapped their life jackets on.

"Should we go in?" Quill asked.

Meg shook her head. "Another fifteen minutes. That's all we need."

Quill turned the *Verity* toward shore and glanced over her shoulder. The clouds from the east were a mass blacker than the night, coming up fast, obscuring the pale moon and the halfhearted light of the stars. At ten-fifteen, Quill said, "I'm killing the lights." She snapped off the running lights. The darkness was intense. Slowly, her eyes readjusted. In a few minutes, she could see Meg at the bow in the faint light from the stars and moon.

Meg unpacked the infrared binoculars, focused, and looked intently toward shore. "I see them," she said loudly, over the roar of the waves and the wind. "They're putting to."

"What are they sailing in?"

"What?"

"I said, what are they sailing in?"

The wind dropped suddenly, and Meg's voice came through clear and too loud. "Just a little twenty footer. Got a big motor, though. At least a hundred fifty horse. It's a cigarette boat, I think. I can even see the name. *Class Act.*" The wind sprang up like an animal surprised, and Meg lost her balance. "Whoops!" She lowered the binoculars. The wind was strong, whipping the wig's black hair into her eyes. She tore it off and stuffed it in the mullet bucket.

She opened her mouth, but Quill could only hear occasional words through the gusts. It was like listening to a radio with static. She shook her head and pointed to her ears. It was becoming harder to see Meg as the clouds advanced across the sky and the moonlight dimmed and brightened erratically. Meg gestured forward, and Quill steadied the bucking boat with one hand on the gunwales, the other moving the throttle against the wave action to keep them steady. They were in a following sea. They moved forward faster than the motor, the waves pushing them inland. Quill did her best to keep steerage, maneuvering the *Verity* slightly ahead of the water. Their father, who'd spent half of his life on the ocean in the navy, had told them both from the time they could walk, *You panic against the sea, and she'll drown you. You accept, moving with her, as you move with a horse, and she won't take you down. Or at least you've got a fighting chance.*

The trouble was that a stiff breeze inland was a wind of twenty knots or more out on the water. And Hurricane Helen—wherever she might be, was at last sending her outriders to plague them on the water.

The red light of the number nine buoy appeared at starboard. Eyes to the binoculars, Meg waved one hand frantically. Quill swung the tiller hard over, slowly, to face into the waves. They were at the mouth of the channel, and she did her best to find the current in the rough water. The light of the buoy bobbed, a steady beacon. The red and green lights of the *Class Act* showed briefly behind the buoy, and then the buoy light was totally obscured as she rounded it.

Meg turned and crawled over the seats to Quill. The redistribution of her weight, as slight as it was, caused the *Verity*'s nose to soar upward. Meg's (or rather Luis's) straw hat had long been blown overboard. Meg pushed her hair out of her eyes and wordlessly handed Quill the binoculars. She took the tiller and Quill raised them to her eyes.

For a moment, all she saw was eerie shadowland. The headland behind the buoy sprang into weird relief. The infrared gave everything a Martian glow. She brought the lenses lower, caught the buoy, missed it, and then focused on Evan Taylor's intent face. Corrigan was at the tiller, and he was a good sailor. He kept the craft steady as Evan reached over the side, a waterproofed canvas bag in one hand, a heavy strap in the other. He lashed the bag to the buoy with swift, muscular twists of his arms, then signaled thumbs up. The *Class Act* motor roared, and the boat disappeared. Quill was left staring at the bag attached to the number nine buoy.

Meg put her lips close to Quill's ear and yelled, "Well?"

Quill gave her the binoculars. "They did it!" she cried. "They left it there."

Meg, her eyes to the buoy, grabbed her hand tight. *"Look!"* she shrieked. *"Look!"*

Quill took the binoculars back. It took her an agonizing length of time to find the marker again. And when she did find it, she shouted, "Hey!"

The heavy seas had torn the packet open. Newspaper plastered the red light, wrapped wetly around the buoy joists, and disappeared into the heaving water.

"There's no money at all!" Meg shrieked. "They stiffed him!"

"We should have a camera!" Quill shouted back. The *Verity* hit a huge wave and she fell forward. Her head hit the seat. She righted herself with difficulty.

". . . get the tote!" Meg screamed.

"What?"

"We have to get the tote! Evidence!"

"Damn." Meg was right. A prosecutor would make mincemeat of their unsupported testimony. She watched the waves glumly. The light from the buoy pitched up and down. Meg was going to have a devil of a time unstrapping the tote from it, even if she could get the *Verity* close enough. A water-soaked tote bag filled with soggy newspaper might not be enough to convict, anyway.

"We've got to try!" Meg yelled.

Quill nodded. The wind had taken her hat off long ago, and her hair whipped wildly around her face. The lights of Palm Beach gleamed less than a quarter mile away.

She shoved the throttle half open and began the slow maneuvering to get the boat to the buoy. Meg sat in the center seat, gripping the sides of the boat, face set. Quill turned to port, misjudged the water, and veered off the back of a large wave headed for the point. She maneuvered starboard, catching the face of the next one. The *Verity* slid forward faster than her motor and it coughed and died. Quill snapped the starter rope; the motor coughed and failed. She snapped it again. The engine caught and held.

With the perversity of distances at sea, the buoy light suddenly showed up portside. Meg crawled forward and waved her hand to the right. Quill moved the tiller slowly, right, then left. The *Verity* pitched like a horse with a burr under the saddle. The red-and-white buoy appeared, then disappeared in the sweep of waves. Meg picked up a line, wound it around her waist and fixed it to the offside cleat. Quill edged the *Verity* closer to the buoy.

Meg leaned forward. "*. . . it!*" Meg yelled. *"I got . . . damn!"*

Lightning flashed in the western sky. The boat jumped as if she had been stung.

Quill swore, turned, and looked into Evan Taylor's desperate face. He sat in the bow of the powerboat. He'd sideswiped the *Verity*. Thunder rumbled. The lightning flickered again. Corrigan was at the tiller.

"Get down!" she screamed. *"Meg, get down!"* She resisted the frantic impulse to jam *Verity*'s throttle wide open. The *Class Act* swung wide, motor roaring, white spume in its wake, and circled to ram them again. Quill eased the throttle forward, turned hard right, and slipped behind the buoy. *Class Act* took the buoy amidships with a thud. Corrigan reversed. The motor whined in protest, stuttered, and died.

Quill blinked, refocused, and scanned the shore. Less than a quarter mile, closer to an eighth. They could swim to safety if they had to.

There was one advantage to the wind, she thought grimly. The howl was so loud it must conceal the sound of their motor, and in the darkness they would be hard to see. She cast a swift look backwards. *Class Act* roared straight for them. Her lights disappeared, obscured by a huge wave. Quill turned the *Verity*'s bow carefully toward the inlet. White spume sparkled in the top of the waves. She tried to recall everything she had ever known about surfing. ''Catch it at the break,'' she muttered, ''catch it . . .'' She slammed full throttle. The *Verity* bucked, and her stern rose into the air. Quill pitched forward, caught herself, and the little boat slid forward, down the face of the wave.

They'd caught it. The wave would bring them in.

She heard *Class Act*'s motor behind them. The *Verity* shuddered. They'd been hit. The portside bulwark rose higher, higher, and Quill tumbled into the sea.

The water reached up and took her. She plunged down, down, the warmth of the ocean a momentary astonishment. She surfaced, gasping, and peered through the darkness for the boat. ''Meg!'' she shouted into the wind. ''Meggieee!''

The clouds swept from the moon, and she caught a glimpse of Meg's face, tight, frightened, determined. Quill raised her arm and pushed forward. ''Go on!'' she shouted. A wave broke over her head and she went under. Her head hit something hard, unyielding. Light shattered.

And then it was dark.

''I'm *fine*,'' Quill said irritably. ''Excuse me.'' She pushed the medic's hand from her wrist. The condominium living room was filled with policemen, medics, at least one FBI agent, and, Quill suspected, a few reporters, since the woman and two men in the kitchen were trying to be as inconspicuous as possible. She was lying on the leather couch in her clothes, which were soaked. What she could see of the wood floor was a small disaster—puddles and mud splashed everywhere.

Jerry Fairchild stood behind the couch and looked down at her. His expression was hard to read. Meg perched on the armrest, smoking one of her rare cigarettes. She'd washed her face and changed into dry clothes. ''You were lucky,'' she said. She stubbed the cigarette out. Her hand was trembling.

"If you're well enough," Jerry said, "I ought to throw you in jail."

"Fine. Go ahead. Bring on the gendarmes."

"She'll be fine," the medic said. She recognized him; it was the same slight fellow who'd ministered to Corrigan when he'd appeared to faint the evening before. "Little waterlogged, and that's a nasty bump on the head, but . . ." He flashed his penlight in her eyes one more time. "No dilation of the pupils, she claims she's not dizzy, and that bump on her head isn't a fracture." His mild brown gaze rested on her, curious. "What's that scar on your shoulder from?"

Quill realized someone had removed her sweatshirt and that the T-shirt beneath was wet. "Bullet," she said proudly. "From another case." She grinned. She sat up. She was shaky. Oddly, she was exhilarated. The past twenty-five minutes had been a confusion of water, wind, and shouting. Predominate was the grizzled face of the fisherman in the Chris-Craft, who'd knocked Evan Taylor out with an oar and dragged her from the water.

Meg came and sat next to her on the couch. "What about some hot tea?"

Quill swallowed. Her nose and throat were dry and stinging. Her eyes were gritty. Somebody had turned the air conditioning either down or off, for which she was grateful. One of the French doors was partly open, and she heard the lash of wind and rain against the windows. The air was warm and damp.

"I'm going to take a hot shower, first, and get out of these clothes."

Meg reached out to help her up and she got to her feet. The room seemed remarkably steady, amazingly bright, after the pitching waves and the darkness.

"We'll wait," Jerry said.

"Wait?"

"If you're all that fine, we're taking you downtown, for a statement."

"Now?"

''Now. Cressida Houghton's going to have sixteen lawyers on my back when she learns her precious pair have been booked for attempted murder.''

''Verger's Taylor's alive?'' Quill said.

''He means you, stupid,'' Meg said affectionately. ''Go on, get dressed.''

''In a minute. Where's the old geez—I mean the old gentleman that pulled me out of the water? He saved my life, Meg.''

Jerry rolled his lips back in what she took to be an attempt at a smile. They were stained brown. He hawked, pretended to spit, and gave a genuine smile at her astonished expression. ''That was *you?*''

''But Jerry, I've seen that old guy out in the boat every afternoon since we've been here.''

''That's Charlie Sinclair. Used to be one of the best defense attorneys on the eastern seaboard before he retired down here to fish. Didn't mind my borrowing his boat, but I had a hell of a time taking his tobacco.''

''Borrowed his boat,'' Quill said. ''Oh, my goodness. Luis!''

''It's not too bad,'' Meg said with a slightly guilty air. ''I got it to the dock, anyway. But there's a couple of dings in the side from getting rammed, and the police have confiscated it as evidence, and I'm afraid we'll have to get him a new one.''

''Oh, dear. And we swore to John that this would be a profitable trip. Well.'' She stood uncertainly and said to Jerry, ''Thank you.''

''You're welcome. Now get changed. I'll wait.'' He raised his voice slightly. ''I'd like this room cleared, please, and that includes you, Monica from channel seven.''

''Jer-ry,'' the woman in the kitchen protested.

''Beat it. I'll give you a statement down at the station. And be glad I'm not pulling you in like Miss Quilliam.''

"Since you've blown my cover, could I just ask her a few questions?"

"No."

"Miss Quilliam, how does it feel to have solved what promises to be the crime of the century?"

"Wet," Quill said cheerfully. "I'll be back in a second."

"Out," said Jerry. "All of you."

Outside, the rain continued in fitful gusts. Quill's euphoria ebbed the closer they came to the Palm Beach County police station. It was situated on PGA Boulevard, across from the Gardens Mall, near the community college. Despite the proximity of these three facilities, the area was blessedly free of the sprawling, neon-lit buildings that seemed to characterize Florida. It baffled Quill that drugstores, grocery stores, and gas stations were placed higgedly-piggedly among golf communities with high stone gates and pot-bellied security guards. The zoning committees must have had unlimited access to rum punches. But the police station was neither tasteless nor intimidating—just a large concrete block building stuccoed over with the ubiquitous white paint and, of course, a red-tiled roof. The building housed the DMV, the tax bureau, and other county offices as well as the jail.

Quill and Meg sat in the back of Jerry's Chevrolet. There was a huge crowd of vans and cars crowded in the parking lot, and a large clutch of people at the door. Some of them carried umbrellas against the rain, but most stood there unfazed by the weather, pale faces dripping, hair lank. To her amazement, Quill saw a few hand-lettered signs:

FREE CRESSIDA'S BOYS! and WE LOVE EVAN.

"My lord." Meg gasped.

"Told you Miss Houghton knows all the tricks." Jerry parked in the FOR OFFICIAL USE ONLY spot and shut off the ignition. "You two ready?"

The next few minutes reminded Quill of the session in the boat. Terrifying, chaotic, noisy, and wet. Hands plucked at her arms, her hair. Voices shouted in her ear. Microphones were thrust under her nose and the lights of video cameras shone in her eyes. She grabbed Jerry's raincoat with one hand and Meg's sweater with the other and they all ducked though the crowd.

Inside, they went through the metal detector at the entrance. The hallways were wide, the floors covered with a beige, rubberized tile. Quill noticed there was no odor of disinfectant or dust—just the scent of damp clothes. There was group of people clustered at the entrance to the county judge's chambers. In the center of the group was a tall, graceful figure in immaculate beige.

Even the reporters kept a respectful distance. Cressida's silvery hair was gathered in a loose bun at her neck. In the strong light, she looked tired, beautiful, and fragile. Her eyes—pale blue, distant—fell on Quill and Meg. She nodded slightly in their direction. The reporters—two of whom Quill recognized as national anchors for evening news programs—turned as if they were one body. Jerry held up his hand in warning. Video cameras whirred, a few cameras flashed. Cressida bent her neck like a swan and said something in a sorrowful tone.

"Cressida's claim is," Jerry said sarcastically, "that you two older women were after the boys' fortune. That this whole kidnapping thing with Taylor was a set-up."

"You're kidding!" Quill said.

"Come in here." He took a key from his pocket and unlocked a side door set unobtrusively midway down the hall. They entered what was apparently a small interrogation room. There were three metal chairs, a square wood table, and bars on the window in the wall.

"The Houghton family is going to try to twist this around to say that we're responsible for Verger Taylor's kidnapping?" Meg said. "Whew! That takes a lot of nerve."

"Takes a lot of money," said Jerry. "But it's not going to work."

"Not going to work?" Meg exploded. "Of course it's not going to work! It's a huge lie!"

"Doesn't mean the defense isn't going to be successful." He looked at them with deeply cynical eyes. "We've got the whole business on videotape, of course. From the drop and the newspapers spilling out to the Taylor kids ramming your boat. There's some great footage of Evan grabbing your hair, Quill, and trying to keep you underwater. Cressy and her lawyers are going to have a tough time defending that."

Meg grabbed Quill's hand and squeezed it hard. "I guess I missed that."

"There's also some good footage of Meg ramming Luis Mendoza's boat into the pier." Jerry laughed silently and shook his head.

"Hah," said Quill. "I don't want to hear another word about my driving."

"Okay," said Meg, uncharacteristically subdued.

"There's got to be more evidence than the videotape, Jerry." Quill ran her fingers through her hair. It was still damp.

"There's the money itself. The twenty thousand dollars that was missing from Verger's office. Evan had it stored in an identical tote in the back of his closet. But . . ."

A tap on the door interrupted him. He frowned. The woman Quill had seen with him the night before—his partner, Quill guessed—came in and shut the door behind her. She gave Quill a brief, angry glance.

"I've already ticked them off about interfering with the investigation, Trish," Jerry said. "And you have to admit that without them, we wouldn't have a charge that would stick."

"We do now," Trish said. "Corrigan just confessed. He says he and Evan staged the break-in to look like a home invasion and shot Verger Taylor twice in the chest with a thirty-eight pistol.

"Where the hell's the body?" Jerry asked.

"That's just it, Jer. He claims they left the body there. Went back to their mother's at seven o'clock and waited for the Quilliams to join them for dinner. Corrigan says he has no idea what happened to Verger's body, and that the kidnapping came entirely from left field."

"What does Evan say?" Quill asked.

"He denies everything. Says his brother was coerced." Her lips twisted. "We've got the confession on tape, Jer. And goddammit, the kid's lawyer was right there. Protesting like anything, but the kid just went on blurting and blurting. We've got 'em. I think we've got 'em. Of course, the thing we all want to know now is . . ."

Jerry grunted, then said, "Where the hell is Verger Taylor?"

CHAPTER 13

The hammering on the front door finally stopped. Meg put her coffee down and said, "Remember that little dead raccoon we found in the woods when I was six?" They'd drawn the blinds down over the French doors and all the windows in the condo. The reporters had arrived in force before the sun was up. Luis didn't get to work until eight. They were barricaded until he could arrive to drive them away.

Quill didn't have to think very hard. The dead raccoon had been Meg's first sight of death. "Yeah."

"All the black flies over it."

"It was October, Meg. I told you that flies are part of a grand plan to . . ."

"Those so-called journalists are just like 'em. The black flies."

"More like Nazis on Krystallnacht," Quill grumbled. "We can't answer the phone, we can't go out, we can't even see what kind of weather's outside, and *don't* tell me to turn on the weather channel. I hate the weather channel."

''You can't hate a whole channel.''

''Well, I do. And the whole state of Florida, as well.''

''Hate the whole state of New York, instead,'' Meg advised. ''That's where the snowstorm is that's delayed Myles and Doreen.''

''That's what we need, Doreen and her mop. She'd take care of that bozo from the *Inquirer* in two seconds flat.''

''Well, I'm going to make us a fabulous breakfast. You're just suffering from post–near death syndrome. All those endorphins were coursing through your system like mad and then, wham. Big letdown.''

The phone had been ringing when they'd walked in the door at one o'clock that morning. Every time Quill plugged the phones back into the jacks, it started again. A flotilla of TV, radio, magazine, and newspaper reporters were pursuing Cressida Houghton's version of Verger Taylor's disappearance: that Meg and Quill, intruders from up North and spurned fortune hunters to boot, had decided to involve her innocent sons in a heinous crime committed by persons unknown. Quill caught about three minutes of the early-morning news and switched the television off.

It was now a little after seven. She'd talked to Myles twice, once last night and again this morning. At nine, she'd call Tiffany to beg off the rest of the week. They'd return the money. As soon as the Syracuse airport opened, they'd leave. Quill had never wanted to go home as much in her life.

The doorbell chimed softly. Quill gritted her teeth. Meg was making an omelet Suzette, with orange slices and Cointreau. Fresh scones were in the oven. She'd peeled and sliced sections of fresh grapefruit, which she'd filched from a tree outside the condo the day before.

''Looks delicious,'' Quill said, ignoring the bell with an effort.

''Those bells are driving me crazy.''

"They'll stop eventually. Whoever it is is pretty polite. There's only been two short rings so far."

"Just answer it, Quill, will you? Tell them go away. Say no comment, all that stuff. But tell them to stop ringing the damn doorbell. If they don't, we'll call the police."

"Who, since they are really, really happy with our interference in their case last night, will be delighted to help us out." Quill smoothed her hair behind her ears and put on a pleasant expression. Channel 7 had run the videotapes they'd taken the night before on the morning news. She'd looked like a drowned rat. Moreover, a drowned rat with a very bad temper. If she was going to be photographed without her consent, she might as well look dignified and presentable.

She reached the front door and opened it with a sigh. "Sorry," she said. "No comment." There was the expected crowd of reporters and the obligatory flashbulbs in her face, but out of the babble came two absolutely dignified and presentable figures: Bea Gollinge and Birdie McIntyre.

"Sorry to trouble you, dear. May we come in?" Birdie said. She was wearing a khaki skirt and a fresh white cotton blouse with a bow. The pearl earrings in her ears were large baroque drops. Quill would have bet a year's pay that they were genuine Renaissance.

"My goodness. Yes, of course. How nice to see you."

Bea snorted. She was wearing freshly pressed jeans and a T-shirt that read CARPE TEDIUM: SONGS FROM THE FORTIES FOR THOSE IN THE NINETIES. A red golf cap shaded her eyes. "I'm sure it's not nice at all, given the adventure you had last night." She turned and raked the clamoring journalists with a fierce stare. "And considering what you are enduring this morning. But Bea and I felt we should talk to you as soon as possible."

Quill led them to the kitchen counter and offered coffee. Meg cast a quick glance over her shoulder and added four more eggs to the omelet she was whipping.

''Hi, guys. Love the T-shirt, Bea. How's about some breakfast?''

''We couldn't possibly,'' Birdie said. ''What are you making?''

''It's an omelet Suzette. I use heavy cream, eggs, sweet butter, and Suzette sauce. Quill, could you get the chafing dish out? And get the scones from the oven, will you? They're about''—the oven timer chimed—''ready.''

Birdie looked hungry. ''Now, omelets. Omelets are low in calories, Bea.''

''Not with heavy cream and sweet orange glaze, they're not,'' Bea said brusquely. ''But I'm not going to pass up the offer of a meal from Chef Meg.''

''It would be rude, wouldn't it?'' said Birdie with a pleased air. ''Can we help?''

''Why don't you set that table over there for four, pour some cranberry juice, and sit down. This'll be ready in three minutes. If Quill gets the chafing dish heated.''

There was a pleasant bustle in the kitchen. Birdie and Bea found place mats, napkins, and exclaimed critically over the sterling flatware. (It was Gorham.) Quill lighted the Sterno under the chafing dish, put out the scones, and began to feel less like an alien and more at home for the first time since she'd come to Florida. The widows sat down at one end of the ornately carved dining room table and waited for Meg to make her omelet.

''Marvelous,'' Bea said, nibbling the scone. ''Cranberry, is it?''

''And raisin,'' Meg said. ''Lot of sweet stuff this morning. Quill needs the energy. Put a trivet or something under the chafing dish, Quill, and bring it to the table. And I need the tray with the brandy, oranges, and sugar.'' She talked as she poured a quarter cup of the egg mixture into the heated pan and watched it puff up, carefully pulling the edges away from the rim with a wooden spatula. She flipped it with an expert twist of her wrist, waited a moment, then slid the omelet onto a plate. "You've heard about what happened last night."

"We certainly did," said Birdie. "That's why we're here." She accepted the omelet, took a bite, and beamed. "We were right, Bea."

"I was right, you mean. I was the one with the idea." She watched closely as Meg sprinkled powdered sugar over her eggs. "Little more than that, dear. That's fine. Thank you. You see"—she turned to Quill—"we want you and Meg to take over the institute."

"That's very kind of you, Bea," said Quill. "But Meg and I are going home. As soon as I tell Tiffany we're resigning."

"You're getting ahead of the game, Bea," Birdie said. "Typical of you. Now you two listen to me." She put her fork down. "Verger's disappearance has made a considerable difference in things."

"His death was a terrible, terrible thing," Quill said. "His own sons. It's hard to believe, but . . ."

"Oh, you're not one of those who believes that nonsense about Corrigan killing him?" Bea crumbled a bit of scone with one hand. "The police coerced that confession from him, poor boy."

"He always was a fragile child," Birdie added. Meg set her omelet in front of her and began on Quill's serving. "Thank you, dear. Do you remember how much trouble Cressy had with him when it was time to send him to school?"

"Wait just a cotton-pickin' minute." Meg shut the Sterno off with a snap of the lid. "You think the police coerced that confession?"

"Well, of course they did! After a good night's sleep, the poor boy came to his senses. He's under the care of a psychiatrist now. Cressy's simply frantic."

"I'll just bet." Meg dumped Quill's omelet—without the sauce—onto her plate.

"Meg," Quill said.

"Hush. Eat your eggs." She scowled at Birdie. "This

is the same poor boy who tried to ram our boat and sink us last night out on the water. The same poor boy who held the boat as steady as he could so that his creep of a brother could try to *drown* my sister! Fragile? Mentally ill? That's the most ridiculous thing I've ever heard in my life.'' She eyed Quill's plate. ''That omelet's raw.''

''I don't want it right now, anyway.'' Quill shoved the plate away. ''So this is the story, is it? This is how the Taylor boys are explaining their attempt on our lives last night? What about the fact that they substituted newspaper for the real ransom money? They can't explain that away, can they?''

''They thought you were the kidnappers, of course.'' Birdie took a few sips of cranberry juice. ''And that business about newspaper being substituted for the money is nonsense.''

''We saw it!'' Meg shrieked. ''We saw it with our own eyes.''

''I'm sure you thought you saw it,'' Bea said kindly. ''No one believes you two would lie on purpose.'' She looked at them solemnly. ''You know they heard from the kidnappers again last night.''

''They couldn't have!'' Meg said. ''There aren't any kidnappers. Verger Taylor's dead.''

Bea shook her head slowly. ''I don't know what you girls were doing this morning. It was all over the news. The kidnapper called with a second ransom demand. Mr. Hawthorne got the call. He's been Cressy's lawyer for years and, of course, he's unimpeachable.''

''We've fallen down the rabbit hole,'' Quill said to no one in particular. ''And what were the kidnappers' demands this time?''

''Nobody knows the details. There's a great deal that's been said, Quill, not that *I* believe for a minute that the police involving amateurs almost cost two more lives in addition to that poor security guard. But a great deal has been said about how you two almost got those poor boys killed. Of course, it is possible that one of you may have been hurt as well. You two and the Taylor boys, messing around in that awful weather last night, each thinking the other was responsible for the tragedy . . . it's a mercy no one was hurt."

Quill looked at Meg. Meg crossed her eyes, looked at the ceiling, and muttered, "We are *not* crazy. We are *not* crazy."

Quill turned to the widows. "We aren't making a bit of headway here. Tell me, Birdie, what do you know about this phone call from the kidnappers?"

"Apparently they were quite upset about the botched delivery last night. And then Verger himself got on the phone, for just a moment, poor man. He said 'they're trying to kill me' and they cut him off, just like that."

Quill opened her mouth, thought the better of it, and shut it again.

Birdie continued. "But it was Verger, no question about it. They did one of those voice thingys—what d'ya call 'em, Bea?"

"They matched the voice over the phone with Verger's voice on a tape and the little thingys matched. The sound waves."

Meg gathered the plates up in a careless heap and stamped into the kitchen. Quill pulled thoughtfully at her lower lip. " 'They tried to kill me?' That's what he said?"

"Yes. We heard the tape ourselves, didn't we, Bea?"

"That part of it, anyway. Mr. Hawthorne gave a press conference very early this morning and they broadcasted live from his home."

"Still in his bathrobe," Birdie said. "He didn't play the whole thing, of course. Said that the whereabouts of this next drop were going to remain secret until Verger was home safe and sound."

Quill couldn't stand it anymore. She leaned forward and touched Bea's hand. "That's what he said at the little speech he made to the board, Bea. Remember? 'They're trying to kill me' or words to that effect."

"Why, so he did," Birdie said.

"I don't remember that, Birdie."

Meg walked the short space from the kitchen to the dining room table and asked, "You think somebody taped it, Quill?"

"I sure do."

Birdie looked at her watch, a Baume-Mercier glittering with chip sapphires. "We've that aerobics class in twenty minutes, Bea. And then the therapy session with Dr. Bittern at noon. Let the girls know why we're here."

"Of course. Well, girls, Verger's disappearance has made a mare's nest of his affairs, as you might imagine."

"Who inherits?" Quill asked.

"That's not the right question," Meg said flatly. "The right question is, who is in control of Taylor Incorporated now?"

"Ernst has full authority," Birdie said, "and he's assured us that everything is going to be handled exactly the way Verger wants it until he gets back."

Meg sat down at the table. "Can Ernst buy and sell any of Taylor's assets?"

"Oh, I don't believe so." Bea looked alarmed at this. "Ernst is a wonderful man, but no one has the talent Verger has. The man's a genius. If Verger's truly gone, then it's time for us to pull our investments out."

"You're selling off your investments in Taylor Incorporated, then?" Meg asked.

"The new ventures, absolutely," said Bea firmly. "That was the very first thing we did last night, after we heard, wasn't it, Birdie? But the existing ones are quite sound, or so Ernst informs me. So we're making no changes there."

Birdie raised her plucked eyebrows. "At any rate, poor Ernst has his hands full, what with trying to do things the way that Verger would want and keeping the empire—that's what Verger always called it, the empire—intact. And he wondered if you two would stay on for a bit. Keep the institute up and running. It's absolute chaos over there—as a matter of fact, that's where Ernst is right now. The place needs a manager, Quill, just for a couple of months. And Chef Jean Paul, Meg, absolutely will not come out of the bread closet."

"What about the chicken people?" Quill asked.

"Oh, that deal wasn't signed. And if it wasn't signed, Ernst said, there's nothing he can do about it. The chicken people are all upset, of course, and as I understand it, Bea, am I right? There was talk of court . . ."

"Court," Bea echoed. Her mouth was full of brioche.

". . . if Ernst doesn't let them occupy the building by a certain date. But that's not going anywhere, Ernst says."

"Let me see if I understand this," Meg said. "As long as Verger is alive, the institute remains in the same state it was in yesterday. That is, no chicken people."

"That's right. And you know who had the idea that you two might help us out for a month or two?" Birdie's eyes were bright. "No, wait. Let me show you what you'll be paid if you accept." She drew a gold Mont Blanc pen from her purse and a pocket notepad. She wrote a number down, then showed it to Meg. "That's each," she said impressively.

Meg tossed the pad to Quill, who took it, read the figure, and managed to keep her face devoid (she hoped) of expression. It was a lot of money.

"Now, guess who made this offer?" Bea said.

"Cressida Houghton," Meg said.

"That's right!" Bea smiled with hope. "So you'll do it? You'll take over *pro tem*, as it were, until Verger is back at the helm?"

"No other message?" asked Meg sweetly. "From Ms. Houghton, I mean? About not testifying against her poor dear boys? Or dropping the charges of assault and attempted murder? Nothing like that?"

"Of course not." Indignation shook Bea from the top of her dyed brown hair to her Bruno Magli shoes.

"Well, we decline," said Meg. She sprang up and walked rapidly back to the center island. Her lips were a thin line in her rigid face. "Thanks all the same."

"No, we don't," Quill said. "You tell Ms. Houghton that we're seriously considering her offer." She ignored Meg's yelp.

Bea patted Quill's bare arm. Her hand was soft and trembled slightly. Quill, looking at her closely, thought that she and Birdie must be well over seventy. Plastic surgery, laser therapy, vitamins—all those things could disguise the outer envelope. But nothing medicine had come up with yet could change a person's eyes. And Bea's eyes were old.

"We knew you'd help out. Well." She rose from the table with a smile. "Come, Birdie. We'll brave that crowd out there and just make our exercise class, if we're lucky."

"They won't pay any attention to old ladies like us, Bea. Goodbye, girls. Don't get up. We'll see ourselves out. Will you two be here when we get back?"

"Here?" Quill asked blankly.

"The first of Dr. Bob's therapy sessions is going to be here at noon. Isn't it, Bea?"

"That's right."

"*Here?*" Meg shrieked.

"Tiffany thought it would be best." Birdie's shrewd old eyes twinkled. "The reporters know how to get here, you see. And she made an arrangement with Luis."

"Swell," Meg said darkly. "That's just *swell.*"

"We'll see you then, I hope. Twelve sharp. Come along, Bea."

"Goodbye," Quill said. "Oh, Birdie? Did you happen to catch the name of the psychiatrist treating Corrigan Taylor?"

"Dr. Bittern, of course. He's quite qualified. Quite."

Meg waited until the front door had closed, then picked up the dirty plates and threw them one by one, with great precision, against the refrigerator door. Quill watched her, arms folded. When the last plate had smashed, Meg bent over and methodically picked them up and disposed of them in the pail underneath the sink. "There," she said briskly. "Now I feel better. Any ideas about what to do next?"

"Oh, yes," Quill said. "Make a call on Verger Taylor's lawyer and attend Dr. Bittern's therapy session. I want to find out what's behind this bribe. And I'm very interested in Dr. Bittern's future plans."

"Tell me, what do you think really happened at Verger Taylor's mansion yesterday?"

"We've got two facts and a supposition. The facts are that we last saw Verger Taylor at six-thirty. The maid confirms he came home at six thirty-five and that the break-in occurred very shortly after. The shooting couldn't have taken more than ten minutes. The devil with the creaky shoes . . ."

"Maria didn't say creaky shoes. She said snap-snap-snap."

". . . anyway, we didn't arrive at Cressida Houghton's until well after seven. From the map, though, Verger's is actually a short walk down the beach, so the boys could've waited for Verger, killed him, and jogged back on home well in time for our invited arrival at seven-fifteen. That's fact one.

"Fact two is that the bridge game so cleverly laid out for us was a ruse, copied directly from the winning grand slam in yesterday's paper."

"I don't think I'd call that a fact," Meg objected.

"I haven't drawn any conclusions yet, Meg! Now the supposition is that the boys were acting when they got that call from the so-called kidnapper."

"I know we can't prove it, Quill, but I'll be damned if that was acting."

"I agree with you. I think the kidnapper was the fire-breathing demon that opened the door on Maria and shut it. *The kidnapping was separate from the murder.* Frankly, I'm so convinced that, at least as working hypothesis, we're going to call it a fact. Okay? And I think the basic scenario is this:

"Evan and Corrigan Taylor planned a home invasion for the express purpose of killing their father and leaving his body for the authorities to find. Someone else came along, found the body, and disposed of it. For a reason we haven't discovered yet, the body snatcher can't have Verger Taylor dead.

"So who's got the best motive?" Quill continued rhetorically. "First, there's Chef Jean Paul. If he knew that the deal with Southern Fried wasn't completed yet, he'd have a chance at finding someone else to run his believed institute."

"I doubt it, Quill. Chef Jean Paul is just like those rabbits. Timid and good only for cooking. Besides, I know three restaurants in New York that would hire Jean Paul in two seconds flat. For an enormous sum of money."

"Okay . . . let's accept that Jean Paul had a motive, but not a compelling one. What about the shrink? Dr. Bittern knew that Verger had made up his mind to prevent Tiffany from going forward with his multimillion-dollar project."

"Again—it's a motive, but not a compelling one. And besides, the man's no idiot. He'd get the same result with Verger dead as Verger missing. Why go to the risk of concealing the body?"

"True," Quill said. "Linda Longstreet, who had the same motive as Chef Jean Paul."

"She's out of it," Meg said. "If she's a murderer, then I'm Paul Bunyan."

"You're right."

"I love it when you say I'm right."

"What about Tiffany?"

They looked at each other and said simultaneously, "Nah."

Meg giggled. "She made it pretty clear yesterday she was much better off being his combative ex-wife. Plus, she's got that spa alibi. You know, Quill, there's another suspect."

"Ernst Kolsacker? According to Birdie and Bea, he doesn't benefit in any way from Verger's disappearance. I can see where his death might benefit him—he could run Taylor Incorporated for a while, but my gosh, guys like that swap corporate jobs all over the country. Like Chef Jean Paul, Ernst could get a good job almost anywhere. Besides, if Birdie's accurate—and have you noticed how sharp she is about money, Meg?"

"No! Really?"

"It's amazing, isn't it? It's how the rich stay rich, I guess. Anyhow, unless we can turn up some reason for Ernst to benefit by Verger's being alive, but out of the picture, then I vote we table him as the body snatcher."

"Agreed. I wasn't thinking so much of Ernst as Mr. X."

Quill groaned.

"I'm serious. That business with the Murex stock bouncing up and down like that is curious, very curious. And you know what? I was so curious I looked at the business section of the paper this morning to track it." Meg reached under the counter and brought out the *Palm Beach Post.* "See that paragraph?"

" 'The alleged kidnapping of real estate tycoon Verger Taylor has resulted in a suspension of the buyout of Murex Limited,' " Quill read.

"This news won't hit the Street . . ."

"The Street?" Quill said. "You mean as in Wall Street?"

"Go ahead. Mock. You'll mock on the other side of your mouth if I'm right. Anyhow, the news hasn't hit Wall Street or the stock exchange yet, but when it does . . ."

"When it does, what?"

Meg's lower lip stuck out and she scratched her head. "I don't know enough yet. But I want to check it out."

"Okay, but I think there's something even more important than our tracking down suspects in this case."

"What's that?"

"Finding Verger Taylor's body."

"Quill, there's no way we can do that. It's a job for the police. And it may not happen for years. It may not happen ever."

"Then we've got to find out who took the body, if not where it is. Because if we don't, we're going to have Cressida Houghton as an enemy for life. And it's goodbye to the inn and our reputations."

"Not to mention hello to our three-hundred-fifty-three-thousand-dollar mortgage. Okay, we're ready. We're committed. We're going to find the body snatcher. Now what?"

Quill held up Verger Taylor's address book. "Jerry Fairchild. We have to give this to the police. It's a terrific excuse to see how things are going from the police end. And then I think we should inquire about hiring ourselves a lawyer. And after that, I want to come back here and check out Dr. Bittern."

Meg, still on track with Quill's first suggestion about finding a lawyer said, "We've got a perfectly good lawyer . . . oh." She looked bemused. "You want to go to find out what Mr. Hawthorne knows?"

"The lawyer for the Houghtons? He won't tell us a thing. Now, Verger Taylor's lawyer? He might tell us a lot."

"Do we even know who Verger Taylor's lawyer is? Was? Whatever?"

Quill tapped the address book. "Franklin Carmichael, of West Palm Beach. It's on Poinsettia Road, which is about ten minutes from the police station. For heaven's sake, Meg, he attended your class with Ernst Kolsacker."

"And you said Dr. Bittern? I thought we crossed him off the list."

"You never know what a shrink knows, Meg. We've

got to look him in the eye and find out if he's concealing guilty knowledge.''

''Fine. There's not anything else to do today, with the institute closed.''

Quill had thrown on a pair of shorts and a T-shirt when she'd gotten up, and she decided to change to a cotton dress. She talked Meg, who protested, into a skirt and blouse. They left the blinds and shades drawn and proceeded cautiously out the front door. The bulk of the reporters had given up; a few stringers hung out by Luis's office door. Quill stopped so fast that Meg plowed into her.

''Luis,'' she said, remembering the catastrophe the night before.

''The boat,'' Meg said. ''You know, the amount of our bribe from Cressida would just about take care of a new boat for Luis.''

They walked across the parking lot to the office. Meg scowled horribly at the stringers, who scattered like seagulls. She rapped on the office door. Luis opened it.

''You!'' he said. ''One moment.'' He slammed the door.

Meg tried again, tapping lightly and calling, ''Luis? Luis? We are really, really sorry about the boat.''

He opened the door again, buttoning his Combers Beach Club coat. ''I apologize,'' he said. ''You caught me in my shirt sleeves.'' He stepped outside and waved to the reporters, who had retreated to a battered Ford Escort parked in the MANAGER ONLY spot. ''You are both looking very pretty this morning,'' he said. ''Would you like the Mercedes again?''

Quill put her hand gently on his arm. ''Luis. We are so sorry about your grandfather's boat.''

''It's fine. Don't worry. Grandfather had it insured.'' He beamed. ''And I,'' he said, ''have a book deal because you wrecked it.''

''A book deal?''

''Well, part of one.'' He looked modest. ''It is to be

called *The Taylor Tragedy: Blood, Sex, and Crime in Exotic South Florida*. I am one chapter. Then there are the talk shows on television. For this, I get paid as well. America is wonderful, Miss Quilliam."

"America is wonderful," Quill mused, pulling into the police station some twenty minutes later. "Do you suppose our wonderful police will believe that we got Verger's appointment book from Tiffany? Will our wonderful justice system let Evan and Corrigan go free? Will *we* be arrested for the sake of making a better book?"

"If you're going to make a speech," Meg said, "I'm walking. And if you don't slow down, I'm walking. Just drive, dammit."

Jerry Fairchild looked as if he hadn't slept at all the night before. He was unshaven, there were heavy bags under his eyes, and his expression was less than welcoming. "What do you two want now?" They were in his office, which was extremely neat and very clean.

"You probably won't believe us," Meg said belligerently, "but we genuinely forgot about this piece of evidence in all the brouhaha yesterday."

Jerry's expression softened a little. "What piece of evidence?"

Quill produced the address book. Jerry took it, flipped through it, came to Verger's rating system, and chuckled.

"I don't think it's funny." Meg crossed her legs and folded her arms across her chest. This further evidence of bellicose behavior seemed to amuse the detective. "The man was a pig."

"But a successful pig."

"You're not hollering at us for concealing evidence," Meg said suspiciously. "I'd feel a lot better if you hollered. What's the matter, Jer?"

He sighed. "I don't know what Verger Taylor's address book is going to tell me that I don't already know.

He had a few meetings the afternoon of the day he disappeared. We're interviewing the people he saw that day—most of them have come forward anyway. Anxious to cash in on the publicity. So consider yourselves hollered at.'' Jerry opened his left desk drawer, took out an evidence bag, slipped the book into it, and labeled it in neat, precise handwriting.

While he was engaged in this, Quill asked, ''You think that the boys had an accomplice—that the clues to Verger Taylor's disappearance—''

''Murder,'' Jerry said shortly.

''The motive for murder lies with his sons? And not in Verger's own activities? What did Evan and Corrigan do with the body?''

''You can buy anything you want around here,'' Jerry said. His eyes looked more tired than ever. ''Want your grandmother raped? There's kids who will do it for five bucks and a bag of cocaine.''

Quill didn't know how to reply to this. She had a glimpse of the day-to-day routine of this man's life, and it made her shudder. She asked quietly, ''Did you really receive another call from the kidnapper?''

''You saw the morning news.''

''As a matter of fact, we didn't,'' Quill said.

''Yes. Hawthorne, that smart-ass lawyer for the Houghtons, got the call early this morning. He taped it. It sounded genuine, but then, the first one sounded genuine. That it, ladies? I've got work to do.''

''We heard about Corrigan claiming his confession was coerced. That he's mentally unstable.'' Meg gave him her most appealing smile.

''As far as I'm concerned, anyone who offs his old man is crazy as an outhouse rat.''

''So you think they did it, too.''

''Of course they did it. We haven't even begun to dig into those kids' financial histories, but they owe money all over the place. And there's preliminary evidence that

Verger had cut the flow of funds off. So they had a motive, all right.''

''Do you think they removed the body?''

''Somebody did.''

''So you're pretty sure they have an accomplice,'' Meg persisted. ''Makes sense. I mean, who else would be making those phone calls?'' She threw out another piece of bait. ''Unless you think that Verger's alive, and that for some reason, he and his kids are involved in an elaborate scam.''

''What I think is that you two ought to go shopping. Or out to lunch. Anywhere but here, butting into this investigation. I'm sure you're familiar with the penalties for civilians mixing in with police work?''

''Nope,'' said Meg pertly. ''In all the cases we've been involved in, the police have been glad for our help.''

''Uh huh.'' Jerry refused to be drawn. ''Thanks, ladies. Now beat it.''

''Ladies. Shopping. Lunch.'' Meg fumed a few minutes later. ''So now what? We find ourselves a lawyer?''

''We find ourselves a lawyer. If he'll talk, we find out who inherits Taylor's money and who's running Taylor Inc. right now. And if the opportunity arises, we explore this business of Murex.''

The traffic patterns in south Florida were becoming familiar to Quill. If you got out on the street fairly early—say before seven o'clock—or late, after dark, it was possible to maneuver through the streets in a reasonable period of time. But after nine in the morning and before sunset, the traffic was horrendous. And all the cars had license plates from northern states. In addition to the jams created by sheer volume, most of the out-of-staters didn't seem to know where they were traveling to. Cars pulled U-turns in the middle of the streets, or even stopped, blocking lanes of traffic, while the drivers figured out that they'd missed the bypass to Oklahoma some three streets back. Quill was beginning to feel some sympathy for the hostile bumper stickers on native vehicles.

They inched their way to the offices of Carmichael, Webster, and Ross (offices in New York and Palm Beach) in about the time it would take to have an emergency heart transplant. Although Hurricane Helen still circled off the coast of Africa, the fringes of the weather system made the air sultry, humid, and sticky. Quill pulled the Mercedes over, unsuccessfully tried to find the buttons that raised the top of the convertible, and it took her twenty minutes just to find a break in the traffic flow to reenter the street. By the time Quill pulled into the underground parking lot, both she and Meg were hot, tired, irritable, and very hungry.

''I still say we should have called ahead,'' Meg said in the elevator. Quill, silently blessing the air conditioning, didn't reply until they reached the fourth floor and entered the carpeted hallway to the attorney's offices.

Then she said, ''Five bucks gets you ten that Carmichael will drop whatever he's doing to see us. And if we get him to talk, who knows what kind of information he'll drop? We'll just tell him we've got a book deal. That'll start anybody blabbing these days. Especially a lawyer.''

Meg clicked her tongue. ''Cynical, cynical.''

The offices of Carmichael, Webster, and Ross had the hush of expensive construction. The pale blue carpets were thick. The gleaming rosewood desk of the receptionist was hand-carved. Pale blue suede covered the walls and—as everywhere in Florida—expensive silk flower bouquets covered most available surfaces.

The receptionist was an icy blonde: slim, tanned, with streaked hair that fell in calculated confusion over her shoulders. She was wearing a neat little black suit, which, if Quill hadn't seen the real thing on Birdie McIntyre, would have passed for a Chanel in bright light. She raised a perfectly shaped eyebrow when Meg and Quill came in the glass door. "Can I help you?"

"We'd like to see Mr. Carmichael."

"Mr. Carmichael is in a meeting." Her eyes flicked over Quill's cotton dress (seventy-nine ninety-five at Kaufmann's) and Meg's skirt and blouse (with Meg, who knew?). There was a distinct edge of disdain to her voice. "Can I ask the nature of your business?"

"I'm Sarah Quilliam. This is my sister, Margaret. We were friends of the um . . . of Mr. Verger Taylor."

Both eyebrows went up. "Oh! Not the two women who . . ." She smiled professionally. "Will you have a seat? I'll see if Mr. Carmichael can be interrupted. He was up all night with this business. He just came in."

She returned, the iciness thawed to at least, Quill judged, sleet, if not above freezing. "It is a matter of some urgency, I presume."

"Yes."

"Then Mr. Carmichael can fit you in. Just for a few minutes. Now, if you don't mind, we just need a little information for our records. If I could ask you a few questions?" She took a clipboard from the corner of the desk and handed it to Quill. It was a questionnaire. The first lines asked the usual questions: name, address, social security number; the remainder looked like an application for a credit card with no limits.

Meg looked over Quill's shoulder, snorted, and said, "Can't you just input this directly? We'll have to write. You'll have to rekey. It'll save some of Mr. Carmichael's time if you open the file up on your server."

"Well." She hesitated and cast a quick look at the office door behind her, which read FRANKLIN CARMICHAEL in gold letters. "Sure." She turned to the keyboard on her desk. It was, Quill saw, part of a larger Unix system. She was vaguely aware that this meant the offices in Palm Beach were systems-connected to those in New York.

"You don't mind if we come around to your side of

the desk?'' Meg said, doing just that. ''It'll take less time if we input for you.''

She ushered them into the attorney's office a few minutes later. From the crumpled paper in the wastebasket and the smell of onions in the air, Quill guessed that Mr. Carmichael had been meeting with a hoagie. A bag of carrot sticks lay on the top of the desk. Empty foil packets of nicotine gum littered the floor. He was wearing yet another three-piece pin-striped suit that must have been miserably hot in any temperature higher than sixty-five degrees.

He rose from behind his desk and extended both hands. ''Miss Quilliam and Miss Quilliam. My sympathies. My profoundest sympathies.''

''We didn't know Verger Taylor all that well,'' said Meg. ''So you can save your sympathies. What we're interested is in saving ourselves. It's why we are here.''

''I see. Please, ladies, sit down.'' He indicated a cranberry leather-covered couch in the corner. Quill sat close enough to Meg to pinch her knee and shut her up, if necessary. Carmichael settled across from them in a matching leather wing chair with brass nailhead edging.

''We find ourselves in need of counsel,'' Quill said. ''Before he . . . that is, before all this happened, Verger spoke highly of you. Very highly.''

''Oh?''

Meg's elbow nudged sharply into her side; Verger Taylor hadn't spoken of anyone very highly. ''To be candid, he spoke of you with less . . . um . . . disapprobation than of others. Besides, we've met before. We trust you.''

Carmichael's teeth gleamed in a brief, insincere smile. He shifted the piece of gum in his mouth. ''That sounds more like Verger.''

''As you may know, we're far from home here, and the events of the last couple days have been confusing. Very confusing.'' Quill waved her hand vaguely. ''The reporters. The book deals. Most alarming, we've just come from the police, and there's a strong indication, Mr. Carmichael, that we may be investigated, too.''

''Ah.'' Carmichael steepled his fingers and nodded. ''Book deals?''

''And other deals. That's our second concern. Meg, as you may know, is a talented chef.''

''Two-star,'' Meg said pathetically. ''I had hoped for the third at tomorrow night's banquet—but . . .'' She trailed off, looking vulnerable.

''And, to get to the point, we've received an offer this morning that's interesting. Most interesting.''

''From a publisher?''

''Well, that, of course. But Meg and I discussed it, and we feel strongly that we need some representation. Some protection in the weeks and months that are to follow.''

He nodded benignly.

The blonde tapped at the office door, walked in, and laid a computer printout of the questionnaire on Mr. Carmichael's desk. His eyes dropped to the bottom of the sheet, which, as Quill was well aware, carried the information about the Quilliam estate's net worth.

He frowned.

Quill was annoyed. She'd tripled her salary and quadrupled Meg's, in the certainty that by the time Carmichael checked on their references, they'd be back in New York. She hadn't counted on the Ethernet system.

''The publicity about this case,'' Quill said, ''is already enormous. The reporters outside our door this morning are already talking about this as the Trial of the Century.''

Carmichael's face cleared slightly. He began to look very interested.

''And, of course, we're finding ourselves at odds with the Houghton family. We thought that if you had represented Mr. Taylor, you wouldn't be scared of taking them on.'' This, Quill thought, was absolutely true. However slick and money-grubbing Mr. Carmichael seemed, he was at least a tough cookie. She did her best to look helpless and feminine.

"At odds in what way?"

"This morning, we received a very lucrative offer to run the Florida Institute for Fine Food for an interim period." Quill thought about the proposed "salary," doubled it, and told him.

He smiled. "And this offer seems to you . . . what?"

"In the nature of a bribe," Meg said bluntly. "Although it's not enough of one, I must say. It doesn't come close to the money we've been offered for the—ah—book."

"Ah. The book. Well. There's no doubt. No doubt at all that you both are in need of—if I may say so in these enlightened days—a strong arm to protect you."

"You may," Meg said sweetly.

"So if we can arrange a suitable retainer, we can get started on the protection right away."

"A retainer," Quill said, dismayed. "How much . . ."

Mr. Carmichael frowned. Clearly, the vulgar discussion of amount would be handled by Miss Ice. "I'm afraid until that's settled, we'll have to reserve any discussion that might be considered confidential."

Quill was silent for a moment, trying to figure how much they could afford to pay for information about Verger Taylor.

"The thing is," Meg said, "we find ourselves a bit short. Before Verger—um, whatever—he'd recommended a stock buy for us and we went ahead and invested most of our available cash in it."

"A stock tip? You invested your savings based on a stock tip?"

"Mr. Carmichael," said Meg earnestly, "who in their right mind would turn down a stock tip from Verger Taylor? We discussed it with Bea and Birdie, of course, before we wrote the check, and they thought it was a good idea."

"Mrs. Gollinge and Mrs. McIntyre? You know them?

What was the stock Verger advised you to purchase, if I may ask?"

"As our attorney, I'm sure it's all right for you to know. It was Murex."

"Murex?" He frowned. "What kind of game is this, anyway? Verger never would've advised you to buy Murex. He hated the whole deal. He was about to . . ." He looked at them for a moment, then rose. "I'm afraid I'm going to have to ask you ladies to leave. I don't know what you're playing at, but you won't play it here, if you please."

"Meg, you idiot!" said Quill, who had been mentally applauding Meg's cleverness in inserting Murex into the conversation. "It wasn't Mr. Taylor, it was Mr. Kolsacker, speaking for Mr. Taylor."

Puzzled, but game, Meg said, "My gosh, so it was. And it was at my cooking class, too. How could I have forgotten?"

"Ernst advised you to buy Murex." Carmichael sat down again. "That I can believe. Although I don't recall that conversation."

"It was while you were boiling the rabbit carcass," Meg said. "You were very absorbed in how to boil the rabbit carcass. I have very few students with your abilities, Mr. Carmichael. I can assure you. You have the makings of a very fine cook."

"Hm." Carmichael looked pleased. "Well. Ernst and Verger were squabbling over that company from day one. And it just goes to show you. The one good thing about Verger's disappearance is that Ernst stands to make a lot of money from Murex." He smiled broadly and snapped his Nicorette. "And of course, so do you."

CHAPTER 14

"So what do you think?" Meg asked as they were once again battling the traffic.

"I think he's having a tough time quitting smoking." Quill gasped, braked, and narrowly avoided colliding with a blue Taurus that had cut into her lane without warning.

"What time is it?"

"Lunch," Quill said. "I hope we get there in time for lunch."

A white Chevy Lumina began backing up in front of the Mercedes. Quill laid on the horn. The woman in the driver's seat looked around, waved apologetically, and continued to back up.

"What the heck?" Quill muttered.

"I think she wants that right turn back there." Meg thrust her thumb over her shoulder. "Better let her go."

Quill decided that if she kept on expecting traffic here to conform to minimal rules of common sense, she was going to work herself into an overnight stay at Dr. Bittern's clinic. She stopped; allowed the Lumina to back up, make a U-turn, and head in the opposite direction; then shifted into drive. She patted the Mercedes' dashboard in sympathy. ''So, how far have we gotten here? I don't think we did all that well.''

''We learned that Ernst profited from the rise in Murex stock, and that the stock wouldn't have gone up if Verger had been around to force the sale. I think that's critical. Critical.''

''I wonder how much money Ernst made?''

''We can find out.''

''How?''

Meg smiled. She patted her skirt pocket on and said, ''Luis.''

''Luis? What about . . . damn!'' She slammed on the brakes, laid on the horn, then waved and smiled weakly as a pair of senior citizens crossed four lanes of traffic on PGA Boulevard with their little dog.

''Luis and his computer. You know that printout of our references for Carmichael's file?''

''Yeah.''

''It's got his E-mail address. His IP/PC code. And they cross-index files by birth dates, Quill. Carmichael's got all of Verger's financial stuff, right? Luis can get us into those files. We can find out exactly how much money Ernst made.''

''So we bag the good doctor?''

''Oh, no. I'm dying to see what this therapy session's like. Aren't you? If we hurry, we'll just make it. And then we'll pay a visit to Luis the hacker.''

''Hurry? I was hoping you'd say that.'' Quill slammed on the brakes; laid on the horn; and swung a wide, wide right turn onto PGA from the farthest left lane, leaving a horde of angry motorists screaming in her wake.

''Gotcha,'' she said. ''That felt good.''

Meg still wasn't speaking to her when she pulled into the parking lot at the Combers Beach Club. She slipped the key card into the security machine at the gate, drove slowly and carefully to Luis's office door, and shifted into neutral with the gentlest of movements.

"We're here," she said brightly.

Meg opened the passenger side door and got out. Luis waved to her through his front window. She waved back.

"Meg? Meggie? I'm sorry. I'm really sorry. All that traffic, being patient. It just got to me."

"Taxis," said Meg flatly. "Taxis, taxis, taxis."

Quill asked what she thought was not an unreasonable question. "How can detectives take taxis?"

"Then I'll drive."

"Meg, you drive like a potato. You are totally inert when you drive."

"At least we're breathing when we get to wherever we're going. Hey, Luis. How's it going?"

"Not so good," Luis admitted. He opened the driver's-side door for Quill and took her place when she got out.

"You don't look very well," Quill said. She bent over and peered at him. "A little pale. Are you feeling okay?"

He shrugged. "My heart is sad." He turned the ignition on and raised one hand in a forlorn way.

"Luis?" Meg said. "We've got a new chapter for you for your book. We need you to help us hack into a computer system."

"No book," he said.

"No book?" Quill looked sympathetic. "I'm sorry. But I hear these sorts of things fall through a lot. Another publisher may come along."

"I don't believe so." His accent, which had been only slightly Hispanic in the discussions Quill had had with him, had deepened. "I had visitors, you understand? There are people who would not like this book. People who tell me if I want to stay in this country, I must not help with this book. So I do not."

"What people?" Meg demanded.

Luis shrugged. "*Que querdo?*"

"You have a green card, don't you?" Quill said.

"I am a citizen."

There was an undercurrent of anger in his voice—very encouraging to Quill. "Then nobody can deport you for helping with a book, Luis. Trust me. It's a basic part of your American freedoms."

"He can trust us," murmured Meg. "I think the question is how far can he trust Cressida Houghton's lawyers."

"Was that it?" Quill demanded. "Did a man named Hawthorne see you?"

"Who else could it be?" Meg said. "Honestly, Quill."

"You have visitors. In your house." Luis put the Mercedes in gear and backed away. "Many women with gold jewelry and fancy cars. I will garage this. Good-bye."

"Luis!" Quill ran a few steps after the car. "Just tell us. Did a man named Hawthorne come to see you?"

Luis hesitated, then nodded.

"Luis," said Meg. "Just park the car and come in to your office for a minute. Okay? We've got a way to get these guys off your back."

"We do?" Quill said.

"The truth," said Meg, "shall set you free. Nobody can stop Luis from his silly book if it's the truth. And if hacking into Carmichael's system can help us break the case, that's going to help Luis, isn't it?" She made a face. "At least it can't hurt."

"True."

Luis parked the Mercedes next to a black Cadillac trimmed in bronze, then walked over and opened his office door. Meg pulled Quill after her, then shut the door against the outside. "Luis. How good are you at hacking?"

He smiled, looking very young. "Not bad. Not too bad."

"Good. See this?" Meg pulled a copy of their client record from Carmichael's office out of her purse. "This piece of paper has this law firm's E-mail address and all other kinds of stuff on it. Can you break into this system and find Verger Taylor's client files?"

Luis took the application and scanned it. His eyebrows rose.

"We lied," said Quill, guessing that he was looking at their phony income statement. "But it'll help a lot, Luis, if you can get to Taylor's financial records and his court cases."

"And his income tax returns and his divorce papers," said Meg merrily. "Whatever. Can you do it?"

"I need a lot of passwords, Miss Quilliam. Do you have them?"

"Passwords? No. No, we don't."

"Do you know who runs the system for the big guy?"

"You mean Verger's system? Um . . ."

"Let me make a few phone calls." He shook his head, brow furrowed over the pages. "La. La. La. La. We shall see."

"Then we'll come and see you after we take care of our visitors. Okay, Luis? You can't let these people intimidate you."

He grinned. "As I said, we shall see."

"You'll just bet we'll see," Meg muttered, stamping after Quill to the door of 110. "Isn't it just *like* the Cressida Houghtons of this world to think they can control the freedom of the press." A stray photographer, either left over from the morning press barrage or the advance guard of the press due for Tiffany's conference at one o'clock, jumped from behind the oleander shading the front atrium to the Combers and shoved his camera in Meg's face. "Get out of the way, you little weasel!" she snapped. She balled one small fist and brandished it in his face. The photographer, wearing a baseball cap backwards and baggy jeans, shrugged cheerfully. Meg thrust her key into the lock of 110's door and growled again, "Beat it!"

"And to hell with the First Admendment," Quill added. Following Meg inside, she almost collided with her.

"What did you say?"

"Honestly, Meg. You can't have it both ways. The press is either free or it . . ."

Tiffany, having apparently heard the door open, came trotting down the hall and came to a full stop. "Oh," she said flatly. "It's just you."

"Just us," said Quill cheerfully. "How's the therapy session going?"

Tiffany was wearing white leggings and a soft white Angora sweater that covered her muscular arms. It had a cowl collar that surrounded her blonde hair with a fuzzy aureole. Her only jewelry was a pair of white pearl earrings. She looked innocent, angelic, and vulnerable.

"I thought you were that little shit shrink," she said.

"Dr. Bob?"

Tiffany whirled and stamped back toward the living room. Quill pulled a face at Meg and followed her.

The living room was filled with beautiful women. Elegantly dressed women. Their hair formed a rainbow of Clairol colors: bronze, sherry, raven, chestnut, and more shades of blonde than had ever occurred in nature. Their skirts were short, showing perfect knees; their suit jackets, blouses, silk sweaters, and knitted tops were tightly fitted, in an astonishing array of reds, greens, yellows, and black. Quill's wholly unscientific estimate of their average weight was ninety pounds.

The air was heavy with perfumes Quill had never smelled before, mixed with the acrid scent of cigarettes. "Virtual *Vogue*," Meg said into the silence. "Wow."

"This is Sarah Quilliam and her sister, Margaret," Tiffany said. She perched on the arm of the leather sofa and lit a cigarette from a pack lying on the table. "Quill? These are the phobics." She waved the cigarette in a semicircle, beginning with a tall brunette slouched gracefully against the kitchen counter. "This is Barb. She's here because she actually took out a Wal-Mart credit card. Then Nicole, the one I told you about, who's got that job in publishing, then next to her is Merry, who thinks she should go to school, for God's sake . . ." She trailed off disconsolately. "Oh, what's the use? There's nobody out there, girls. Just some reporter from the local Pennysaver."

"Where *is* Dr. Bob?" asked Quill gently.

Tiffany stubbed out her cigarette and lit another one. "It looks like he's not coming, doesn't it? I swear I'm going to report him to the AMA. How dare he leave us hanging like this? How dare he!" She narrowed her eyes through the smoke. "You know what happened, don't you? You know who got to him, right? That caviar-wouldn't-melt-in-her-mouth Miss Idol-of-America Houghton. He's ditched us. Abandoned us completely."

CHAPTER 15

"Okay, Luis," Meg said, "power up." She pulled a chair next to his desk and sat down. Quill prowled nervously around the office. She tapped at the keys to the units hanging neatly on the wall, flicked aside the window blind to look out at the darkening sky, and switched the radio on. The announcer was forecasting the arrival of Hurricane Helen the next day. She flicked the radio off.

Luis reluctantly took a seat in front of his PC. "You're sure this is legal?

Meg shook her head. "No, it's not legal. But you want another chapter in the book, don't you?"

"Well . . ."

"Of course you do. You're helping us catch a body snatcher. Maybe. Come on, Luis, cheer up. Log on."

"Log on? I am logged on. All the while you were with your guests I am hacking. I have the gateway. I have the passwords. I have . . ." Luis typed, swore in Spanish, deleted, and typed again. "Okay." He input rapidly, the keys clicking. "Okay. Now, you're sure about this? You want me to break into this man's files?''

''Hack away,'' Meg said firmly. ''Now what?''

''We try to log on the system as 'anonymous.' This is stupid as an account name, but very usual.'' He input. ''This does not work. So we try to log on as 'guest.' This is also stupid, but usual.'' He input a second time. ''No. No good. Third time lucky, as they say here in America. What is this man's name?''

''Franklin Carmichael,'' Quill said.

''And . . .'' Luis sat back. ''*Hola!*''

The screen asked FILE NAME?

''Hooray!'' Meg yelled. ''Okay, this law firm cross-references by birth date of the principal clients. Try Quill's.'' She gave him the numbers. Within seconds, the application they'd filed that morning with Carmichael appeared on the screen.

''Whoop!'' Meg tapped Luis aside. ''Mind if I take it from here?''

''I don't mind. I think that maybe I will take a walk outside, and that maybe you have borrowed my computer without my permission.''

''Now, Luis,'' Meg said. ''This is fun.'' Her fingers flew over the keys, scrolling through the file. ''Why, the little creep!''

''What little creep?'' Quill came to peer over her shoulder. After they'd left his office, Carmichael had added a few notes about them. The most interesting was 'QUERY: criminal charges re: VT's disappearance? Probably. Inquire Stan at WPBPD.' ''

''Who's Stan?'' asked Luis.

''Who cares?'' said Meg. ''Quill, Carmichael thinks *we* did it.''

''Oh, dear. Let's try for the Taylor file.''

Verger Taylor's birth date was known to half of America, principally because he'd been born on the fourth of July fifty-five years before and used this as evidence of his commitment to American *laissez-faire*. Meg keyed in the numerics. A long list of file names scrolled across the screen. "Jeez," said Meg. "Here's the file on his divorce from Cressida."

"No," said Quill. "It's private."

"Quill, all this is private!"

"I don't care. Don't open it."

"And here's the file of the divorce from Tiffany . . . yikes, this reads 'pat. suit: Amber St. Clare.' You don't suppose . . ."

"Just look for Murex, Meg."

"Okay, okay. I'll have to scroll back, then; they're alphabetized. Yep! Here is it."

She clicked on the file name, and a document scrolled across the screen. "Good lord," Meg said in disgust. "This thing's huge. Help!"

"What are you looking for?" asked Luis, who had not carried out on his threat to leave the room.

"I don't know." Meg sat back and ran her hands through her short, dark hair in frustration. "Carmichael said Ernst profited from the rise in stock, but how?"

"Search for anything in the Murex file related to Kolsacker," Quill suggested.

"Brilliant, Watson."

"Obvious, Watson."

Meg requested a search, typed in Kolsacker, and the hard drive hummed. "Purchase price, stock option, buyout," Meg read. "Let's try buyout." She moved the mouse, clicked, and the screen filled with type.

Quill read with Meg, over her shoulder, and was the first to say, "Ha!"

"Ha? You have found something?" Luis asked.

"Ha!" said Meg. "We sure have!" She looked around. "Can we print this sucker?"

Luis nodded. "Sure."

Meg selected PRINT and the printer burped, whined, and subsided to a steady hum. Paper began to feed, and Meg leaned back with an exclamation of triumph.

"So what did you find?" Luis asked again.

"Verger and Ernst sold Murex last year to a German

company. Part of the deal was a staged payout, with stock options coming due at six-month intervals for eighteen months. Ernst was due for a payout on stock yesterday afternoon. And it was a lot of money, Luis—he stood to gain over ten million dollars.''

''Ten million!'' Luis said. ''Do you know what I could do with ten million?''

''Lots,'' Meg said briefly. ''Anyhow, Verger decided to buy the company back a month ago, at least according to the information in *The Wall Street Journal*. The German company was going to litigate. As all of us know, litigation is costly, and the news of the suit made the price of the stock go down, down, down—until Verger's disappearance, of course. Now the stock is going up, up, up. It took a nice hike yesterday—and Ernst cashed in.''

''But why is Verger's disappearance an advantage,'' Quill asked, ''and not his death?''

''The document says that in the event of Taylor's death, Carmichael will execute any standing orders. Doesn't say a word about what happens if he just beats feet. As Birdie and Bea told us this morning, Ernst is in charge until Verger comes back or is proved dead. So Ernst had enough time to cash in. Which maybe was all he wanted.''

''We've got a motive,'' Quill said, ''but we don't have any evidence. If it's true, how the heck do we catch him?'' She sighed. ''And still get home in time for spring.''

Meg grinned. ''See this? The next payout's due in thirty days. What if we we E-mail Carmichael—with an electronic order from Verger to press the Murex suit forward. That'll drop the stock price again for sure.''

''What's that going to do?'' Quill said, exasperated.

''Think about it, Quill. You're Ernst Kolsacker. You illegally moved and/or otherwise disposed of your partner's body. Everything's fine until he starts to speak beyond the grave. All of a sudden, you've lost any advantage you might have keeping your partner alive, but absent. It is highly advantageous to your future to have him turn up dead. Quill. That means the police will have to find the body. You see.''

''I see that. What I don't see is how that's going to implicate Ernst Kolsacker any more than he's implicated already. And that's *nada.*''

''Hey,'' Meg said. ''It's the physics of murder.''

''The physics of murder?''

''For every action, there's an equal reaction. The more Ernst has to act, the higher his chances of exposure. And of course, there's one more thing. Ernst is going to be able to track where this order came from. I mean, he can backtrack from this message into our system just as easily as we broke into Carmichael's. So. Is Ernst going to run to the cops and tell them we're interfering with his ability to make a profit on Murex? Not likely. That's risking too much exposure. As soon as he finds out where this order originated, he has to act. Most likely,'' Meg said sunnily, ''he'll come roaring after us. Tonight.''

''You mean me,'' Luis said in alarm. ''This is my computer. I think I'd better go visit my cousin.''

''We'll make sure he knows it's us, Luis,'' said Meg. ''We'll use an address like gourm.det.quill.meg. Right, Quill?''

''*Pfui*,'' Quill said, in the best Nero Wolfe tradition. ''This is nuts, Meg. I absolutely refuse to put either one of us at risk.''

''It's not much of a risk. We input this order. We wait. Ernst shows up at our condo tonight. I threaten him, recording his confession with a concealed tape recorder of course. He agrees to pay blackmail. I agree to take the money. We get it all on tape.''

''It's too dangerous.''

''It is not too dangerous! Ernst is a body snatcher. That's a far cry from murder, Quill. He just took advantage of the situation that presented itself. He's no killer.

Gosh, the man's sixty-two years old with a heart condition. And he loves to cook. I refuse,'' said Meg, with an utter disregard for the rational, ''to consider anyone who's a good cook a killer.''

''Oh, Meg.''

''Let's put it this way. You want to go home, right? Sometime before next Christmas? You know perfectly well what's going to happen if we don't expose Kolsacker. We don't expose Kolsacker, we may never find the body. No body—no conviction for Evan and Corrigan. If we ever do get back to Hemlock Falls, we'll be dragged back here for depositions, testimony, and God knows what all. Month after month. It may even take year after year. You can just bet that Cressida isn't going to miss a trick to save her boys from a murder charge, and legal tricks take weeks. Months. Years. You want to tie yourself up that long? I mean, we do have a life.''

''What if he doesn't show up tonight?''

''He'll show up,'' Meg said confidently. ''Trust me on this one.''

''We should at least tell Jerry what we're doing. He could give us some protection.''

''As if!''

''Why don't we turn this information over to Jerry? He can trap Ernst if he wants to.''

''Because the police can't entrap citizens, Quill,'' Meg said virtuously. ''It's not legal. If you just presented the cold facts to a judge—where's the wrongdoing? We have no physical proof that Ernst snatched the body . . .''

''We don't know that he did, either,'' Quill pointed out.

''And in the absence of proof, all he has to say is that he—sorry about that—took advantage of his dear friend's absence to make a little money. And who on the jury is going to dispute that? Especially down here? Everybody wants to make money down here. No, Quill, we have to have some proof. This little blackmail scheme will provide us proof. I'll tell you what. We'll even let Ernst know that we know where the body is when we talk to him."

"But we don't know where the body is."

"He doesn't know that. Okay?" She sat at the computer, her fingers poised. "All I've got to do is use the E-mail to get word to Carmichael. Carmichael's obligated to pass word of this on to Ernst." She cocked her head. "Don't look so worried. I mean, it's much more realistic if we go ahead and prove that we have this knowledge and can pretend to be Verger Taylor and give orders for a while, by sending this phony buy order from Verger."

"Be quiet a minute, Meg." Quill dithered. She bit her nails. She pulled her hair. Finally she said, "Okay. But. If anything, anything happens to either me or Meg tonight, Luis, you go to the police. Agreed?"

"Can I put all this in the book?" Luis asked. "After you've captured him, of course."

They waited all night. Ernst the body snatcher never showed up.

CHAPTER 16

"What do you think I should wear tonight? It's black tie." Quill yawned, shook a long black jersey dress free of its hanger, and held it up to herself. "I always feel like a cellist in this. Meg?" She stuck her head out into the hall. "Meg!" She walked into the living room. It was just before lunch. Tiffany had called in great excitement. The electrical problems were fixed, the banquet was on, and the hurricane wasn't supposed to hit until tomorrow. Everybody was coming. And—although it might not be nice to say it—the interest in Verger's disappearance had heightened, if that were possible, and nothing at all had happened for the last twenty-four hours, so they could count on excellent media coverage. She, Tiffany, was going to wear black.

Quill looked at the sky dubiously. She'd rapidly become accustomed to Florida's insistently sunny weather. It was gloomy today. And those looked like genuine cumulonimbus thunderheads stacking up in the east. The living room was unaccustomedly shadowy.

Meg, curled up into a small ball in the corner of the

couch, was wearing a T-shirt that said NO GUTS, NO GLORY.

"Hey." Quill greeted her. "You talked to Doreen and Andy? The airport in Syracuse is still snowed in, I take it."

"Yep, I talked to Andy. Noreen had her baby. C-section. It was quite an operation, Andy said."

"Myles is still out helping with the blizzard victims?"

"Yep. He sends his love, though."

"I'm homesick," Quill said.

"Me, too."

"But thirty-six inches of snow in twelve hours with a wind chill factor of six below sounds positively gruesome."

"That it does. What else have you got to wear besides the black?"

"Nothing."

"Then I guess you'll look like a cellist."

"You all right?"

"Yeah. Tired, though. Jeez, I thought he'd show up. I was sure he'd show up." She rubbed her face with both hands.

Quill yawned again. "Look, as I told you about sixty times, Ernst probably won't get the message until this morning. I'm convinced we're right, Meg. No one else had sufficient motive to take Verger's body anywhere."

"Mr. X," Meg said glumly. "This may be the first case we fail to solve."

"I doubt it. I'm taking the tape recorder, and we'll keep an eye out for Ernst. At the first opportunity, I think we should get him into a secluded corner . . ."

"We've been over this about a million times," Meg grumbled.

"We'll go over it once more, just to be sure. I think the best place is the charcutiere kitchen. It's isolated, all your dishes will have been sent downstairs long before the banquet itself starts, and you'll be crawling the walls waiting for the *L'Aperitif* people to fall over in delight over your dish—which they will, Meg. Guaranteed. Anyhow, we back him into a corner at the earliest opportunity and get him to admit the heist.''

''The heist?''

''Whatever. And bingo, we're free and clear to go home.''

''I've got to psych myself up for this thing tonight. All the challenge has gone out of the banquet, though.''

''That's because you don't have enough to do,'' Quill said. ''Just supervising the main course presentation isn't nearly enough. Usually about this time, you're in the middle of the kitchen at home, flinging pots against the wall, singing and yelling. But that was the point, wasn't it? Didn't we say something about easy money and the time of our lives and fabulous weather?''

Meg stretched her legs out, wiggled her toes, and looked dreamily at the ceiling. ''If we were having a competition this size at home, and I was in charge, I'd be flying around the room right about now. But instead, I'm sitting here like a big fat lump.''

''You know what it is? It's the fact that the barometer's dropping. With any luck, we'll be out of here by tomorrow morning before Hurricane Helen comes roaring in, but there's this low pressure system in front of it, and that's why you feel so miserable. I'm a little depressed myself.''

''It isn't a low pressure system that's making you feel depressed. You're scared.''

''I'm not scared,'' Quill said indignantly. ''How dangerous can a five-foot, three-inch body snatcher with a potbelly be? My gosh, Meg, the two of us outweigh him by thirty pounds.''

''You've got a point there, pal. So, I'm not scared of Ernst the body snatcher.'' She brightened. ''I'm nervous. I'm nervous that the darn rabbit will taste like mung, I'm nervous that the editor from *L'Aperitif* is going to hate Jugged Hare a la Quilliam and I'll get skunked and end up with no stars instead of three stars.''

She jumped to her feet. "At home I'd be in my own kitchen with my own stuff and Andy to look forward to at night. Tell you what—pack up the dress and we'll go to the institute early. I need to cook something. Anything."

"And what am I going to do?"

"Take your sketch pad. You can do a charcoal of Ernst and sell it to the publisher of Luis's book for the cover. You'll make a million bucks. Besides, it'll make a great place to conceal the tape recorder."

The activity at the institute was both familiar and soothing to Meg and, by extension, Quill. Le Nozze had been closed for the day, and the students were busy setting up tables, decorating the ceiling with swags of white roses and eucalyptus, and polishing all the available woodwork.

Meg went up to the pastry kitchen to try a variation on crème fraîche that had just occurred to her. Quill helped for a bit with the tables, folding napkins into tulip shapes, and then, when the hour for the cocktail party approached, went into Linda Longstreet's former office to change. She eyed the black jersey dress in the mirror. Myles had told her that the dress did make her look like a cellist—but a very sexy cellist. It fitted smoothly over her shoulders, breasts, and hips. The skirt was full and swinging from the hips on down, but she could hardly strap the tape recorder around her waist. Despite Meg's suggestion, she'd left the sketch pad at home and carried the tape recorder in her leather purse. To her dismay, it wouldn't fit into her evening purse.

"Meg'll just have to do the recording," she muttered.

The door swung open and she turned, tape recorder in her hand. Ernst Kolsacker stood there. He was dressed in white tie. He was sweating freely. Quill wanted to scream, didn't, and hastily thrust the tape recorder down the bosom of her dress, where it made a peculiar-looking bump.

"Sorry. I thought the office was empty." He averted

his eyes. "Um. Yeah. Look, I'll catch you later."

He really was, as Birdie had said, a dear, teddy bear sort of a man. Quill was almost sorry for him. "Ernst," she said. "Wait."

He turned back. He was breathing with difficulty. Quill advanced toward him, her hand stretched out. "We know," she said. "We know everything."

His gaze sharpened. He stopped looking like a cute little bear and looked a great deal like a very competent business executive. "Know what?"

"About Murex. About Verger. About the body."

"Whose body?"

"Verger's body, Ernst. The penalties for removing a body aren't nearly as severe as you might think. You're looking at a year or two suspended sentence. Unless you've done it before. Which I'm sure you haven't."

Ernst not only looked angry, he looked completely bewildered. "What in the name of God are you talking about? If it's Murex, screw Verger, wherever he might be. I was free to sell the stuff if I wanted to."

"We knew you'd say that," Quill said sympathetically.

Meg appeared at the open door. She was wearing her dress tunic, the one with the gold buttons and the flowing sleeves. She looked smaller than usual inside the folds. Her face was paper-white. "Quill," she said. Her voice was barely above a whisper. "Come with me. Right now."

"Ernst is right here," Quill said brightly. "We were just about to . . ."

"He didn't do it. Come with me. Both of you, come with me. No. Ernst, you call the police."

"Meggie, are you okay?"

"No. No. I am definitely not okay. Just come with me, now. Ernst, please. Call Jerry Fairchild."

"Meggie, you're shaking."

"Come on."

"I can't hear you."

"I said, come on!"

They passed the archway into Le Nozze. Meg hurried up the stairs ahead of her. Quill paused for a moment. The room was filling up with formally dressed guests. Tiffany was in the middle of a group of three men, two of them in ten-gallon hats, flirting madly. She was wearing lilac, which did remarkable things for the color of her eyes. Quill waved at Franklin Carmichael, who smiled and waved back.

"Quill." Again that weird, strained whisper from Meg.

Quill, by now recovered from the near faux pas with Ernst Kolsacker, was becoming alarmed. She followed Meg down the empty halls to the charcutiere kitchen. All of the banquet preparations were being made, of course, in the Le Nozze kitchens. Quill wasn't surprised to find it empty. It was dark, though, and the light from day had gone. "Is there something wrong with the potted rabbit?" Quill asked again. It would typical of Meg—as much as she claimed to disdain this evening's banquet and its consequences—to call the police if something had happened to her precious rabbit.

"Come in here, Quill."

Quill followed her into the storage cupboard. As soon as she stepped over the threshold, Meg flipped on the lights. The shelves were the same untidy mess they had been when Quill toured with Linda Longstreet. The empty shelves at the bottom had recently been filled. Forty or fifty quart jars of potted rabbit? Quill thought. How odd.

Meg pointed to the first jar. Quill looked at it more closely, then sprang back with a shriek. A small foil square floated among the potted meat. An empty square of nicotine gum.

"Snap-snap," said Meg. "That's what Maria was trying to tell us. The body snatcher was chewing gum."

"Franklin Carmichael?" Quill whispered. She looked at the quart jars of meat. For a moment, she was sure she'd faint. ''He . . . oh my God. Verger!''

''Oh my God, indeed,'' said Franklin Carmichael.

Quill whirled. He stood there in white tie, holding a small, efficient-looking gun.

''It's too late,'' Quill said. ''We've already called the police.''

EPILOGUE

Quill sat in the lounge at the Inn at Hemlock Falls, watching the news. Hurricane Helen was hitting the south coast of Florida with brutal force. The palm trees lining the channel to the Port of Palm Beach were horizontal with wind. A buoy flew past the camera lens, there was a wash of spray, and the camera tilted.

The station cut back to the announcer. *''Hurricane Helen continues her rampage across Florida's southern coast. Seventy-mile-an-hour winds have devastated much of the vaunted Gold Coast at Hobe Sound. Next, another sensational revelation in the murder trial of accused killers Evan and Corrigan Taylor.''*

Quill grabbed the remote and turned the television off. She was sitting at one of the small tables for two next to the mahogany bar. Nate, the bartender, was restocking the shelves with a shipment of liquor that had just come in. Outside, the sun sparkled on snow. The sky was a clear, frosty blue. The inn was going to reopen tomorrow, unless another storm blew in.

Quill put her feet up on the chair across the table from

her own and sighed. It'd been a long trip home.

The door facing the perennial gardens opened, and Myles walked in. He pulled off his heavy parka, and Quill looked at his shabby sports coat with a surge of affection. "I ought to sew those buttons on for you."

Myles laughed.

"What?" she demanded.

"Just wondering how long this excess of sentiment is going to last. No. Don't get huffy. I love it." He bent over her chair and kissed her hair.

"Did you straighten things out with Jerry?"

Myles nodded, eased her feet off the chair, and sat down. His eyes were very gray in his weathered face. Quill thought she noticed more silver in his dark hair than there had been before. She took his hand and held it. "Is he still furious with Meg and me?"

"He's making loud noises, but I think he'll come around. He's right, Quill. Fooling around with someone like Franklin Carmichael could have been very dangerous."

"I told Ernst to call the police."

"But Jerry didn't get there until after Ernst tackled Carmichael and got the gun away from him. And if Ernst hadn't had a black belt in tae kwon do—" His hand tightened on hers. "Well, I'm just glad he did."

"Has Carmichael confessed?"

"No one's confessed. But it took Carmichael almost eighteen hours to—er—prepare those quart jars, and he's having a lot of trouble coming up with an alibi that the prosecution's going to buy. My guess is that he'll plead and get a suspended sentence."

Quill straightened up in horror. "After what he did? He *canned* Verger Taylor's body! And it was just for the percentage he got selling that stock for Ernst?"

"He cleared close to a million dollars on it, Quill. And he was running with an expensive crowd. Anyway, it's pretty clear Verger was already dead when he got there. He was Verger's personal lawyer, remember—he wouldn't have had a slice of Ernst's business after Verger's death. The heaviest charge Jerry can come up with is interference with the disposal of a body. The risks were pretty small. And, of course, the fee Carmichael collected for the stock sale belongs to him. It was all perfectly legal."

Quill shuddered.

"So. I talked to John this morning. Convinced him that the inn can do without you for a few days. That the two of us should take off for a long weekend. Someplace warm. What do you think?"

Quill looked at him. "They say that Toronto is absolutely fantastic this time of year."

"Then Toronto it is."

About the Author

Claudia Bishop is the author of five mystery novels featuring the Quilliam sisters. She is at work on a sixth, *A Touch of the Grape.*

After the sale of her consulting business to a large advertising firm, Bishop retired to write full time. She divides her time between a farm in upstate New York and West Palm Beach.

After the events in Palm Beach, Meg, of course, will never make potted rabbit again. Here is her recipe for Omelet Suzette.

QUILLIAM'S OMELET SUZETTE

Per individual omelet:

2 eggs
1 teaspoon flour
1 tablespoon sweet cream
¼ cup freshly squeezed orange juice
2 tablespoons granulated sugar
1 teaspoon Cointreau
confectioner's sugar

Beat the two eggs together with a wire whisk until creamy. Add flour and tablespoon of cream. Whip until frothy. Set aside.

Caramelize the granulated sugar in one teaspoon butter. Add orange juice and Cointreau. While mixture is reducing, prepare omelet. Heat one tablespoon butter in the bottom of an omelet pan until brown and sizzling. Pour egg mixture into pan. Let omelet sit and cook for a minute, then carefully lift the edges with a wooden spatula, letting the uncooked egg run underneath the omelet. Flip omelet, cook through on opposite side, fold, and remove to a warmed plate.

Pour the orange sauce over the omelet and sprinkle with confectioner's sugar to taste.